DRAGON
BOUND

DRAGON BOUND

CHELSEA M. CAMPBELL

SKYSCAPE

SKYSCAPE

Published by Skyscape, New York

www.apub.com

Amazon, the Amazon logo, and Skyscape are trademarks of Amazon.com, Inc., or its affiliates.

ISBN-13: 9781503936096
ISBN-10: 1503936090

Cover design by Kirk DouPonce, DogEared Design

Printed in the United States of America

For Chloë, who made me believe in this book

1

PUTTING THE "VIRGIN" IN VIRGINIA

I want to punch everyone at this party in the face.

The girls for snickering behind my back. And for how they all fit perfectly into their corsets and ball gowns.

The boys for how they ignore me. I'm a freaking *St. George*. At the very least, that makes me some pretty good breeding stock. They should be more interested.

The old men milling around the party, because they keep looking at me like I'm a cow at an auction. And not even a prize cow or anything. More like one that's only so-so, but that they're getting at a huge bargain.

There's also my older sister, Celeste. This is her party, yet another celebration of how wonderful she is. She slayed the dragon whose head is currently hanging on the side of the paladin barracks overlooking the courtyard. A purple dragon, one of the worst clans. It's right next to my window, and it smells sickeningly sweet, like decay and death and blood. Flies swarm around it, and I can hear them buzzing while I sleep at night. Celeste is the epitome of what a St. George should be. Magic?

Check. She can use the family power like nobody's business. Good with a sword? I think the scaly severed head staring down at all of us is proof.

Then there's my father. He's the one who invited all the old men from out of town. They're not paladins, not from any of the Families, so I know they're outsiders. Most of them are his age, and fat, balding, and somehow also way too hairy. He keeps pointing in my direction while talking to them, like they're discussing how many actual cows I'm worth. Or, more likely, my father is trading me for weapons and armor. It's a smart move, if I'm being completely impartial. Trade the useless daughter for tools that will help better the whole community. *Think of how many dragons could be slain with the haul Vee will bring in.* That's probably what he's thinking. And it's not like I don't turn seventeen in two weeks. My deadline's almost up.

And that brings me to the person I *most* want to punch in the face. That would be my best friend, Torrin, who's spent this whole party by my side—plus five points for loyalty—but whose eyes have been on other girls. Mostly Mina Blackarrow and Ravenna Port, who are both tall and blonde and weigh about twenty pounds less than me, and it shows. But still. Minus ten points for ogling those girls, who, like pretty much everyone here, I'm not on good terms with. Minus *twenty* points for never looking at me like that. Especially tonight, when I'm probably going to be sold off to the highest bidder.

"Torrin," I say, "can you do me a favor?"

"What's that?"

"Will you kindly inform everyone at this party that I intend to punch them in the face?"

He laughs, the corners of his mouth jumping up into a smile.

"I'm serious." To show him just how serious, I make a fist.

"Uh-huh. Your thumb goes on the outside, by the way. Don't hold it under your fingers like that or you'll break it. *If* you were actually going to do all the punching you say you are." He picks up two miniature chocolate cakes from the dessert table and offers me one.

Plus three points for generosity. But he's still at negative twenty-two by my count.

There's a moment where we're quiet, eating our cakes and staring at the festivities. Ravenna Port laughs really loudly at something George Marks just whispered in her ear. She sounds like a horse, but that doesn't seem to bother him, especially when she takes his hand and leads him to the dance floor as the string quartet eases into a slow, romantic song.

"They're here for you, you know," Torrin whispers.

I almost drop the last bite of my cake. A couple dark crumbs spill down the front of my white dress. I swipe at them without thinking and end up smearing frosting across my chest. I shut my eyes and bite my tongue, silently cursing my father. He's the one who made me wear this stupid white dress tonight. To emphasize how pure and pristine I am to my new suitors, no doubt. Putting the "virgin" in Virginia, that's me.

"Who?" I ask, my voice shaking. "Who's here for me?"

"I think you know," Torrin says. He jerks his head in the direction of a couple of the old men. One has a beard so long it's tucked into his belt. The other has huge sweat stains around his armpits.

"Yeah, *so?*" I grind my teeth together, even though Celeste would roll her eyes at me and tell me how bad it is for me. But thinking about that just makes me grind them even harder.

"They're not from around here." He gives me *a look*. An annoyingly knowing sort of look. Like he has the nerve to be concerned for me. And yeah, okay, best friend and all that, but it's not helping. "How long has it been since you left the barracks?"

I glare at him. Teeth cracking apart from grinding in three, two, one . . . "That's what you're worried about? My father is pretty much having a silent auction for me right now, and *that's* what you—"

"How long, Vee? Four years? Five?"

"Four and a half," I whisper, but not to him. He's pissing me off too much, so I say it to my feet. My wonderful feet, who have never brought up uncomfortable facts exactly when I didn't want to hear them.

He takes a deep breath and slips his hand into mine and gives me a reassuring squeeze. For a moment, I don't feel quite so alone in this. But then I pull my hand away because, the truth is, I *am* alone. I'm the one with no magic, the one who can't fight dragons, the one who has to be married off to some foreigner. Torrin's a Hathaway. He fights almost as good as my sister, *and* he's fireproof.

And did he watch his mother get ripped to shreds by a dragon in the marketplace? Did he have to just stand there, helpless, hearing her screams, the crunching of bones, and the ripping of flesh? Does he still wake up in the middle of the night, years later—four and a half, to be exact—and still smell her blood and the stink of her charred skin?

The memory makes a cold, sick feeling ball up in the pit of my stomach. I shudder just thinking about it.

But the last thing I want is Torrin getting misguided and thinking he needs to feel sorry for me, so I push the shuddery feeling away and latch on to my anger. "And what, exactly, is so wrong with staying in the barracks? You know what the barracks has going for it?"

"Vee, wait, I didn't mean—"

"No dragons. Not in dragon form, not in human form—none. Zero. This place is crawling with paladins like you and Celeste who'd kill any of them that so much as thought about stepping foot in here. Out there"—I point a shaking finger in the direction of the entrance to the barracks that leads to the rest of town, and, more importantly, to the marketplace—"you can't trust *anyone* out there."

Anyone could be a dragon. After all, my mother knew her killer, and she never suspected a thing. She married into the St. George family, she wasn't born a paladin, so she didn't stand a chance against him when he turned on her. Some people blame my "condition" on my father for marrying an outsider and diluting our bloodline. Celeste inherited everything she was supposed to, all the skills needed to become a hunter, and there was nothing left for me.

"I might not like most of these people," I go on, gesturing to the other partygoers, "and some of them might even hate my guts, but at least I know who they are. We grew up with them, so even if I can't trust them to not talk about me behind my back, I can still trust them not to transform into my worst nightmare and go on some murdering rampage. Inside these walls, me and the people I love are safe. Outside . . . anything could happen."

"I know, okay?" He puts his hands up, palms out, pleading with me. "That's what I'm trying to say. You *can't* marry one of these guys. You'd have to leave. And . . . you can't."

I laugh. "Well, you know what you can do to stop them."

He goes quiet and looks away, shifting his weight from one foot to the other. An uncomfortable silence falls between us. Doesn't he know that I was *joking*?

Okay, half joking.

Marrying Torrin would be about a hundred times better than getting sold to some guy three times my age. So what if he's not in love with me? Normally I'd say that was a big factor I'd look for in a husband—does he love me, yes or no?—but in this case, it's kind of moot. I mean, this is my life on the line here. Maybe it's not life or death, but when I think about having to spend the rest of my life with some stranger, someone who won me in an auction because I can produce paladin children for him, it makes me sick to my stomach.

In two weeks, I'll be married, and one of these old men will be sweating and heaving on top of me. Touching me in places I'd never let them anywhere near if I had a choice.

My eyes are starting to water, so I close them and take a deep breath. I'm not going to think about two weeks from now.

I get ahold of myself—I'm Virginia St. George, and someone might steal the rest of my life from me, but they are *not* taking what time I have left—but when I look up, I accidentally make eye contact with one of my suitors across the courtyard. I glance away, but too late—he's already coming over here.

"Vee," Torrin says, his cheeks still red, "you know I—"

"Save it." I grab his hand. "You're asking me to dance. *Now*."

He catches on, glancing in the direction of the old man making his way over here, and puts a protective hand on my arm and leads me to the dance floor.

The romantic song is over, and the band is in the middle of a sad war ballad that sounds absolutely heartbreaking on their stringed instruments. Figures.

At first we don't say anything. We just dance, performing the steps we've had to learn by heart since we were kids. This isn't the first time I've danced with him, but it is the first time it wasn't for practice. I try not to think about the times I've seen him dance with other girls. I wonder what else he's done with them, once the parties are over, but I wince and try not to think about that, either.

Instead I look into his eyes, not wanting to risk making eye contact with anyone else. In my head I concentrate on counting out the dance steps—one, two, and-three-and-four, one, two, and-three-and-four. And if I enjoy the warm weight of his hand on my waist, or the way we're close enough that I could easily rest my head against his chest, well, who can blame me?

Then he ruins it all by leaning in close and whispering in my ear. "You know I can't marry you."

There's a bad, bitter taste in the back of my mouth. I swallow it down, trying to wash it away. But my heart is pounding and my fingers clench up, digging into his skin like a cat flexing its claws.

Great job. Way to not give yourself away.

"I know," I tell him, letting myself sound as annoyed as I feel, which, in case it isn't obvious, is a lot. "Of course I know that."

"Ahem." There's the sound of a man clearing his throat behind us. We both pause to stare at him. He's the old man I accidentally made eye contact with, the whole reason Torrin and I are dancing in the first place. He smells like sour sweat and fried fish. His clothes are dyed a deep blue, so I know he must be from one of the southern cities, where they grow the best indigo. When he speaks, his voice is gravelly and low. "I'm cutting in."

Like hell he—

"Like hell you are," Torrin says. "She's busy. With *me*."

"Psst," I hiss, getting Torrin's attention. Then, quietly, out the side of my mouth so only he can hear, "Punch him in the face."

Torrin ignores me and puts himself between me and my suitor.

The old man looks Torrin over, sizing him up. "Lord St. George said she was available."

"Clearly she's *not*."

"Yeah," I add, "dancing with me is by appointment only. If you didn't put in your request, like, three weeks ago, you're out of luck. It's not fair to everyone else who followed the rules and waited their turn."

Both Torrin and the old man glance at me like I'm completely nuts. It's like they've never heard sarcasm before.

"Fine," the old man says. "I've seen enough, anyway." Then he storms off.

"Can I put you down for three goats and two cows for a bride-price?" I call after him.

"*Vee!*" Torrin warns.

"That's funny," I say. "I thought he was interested. What changed his mind? Was it the chocolate stains down my front? The way that, even with this corset on, I'm a little lacking in the chest department? It's not my wonderfully refined manners, I'll tell you that."

"This is serious."

"I know. And thanks for, you know, getting rid of him." Though if it's not him, it's going to be one of the others. I'm not exactly saved or anything.

"Yeah, well . . ." He sighs. "I can't get married. Not to you, not to anyone. At least, not right now, while I'm in training."

Paladins in training have specific vows they have to make. They're not allowed to go around making vows to other people. He'd be giving up his whole career if he married me right now, plus shaming his family, and I know that would be asking a lot. I mean, it would be a huge sacrifice even if he did feel that way about me. But asking him to do that *and* spend the rest of his life with someone he isn't in love with? It kind of makes me just as bad as the suitors who are here for me tonight.

Well, *almost*. And I might have chocolate smeared across my dress, but at least I don't smell. As far as I know, anyway. And, unlike them, it's not like I'd *make* Torrin sleep with me if we had to get married. If he felt obligated, I wouldn't protest too loudly or anything. But that's different.

"It's okay," I tell him, letting out a deep breath. "It's not your problem."

"I'm not saying that. Don't make it sound like I don't care what happens to you, because I do."

"And I care what happens to *you*. So, even if you were offering to marry me, I couldn't let you throw your life away like that. I'd have to turn you down. So just save us both the embarrassment and—"

"Excuse me, Miss St. George?" *Another* male voice interrupts us. I whirl toward him, ready to tell another old man where he can stick it, but I stop short when I see him, because he's not at all what I expected. For one thing, he's young, maybe only a few years older than me, if that. But I've never seen him around before, so he's not from one of the Families. He's tall with brown hair and deep blue eyes. He looks directly at me, like I'm the only person in the world, and flashes me the most inviting smile I've ever seen. He takes my hand, raising it up to his lips, and very softly kisses my knuckles, making my skin tingle. "It would be my pleasure to have this next dance with you. If you're not preoccupied." His accent is rhythmic and clipped. I can't place where he's from, but the way he talks makes every word sound absolutely *fascinating*.

8

"Obviously she *is*," Torrin snaps. "Can't you see we're in the middle of something here?"

The new guy ignores Torrin, simply raising an eyebrow at me.

"It's all right," I tell Torrin. "I think we were done here, anyway." I smile at the new guy and add, "I'd love to."

"Excellent." The stranger shoots me a warm smile and offers me his arm.

I'm about to take it when Torrin blocks him, then steers me a few steps away and whispers, "I've got a *bad* feeling about this guy."

Uh-huh. "You mean because it's crazy for someone to actually want to dance with me? Is that your 'bad feeling'?"

"I don't trust him. Something's off. He's not like the other guys your father invited here."

"He's not old and fat, and he doesn't smell like a garbage heap, you mean? No one who doesn't have sweat stains pouring from their armpits and a carpet of scraggly back hair could actually be interested in someone like me, right?"

Torrin shakes his head. "You're a St. George. You *know* why he's here. He doesn't want you—he just wants a paladin bloodline!"

I could slap him. Or kick him in the shins. I probably should, but instead I stand there in shock, stinging from his words.

Torrin looks shocked, too, like he can't believe he said that. Like he knows he went too far. "I'm sorry. I didn't mean—"

"You think I don't know why he's here? Why they're all here? You think I don't know that the only reason any guy would ever want me is because of who my father is? Let me ask you something, Torrin Hathaway. If you weren't in training, would you marry me then? To save me from people like him who only want me for my oh-so-precious golden eggs?!"

His face goes bright red, and he sucks in his breath too fast and starts coughing, choking on his own spit. "Not fair, Vee. You know I care about you."

"That's not what I asked. It's a simple question with a simple answer. *Yes* or *no*?"

He looks anywhere but at me. "Don't make me say it."

"Then don't lecture me on who I should be dancing with." I elbow him in the ribs as I shove my way past him and toward the stranger who may or may not be my future husband.

Okay, so I take back what I said. Maybe I don't want to punch *everyone* at this party.

When I go on my punching spree, I'll spare my new dance partner. Who I don't have a bad feeling about *at all*. In fact, the way he keeps all his attention on me, like I'm the only other person here, gives me some really *good* feelings. So Torrin can just take his warning and shove it, because he's not the one who has to leave the barracks for the first time in almost five years and marry a stranger. And if the one suitor here who doesn't smell like week-old garbage wants to dance with me, I am *not* going to argue.

"I didn't catch your name," I say, because I might need to know that kind of thing. So when I look at my father's list of potential husbands, I can point to the right one.

"Prince Lothar," he says.

I blink at him. Did he just say he was a *prince*? Or is that, like, his first name and Lothar is his last name? There is *no way* a prince wants to dance with me. His kingdom must be completely infested with dragons. He's got to be super desperate for some paladin children.

He's just staring at me, waiting for my reaction, like his name was supposed to mean something. Like maybe I'm supposed to know who he is already, but, as Torrin so helpfully pointed out, it's not like I get out much.

"I'm Virginia St. George," I say, on the off chance that he didn't know that. That he didn't come here specifically to check out the auction tonight.

Or maybe he didn't. Maybe he's here for Celeste and got confused. But my sister might have finished her training and be a full-fledged paladin, but she's too valuable to be allowed to marry outside the Families. So if he did come here looking to woo her or whatever, he should think again.

"St. George," he murmurs, my last name sounding beautiful in his accent. He leans close and takes a deep breath, and if I didn't know better, I'd think he was savoring the way I smell.

Must be the chocolate I smeared across my chest. Boys can't resist.

"So you're a paladin," he says. "With the family talent."

"I'm a St. George, aren't I?" He's referring to my family's ability to bind a dragon's powers and keep them from working any of their evil magic. Which includes transformations. If I'd had the power, like Celeste, I could have stopped that dragon in the marketplace. As soon as I saw him start to change, I could have trapped him in human form. But I don't have magic like she does. Not that Prince Lothar needs to know that. If my father didn't tell him this auction was for an as-is dud, I'm not going to spill the beans.

"And you're a . . . a prince?" I try not to sound so skeptical. It's not that I don't believe him. It's just that, well, it's unbelievable.

"It's a small kingdom," he says, lifting my arm and twirling me around as the music speeds up. I remember practicing twirling with my mother when I was little, because I thought it was the most amazing dance move ever invented. And yet this is the first time in my life anyone has ever twirled me in a non-practice kind of way. "In the Hawthorne Valley."

I suck in my breath and hope that when he wraps his arm around me to pull me close for the next dance step that he doesn't notice the slight shudder of fear that runs through me. "That's in the middle of nowhere." And by *nowhere*, I mean it's in the middle of dragon country.

"Is that a problem?"

"You must have a lot of dragons." My voice shakes. At least three separate clans live in that valley. Even Celeste has only been to the outskirts. "A lot of attacks." He was starting to seem too good to be true—of course there had to be a catch. His strong arms are around me, his body so warm and so close to mine. The kinds of things that should make me feel safe. Protected. Like they do when . . .

Like when I'm with Torrin. Good old fireproof Torrin. But I'm not going to think about him.

Prince Lothar draws me close, ignoring the dance, and gazes into my eyes. His voice is dead serious when he says, "Believe me, Virginia, no one—dragon or human—gets in or out of my kingdom without my permission. *No one.*"

He really sounds like he means it. I nod my head, acknowledging his statement, but I don't know how it could be true. And if it is—if he really can keep dragons from preying on his tiny, unknown kingdom in the middle of a dragon-infested valley—then what does he need *me* for?

He relaxes, sliding his hand to my waist to continue the dance, but I hold back.

"That's . . ." I swallow, not sure if I should even believe him. Nobody's security could be *that* good. "That's a pretty big claim."

"It's not a claim. It's the truth."

"But . . . Dragons could look like anyone. How can you be sure?"

He grins and leans in close, whispering in my ear, "That's a secret. But maybe I'll get the chance to show you one day. If you come to live with me."

A shiver runs down my back. Is he saying what I think he is? He's really here for me, and he already has all the protection he needs from dragons, so . . . I take a step back, looking him over, watching his face for signs that this is some elaborate prank. "Who are you? Did Ravenna put you up to this? Or Justinian? Or . . ." Or anyone at this party. I should have known a handsome stranger who's supposedly a prince and has a kingdom safe from dragons would be too good to be true.

A hurt expression tugs on his features, wrinkling his forehead and giving his mouth a sad, pouting look. "I am who I say I am. Prince Lothar, of the Hawthorne Valley."

"Then you're lying about your security. If you're here tonight, it's for one reason, and that's that my *loving father* put me up for sale. You don't know a damn thing about me except for my bloodlines, so don't tell me that's not why you're here. Or why you're pretending to be interested in me."

"Oh, he's not pretending."

Both Prince Lothar and I turn to see who just spoke. There's another guy standing there, about my age. He's got messy black hair, with one streak dyed bright red in the front.

Recognition flashes across Prince Lothar's face. "Amelrik," he growls, his eyes narrowing. "I should have known. Back from the dead, I see?"

"Well, I guess you two know each other," I mutter.

The guy with the red streak in his hair—Amelrik—looks me up and down and raises an eyebrow. He speaks with the same clipped accent as Lothar. "This is how you like them now, eh, Lothar? Soft and covered in . . ." He glances down at the stain on my chest. "Well, I hope that's chocolate."

Prince Lothar grabs my arm, jerking me toward him, his fingers digging into my skin.

"Hey!" I shout.

"She's mine," he snarls, ignoring me and speaking only to Amelrik. "I got her first. And, besides, you're *dead*. Or supposed to be. I don't know what my father was thinking, letting you go, but I'm happy to correct his mistake."

Amelrik swallows, the muscles in his face tensing. But it only lasts a second, and then he's smirking at Lothar, as if his threat didn't bother him at all. "It's going to be awfully hard to kill me if you're dead."

Lothar's grip on my arm tightens. "Let me go!" I scream. I stomp on his foot as hard as I can, and I'll admit my stomping skills might not be up to Celeste's level or anything, but it should still hurt. Except he doesn't even flinch, just wrenches my arm instead, dragging me even closer to him with a strength I wouldn't have thought possible. It feels like my arm's going to break.

People have started to notice what's going on. There's murmuring around us and gruff voices and Torrin shouting, "Vee!" from across the courtyard.

"You can't kill me," Lothar tells Amelrik, his nostrils flaring in a smug expression that makes me want to barf. I can't believe I ever liked this guy. You know, thirty seconds ago, when I was young and naïve. I've matured a lot since then.

"No, I can't," Amelrik says. "But *they* can. Or did you forget you were surrounded by paladins?" He reaches into his leather vest and pulls out a dagger. It happens so fast, I blink and almost miss it. There's a flash of metal in his hand, and then he's shoving me out of the way and plunging the dagger straight into Lothar's chest.

2

A PIECE OF ADVICE

There's a horrified murmur running through the crowd. Paladins shouting and surging toward us all at once. Time slows as I watch the blood flow from Lothar's chest, soaking his clothes, his hands, the stone courtyard around him. His eyes are wide, shocked, as his life seeps out.

I feel like the whole world just turned upside down. I don't know if I'm going to throw up or scream or huddle in a ball in the corner. I haven't seen this much blood since my mother died.

Amelrik grabs my arm, dragging me into the crowd and away from his victim. "Listen—"

"You *killed* him!" I shriek. "You just freaking killed him!"

"A piece of advice." Amelrik bends down a little so his eyes are level with mine and says, *"Run."*

I twist out of his grasp. "Don't touch me!"

He lets me go, holding up his hands and backing away. "Fine. But don't say I didn't warn you." Then he turns and hurries toward the front gate, following his own advice and shoving terrified partygoers out of his way.

I'm watching him go when there's this horrible wet crunching sound behind me. Followed by the sound of skin ripping and tearing. Noises I haven't heard in four and a half years. My stomach twists into a tight knot, and my blood freezes in my veins, because I know I have to turn around and look.

I hope I see a human boy, even if it means he's bleeding to death. Because that would be better than the alternative.

But when I turn around, there is no Prince Lothar. It's like I dreamed him up. At least, there's no *human* version of him. Instead there's a purple-scaled dragon rearing his head. I look for the wound where Amelrik stabbed him, but it's already healed.

Amelrik knew him—he knew what he was. That's why he told me to—

Lothar's eyes gleam as he looks right at me. I feel like he can see through me, like in this form he knows all my secrets. How I froze when the dragon attacked my mother. How I'm freezing now.

He rears back his head, and somewhere in the back of my mind I know what's coming, but I stand there anyway, gaping like an idiot, unable to move.

"Vee!" Torrin shouts. He lunges toward me, pushing me to the ground and landing on top of me just as Lothar breathes fire over the crowd. The flames crackle around us, scorching hot. People scream. The acrid stench of burning hair and skin fills the air.

Torrin's fireproof body is the only thing keeping me from frying to a crisp.

Swords *shink* as paladins draw their weapons. I hear Celeste's voice loud and clear over all the craziness. "Follow me!" she shouts, and I feel a wave of relief. My dragon-killer sister is here to save the day. Father can hang Lothar's head right outside my room for a *month* if he wants, and I'll ignore the stench and the flies and how creepy it is having a dead dragon's head five feet from my bed. Just as long as Celeste makes this nightmare stop.

"Come on," Torrin says. The flames have ended, at least for now. He gets up and grabs my hand, not daring to leave me to fend for myself.

And yeah, okay, plus one hundred points for saving my life.

He pushes through the crowd, dragging me toward the edge of the courtyard.

"Get back here, you little coward!" Lothar's deep dragon voice rumbles into the night. At first I think he means *me*, until he adds, "You can't run this time, Amelrik—you're *dead*. You hear me?!"

Torrin swears under his breath. He shouts for someone to bring him his sword. "Vee, get inside. You'll be safe there."

Yeah, right. Lothar is here because of me. This whole disaster is because of *me*, and I'm not just going to run inside and hide like it doesn't matter. Like I don't care what happens to Torrin or Celeste or anyone. Even if I just stand here, like an idiot, I'll risk my life like everyone else. I have to see how this plays out.

Lothar lunges at Amelrik, who's trapped inside the just-closed front gates, unable to make his escape. If he hadn't told me to run, he might have made it. Everyone screams and moves out of the way. A circle of space opens around Amelrik, probably because nobody wants to be anywhere near the guy a dragon just threatened to kill.

"Show your true form and face me!" Lothar shouts.

Your true form. That means there isn't just one, but two dragons here tonight. Here, at the barracks, invading my world. This is the one place that's supposed to be safe. There's a reason I haven't stepped foot outside of it in four and a half years.

The dragons were never supposed to get in here. They weren't supposed to come to *me*.

As I feel my world shrink, my bubble of safety popping and disappearing, I watch the fight playing out before me. Someone shoves me on their way into the barracks, probably to hide. I stumble and almost trip over an abandoned glass, spilling punch across the stones.

A spear flies through the air, hitting Lothar in the back of his right thigh, but he shakes it off. He lunges at Amelrik again, jaws snapping. Amelrik's face is pale, panicked. But he stays human.

"Come on," Lothar bellows at him. "Take your true form!" He laughs, like there's some kind of joke none of us is in on.

Amelrik ducks as Lothar takes another swipe at him. One of the paladins thrusts out her hands and shoots a blast of magic straight at Lothar. He scrambles backward, out of the way, letting it hit the stone wall in front of him. The stones shatter and crumble. But he doesn't even glance at his attacker and instead keeps his focus on Amelrik. Because apparently that's more important than the dozen paladins trying to kill him.

Celeste's voice rises above the noise, shouting orders for the others to cover her while she casts the spell that will bind a dragon's powers and force him back into human shape. Our family's specialty.

Lothar must hear Celeste, too, because he seems to recognize that this is over. He makes one last lunge for Amelrik, who drops to the ground and rolls away just in time not to get mauled to death. Lothar shouts something angry and guttural in a language I don't know, and then he's a blur of purple scales and flapping wings, launching himself into the night sky. The air whirls around us, getting dust in my eyes and making me squint. The smell of sulfur prickles my nose as Celeste finishes casting. There's a flash as the magic leaves her hands, followed by a crackling sound as it fizzles out and dies, its target no longer there.

Amelrik gets up from the ground, ready to run, but Torrin grabs him and forces him down before he can escape. The other paladins rush to help, and Celeste holds up her hands to cast again, though she looks tired now and sweat drips from her forehead. Magic takes a lot out of you—or so I'm told—and I swallow, painfully aware that it should be me casting this time. I should be able to take some of the burden off of her.

But if I could, Father never would have opened up this party to outsiders, and none of this would have happened.

There's another flash of magic as Celeste finishes casting, binding Amelrik's powers so he can't change forms. But it seems to me that if he was going to change, he would have done it by now. Either to fight off Lothar or to fly away or whatever.

Not that I care.

Celeste's voice rings out, echoing across the courtyard. "Prince Amelrik of Hawthorne clan, I, Celeste St. George, hereby declare you under arrest."

Prince? There were not only two dragons at this party tonight, but they were both *princes*?

The crowd cheers. Medics show up to tend to the wounded. The other paladins gather around Celeste, congratulating her as they haul Amelrik down to the dungeon.

Everyone except Torrin. "I told you I had a bad feeling," he says, grinning playfully at me to soften his words.

"I was this close to *marrying him*." I pinch my fingers together to emphasize just how close.

"Nah, that wouldn't have happened." He puts his arm around my shoulders.

"You're right. He probably would have ripped me to shreds before then." My throat is dry. I try to swallow, but with no saliva, and that just makes it worse. "If Amelrik hadn't shown up, if he hadn't tried to kill Lothar . . ." But why *had* he tried to kill him? It seems to me that Amelrik didn't want anyone to know he'd been seen. So why did he show up to this party and reveal himself to Lothar in the first place? Was he here to rip me to shreds, too? But if he was, why did he tell me to run?

"You're lucky." Torrin whistles and raises his eyebrows.

"Yeah, I know. I could have been killed." If he and Celeste weren't around, I probably would have been. A couple of times.

"You met one of the most dangerous criminals I've ever heard of. He's fooled a lot of people, going around in human form like that, and he's wanted for a list of crimes three miles long all over the five kingdoms."

I remember Prince Lothar's charming smile and his sexy accent. And then I feel sick for even thinking such a thing. "All these years, I was right. I can't trust anyone."

"Except me," Torrin whispers. "You can trust me."

"Now all I need is for you to follow me around, in case of dragon attacks. Whoever ends up marrying me will just have to accept that you're my bodyguard and that you can't leave my side day or night. That'll go over well, don't you think?"

"Don't be so hard on yourself. None of us knew. If Lothar hadn't pointed him out, we'd never have caught him."

I blink, taking that in. "What do you mean, if *Lothar* hadn't pointed him out? You're telling me the dangerous one *wasn't* the one breathing fire at us?"

"Hey, I'm not saying he's harmless."

"Maybe a little dragon fire isn't such a big deal to *you*, but to me, it's kind of fatal."

"I'm just saying that Lothar's your average dragon. Amelrik's the one you've got to really watch out for. A lot of people have trusted him and ended up dead."

Great. I mean, not that it should surprise me that he's dangerous. He did stab Lothar right in front of me. I shudder, thinking how close I came to both of them. How easily I could have trusted Lothar and agreed to marry him. Not like I didn't have doubts—he *did* seem too good to be true—but it's not like I had a lot of other options. And Amelrik . . . Technically, he saved me from him. He made Lothar reveal what he really was and told me to run. So is he really as dangerous as Torrin says?

"You saved my life," I tell Torrin, as if this is news. As if he doesn't already know that.

"It was nothing," he says, trying to shrug it off.

"I like to think that me still being alive isn't *nothing*."

"You know what I mean. Like I said, you can trust me."

I nod, because I don't trust my voice. Because if I speak, I might start crying in front of him, and I don't want that. I don't want him to think of me as the pathetic girl he had to save and then comfort when she burst into tears. I'm supposed to be a paladin. I might not be able to do magic or fight dragons, but I can still act like one.

"Thanks," I say, managing to get out that one word without letting any tears fall. I take a few more moments to get ahold of myself before adding, "At least one good thing might have come out of this."

"What's that?"

"I think that dragon scared off all my potential suitors. They're probably all running home in fear. My father's going to need the help of St. George himself to get me married off now. Which means I'm not leaving the barracks in two weeks. I'm not leaving them *ever*."

Torrin frowns. "Vee, that's—"

I hold up a hand to stop him. "I don't want to hear it. Whatever you're going to say, just don't. You weren't the one who was going to have to marry one of those guys and leave behind everyone and every-thing you've ever known. You weren't going to have to sleep with one of them and bear his children. And you weren't the one who almost got burnt to a crisp tonight by your worst nightmare. So don't you dare lecture me about staying inside forever, where it's— Damn it, Torrin, it's not even safe here! I can't say that anymore, not after tonight. But it's the safest place I know, and let's face it, we both know I'm not going anywhere. I *can't* leave."

"Oh, come on," he snaps. "If you *wanted* to leave, you could. You just *won't*."

I glare at him, my mouth hanging open in shock. That's easy for him to say. He doesn't feel icy hands of dread clenching up his heart and his guts every time he gets too close to the gate. Every time he even thinks about the marketplace or about what it would be like to step foot outside the barracks. His throat doesn't close up, his knees don't wobble. He doesn't feel the bile rising in his throat, and his vision doesn't get blurry.

It's easy to be fearless when you've never felt real fear.

He sees the way I'm glaring at him—like I hardly even know him—and starts to apologize. "I'm sorry," he mutters. "I didn't mean it. I—"

"No, Torrin Hathaway, you *did* mean it. And maybe I can't walk out of this place, but I can walk away from *you*."

I turn my back to him and storm off into the barracks, my fists clenched and my footsteps heavy with anger. He calls out another apology but doesn't come after me, and I'm pissed both because he has the nerve to try to apologize—as if his words didn't cut me, as if they can just be taken back and forgiven—and because he's not trying harder to stop me and make this right.

Saving my life doesn't give him the right to insult me. And even though he's at seventy-eight points for the night, he can consider himself disqualified.

3

MAYBE HE HAS A SON MY AGE

Celeste bursts into my room in the morning like she owns the place. I pull my covers over my head, hoping she can take a hint. I haven't been ignoring the sunlight streaming in through my window or the stench of that rotting dragon head hanging outside for nothing. Sleeping in isn't always easy. Sometimes it takes real effort.

"Virginia St. George!" she shouts, grabbing the edge of my covers and yanking them away. "Do you know what time it is?"

Golden sunlight catches in Celeste's blond hair, making her look shiny and brilliant, like some kind of angel. She scowls at my discarded dress from last night lying on the floor and picks it up, smoothing it out and setting it on the chair with a sigh.

I grab my covers back while she's preoccupied. "Go away," I tell her, fighting and losing against a yawn. "Try me again tomorrow." Not that she'll get anywhere with me tomorrow, either. As far as I'm concerned, I never have to leave this room again, let alone this bed.

"Father's not going to be pleased."

"He's *never* pleased." Especially with me. "He's the one who let strangers in last night. It's not my fault a dragon attacked."

"Two dragons," Celeste corrects me. She hesitates, then sits on the edge of my bed, resting a comforting hand on my back. "Are you okay, Vee? I should have been paying closer attention to everyone. I should have been watching."

No, I should live up to my family name and be a better paladin. Right now I'd settle for being one at all. "Torrin was there, and he didn't know." Not *really*. Having a bad feeling doesn't count.

Thinking about him makes me clamp my teeth together. He might have saved my life, but I haven't forgiven him for what he said.

"We only got one of them," Celeste says. "Lothar got away. He's still out there somewhere. But if he tries to come back . . . We're all on the lookout, you know?"

I sit up, nodding and biting my lip. "I still don't get it. Why he'd risk coming here, and for what? To try and marry me?" The thought sends a shiver down my spine.

Celeste looks away, and there's something funny about her voice when she says, "I don't know," so that I don't quite believe her.

"What is it?" I ask, my voice coming out a whisper. "If you know something—"

She shakes her head. "He saw an opportunity to attack a St. George. That's all it was."

But that doesn't add up to me. He didn't know I don't have the family power. He didn't know I'm not just as dangerous as my sister. And he didn't attack until Amelrik showed up and made him change forms.

"At least we got the other one," Celeste says. "He's locked up in the dungeon with a dragon ring around his neck."

"Torrin says he's on a bunch of most-wanted lists. Is he really that dangerous?"

She wrinkles her forehead, questioning my sanity with a look. "You're asking me if a dragon is really *that* dangerous?"

My face gets hot, and I turn away. I feel guilty and ashamed for even asking. He's a dragon. Of course he's evil. I know that better than anyone. "No," I mutter, staring into my lap, "I just thought it was weird that he never changed forms. He could have gotten away."

"All the more reason to be suspicious. But don't worry, we've got him under top security while we interrogate him." She pauses a little on the word "interrogate," and I know her and the other paladins will drag out any useful information they can get from him, using whatever means necessary, no matter how ruthless. Not that it isn't what he deserves. He's a wanted criminal, after all. A *dragon*.

He might have told me to run, but he didn't save me. Torrin did. And if anything, Amelrik put me in danger. He's the one who stabbed Lothar and caused all the chaos. Though, if he hadn't done that, I might never have known who—or *what*—Lothar really was.

"And after that?" I ask.

Celeste cracks her knuckles. "When he's no longer useful, he'll die by public execution. We haven't had one of those in a long time. Anyway, Father is demanding your presence downstairs."

"He thinks it was my fault." Of course he does. Just like he blames me for Mother's death. And maybe that *was* my fault, in a way, but did it have to mean he stopped caring about me? "Why can't he just leave me alone? No one's going to want to marry me now, not even some idiot from out of town, so— What, Celeste? What's *that* look?"

She pales a little, not meeting my eyes. "He found someone."

I hear a rushing sound in my ears, and my blood runs cold. "He *what?*" After the attack last night, I thought all the suitors would be long gone by now. Not only am I useless in a fight, not only do I not have the family power, but I apparently *attract* dragons. My hands clasp at my bedcovers, gripping them so tightly that even the soft fabric feels rough against my skin. "Who?" I ask, and I'm both dreading and dying to know the answer.

But Celeste just shakes her head. "Come on—get dressed. You'll find out soon enough."

Celeste marches me through the Hall of Heroes like I'm her prisoner. Which I kind of am, because if it was up to me, I'd be anywhere but here right now. Even though I'm curious to see who my father could have possibly found to marry me. Maybe one of the old men from last night fell asleep during the dragon attack and doesn't know what went down. Maybe he woke up this morning, the only suitor left, and thought he'd lucked out.

I glance at the suits of armor that line the walls as we walk by. The silent tributes to the paladin heroes of the past. Celeste's armor will be in this hall someday, but I've never even been fitted. I start to feel a pang of guilt and envy, and then we pass by a suit with a giant tear across the chest, right over the heart. I don't look long enough to see the details, but I imagine there are bloodstains. I picture that paladin's gruesome death at the claws of a dragon. The other suits might be more intact, but that doesn't mean their owners escaped their fate. There's a drawback to being one of the Families' best and brightest.

"You want to watch it with that iron grip there?" I ask Celeste. She's got her hand clamped around my upper arm like a vise. "I'm not one of your prisoners."

She sighs and loosens up a little. "It's not that I think you're going to run."

Which is kind of foolish of her, because I'd run the second I got the chance. That is, if I had anywhere to go other than hiding under my covers.

"I was just thinking," she goes on. "I told Father he should reconsider, but . . ." She glances over at me, then shakes her head. "Listen,

Vee, you're not seventeen yet. I don't care what anybody says—you're a St. George. You have the family blood, same as me."

"Just not the family power."

She pulls me aside—right next to a charred suit of armor that doesn't exactly inspire confidence about the family business—and grabs my shoulders. "I don't believe that. You shouldn't, either."

I sigh and take a step back, slipping out of her grip. "I've tried. Whatever makes you and Father so amazing just isn't in my repertoire." I shrug. "I don't have the magic."

Celeste glares at me. "You don't *want* it, you mean."

She's starting to sound like Torrin. "Yeah? And so what if I don't? Why should I?" I gesture to the charred suit of armor looming next to us. "So I can end up in here? So a new generation of paladins can stare at what might as well be my mangled corpse and be inspired to go get themselves killed, too?"

"They were killed protecting the kingdom, our *home*. You want to hide in these barracks all the time and rely on other people to keep you safe? *Fine*. But don't forget that people like them"—she waves at all the suits of armor lining the hall—"and people like me are the only reason you have that luxury. It's a dangerous world out there, and some of us have to live with that."

"If I wanted a lecture, I would have asked Father."

"You have to *want* the magic. If you wanted it badly enough, you'd find it."

"Right. It's my fault I'm a dud because I just don't want it enough. Being defenseless against my worst fear is *my* choice. I *want* everyone to make fun of me and for Father to have to raffle me off to the highest bidder because I'm not good for anything else."

"You've still got two weeks until your birthday. Father's made up his mind, but if you had the family gift, if you had real magic, he couldn't force this on you."

"No, then I'd just have to go out dragon hunting and risk my life on a daily basis. Until I came back gutted or maimed or burnt to a crisp. And don't tell me that wouldn't happen, because *you* might be able to survive out there, but even with magic, I'm not cut out for hunting dragons. So, let's face it, Celeste, this marriage is kind of my only option."

Celeste tilts her head and gives me a look, but she doesn't say anything and instead marches me onward toward my fate.

We turn the corner and move past a few more suits of armor—these ones are intact and have been polished to such a bright sheen that it almost hurts my eyes—and then through the heavy wooden doors and into the Ceremonial Room at the end of the hall.

The room is structured kind of like a chapel. There are ornately carved wooden benches lining both sides, with an aisle running between them that leads to a stone dais. This is where the Families gather to hold elaborate ceremonies to honor their heroes. It's where the last rites are given over the bodies of those who don't come back alive. It's also where we hold weddings.

A fact that isn't lost on me as I trudge down the aisle with Celeste, toward our waiting father and my new husband-to-be. I gulp down a mouthful of air, suddenly feeling like I can't breathe. It's worse than I thought. *He's* worse than I thought, because standing there, next to my father, is a thin, bony old man. He's completely bald, with a wispy white beard that hangs off his chin in tufts. He's dressed in a tailored suit and stands stick straight, his mouth a grim line as he watches me approach. Appraising me with cold, hard eyes.

I've seen him before—one of Father's friends—and my mind races, trying to remember his name, but the more I scramble to remember, the more I draw a blank.

"Virginia," my father says, "you remember Lord Varrens?"

"Of course," I lie. For a moment, I think maybe this isn't really happening. Maybe he has a son my age—or at least closer to my age—and that's why he's here. He can't possibly intend to marry me himself, can he? "Is your son here?"

Celeste elbows me hard in the ribs, and Father purses his lips in a scowl.

"I have never been blessed with any sons," Lord Varrens says in his reedy old-man voice. "Many daughters, but no sons."

"Silly me," I mutter. "Your grandson, then?"

"Vee!" Celeste hisses, her eyes going wide.

Father's eyes narrow until they're just two little dark beads staring down at me. Lord Varrens must be hard of hearing—no wonder, at his age—because he doesn't seem to notice I said anything.

Father clears his throat. "Lord Varrens has graciously offered to take your hand in marriage. This way you won't have to go far from home. It's the perfect match."

Lord Varrens nods, looking me over. "Perhaps she can give me the son I've always hoped for."

"Yes," Father says. "A good strong paladin son."

This guy? On top of me? I don't think so. "Was there seriously no one else?"

"What?" Father says, sounding incredulous. Like he can't believe I would be so bold.

"I said, was there no one else? No other suitors? You didn't have any other friends who were closer to my age that you could pawn me off on? Any that were still breathing?"

"Virginia!" Father's face turns bright red.

This time I know Lord Varrens heard because his mouth drops open and he looks from me to my father in disbelief.

Father takes a step toward me, his voice low as he speaks through gritted teeth. "After that debacle last night, you're lucky to have anyone willing to even consider asking for you."

"*Asking* for me. Right. Like I don't know you're behind this. How much did you have to promise him? How much gold and armor? Or was my blood enough?"

"How dare you speak to me like that!"

"And how dare you sell me to someone like him! I know you hate me—ever since Mother's death—but *this*? Did you at least tell him I'm a dud? That I don't have the family magic?"

"Virginia!" Father raises his hand, ready to slap me.

I brace myself, almost wanting it to happen. To let everyone see how much he hates me. And yet part of me—a big part—really hopes Celeste will come to my rescue and intervene.

But it's Lord Varrens who grabs Father's hand to stop him, while Celeste only gapes at me. "Please," Lord Varrens says. "I only want a son before I'm gone. I don't care about his bloodline."

So that's it. He doesn't even want me for my family. Which I should be relieved about, but somehow it just makes me feel even more useless. I glare at my father, my face hot with shame, tears prickling my eyes. "How could you do this to me?" I turn on my heel and walk away from him.

"Virginia! Don't you dare!" he shouts, but he doesn't lift a finger to stop me.

Celeste grabs my arm. "What do you think you're doing? You can't just walk out!"

"Watch me. I didn't see you trying to stop Father just now. So don't try to stop me, either." I twist out of her grasp, just as pissed at her as I am at Father, and make a run for the door.

4

I'VE ALWAYS HAD A SOFT SPOT FOR VIRGINS

I can't hide in my room, because that's the first place everyone would look for me. And the last thing I want right now—besides marrying Lord Varrens, obviously—is to have Celeste find me sobbing under my covers and tell me I have to honor my duty as a St. George. Being a St. George is all great and wonderful for her, but not so much for me. And she might be brave enough to fight dragons, but she's too scared or just too blindly obedient to ever stand up to Father.

So when I get to the staircase, I don't go up to my room. It's only a matter of time before Celeste comes to drag me back to my fate, and I hate the idea that she knows exactly where to find me. Or at least that she thinks she does. I go down the stairs instead, down to the dungeon, the last place anyone would ever think to look for me.

A few torches line the walls, their light dim, and I'm grateful for the darkness as the tears start to fall. I wish I could be stronger and braver, like Celeste. If getting married off to some bony old man was her lot, she'd take it with her chin held high. No running and no tears. She definitely wouldn't be hiding in the dungeon, feeling sorry for herself.

But I am *not* my sister. And now that I'm alone, hot tears fill my eyes and spill down my cheeks. My shoulders shake, and a loud sob escapes my lungs, echoing off the dungeon's stone walls and empty jail cells. I lean against one of the walls, my hands pressed to my face. The stones are cold and harsh, unforgiving, just like everything else in my life right now.

Then a chain jingles in the cell to my left. Metal scrapes across the floor. Cold fear floods my entire body and makes my heart race.

Great. Just when I thought I was alone with my misery. If there's anything worse than Celeste finding me crying my eyes out, it's got to be this. Because I know we've only got one prisoner right now. One I thought would be in an interrogation room with a crew of paladins extracting information from him. Not here, in a cell, listening.

Amelrik comes up to the metal door, right up to the barred window, and I hear him *sniffing* the air. My tears are all dried up, replaced with terror. I'm frozen against the wall, unable to move. And then I remind myself that he's chained up and locked in a cell. He can't hurt me, and even if he could . . . isn't he the one who told me to run last night? Didn't he try to save me from Lothar?

"Virgin," he says, in that sharp accent of his, and I can hear a surprised smile in his voice. "You're still alive."

"It's *Virginia*," I snap. "And don't sound so shocked."

"Is that any way to talk to me? I saved your life last night."

"You're a dragon and our prisoner—I'll talk to you any way I want. And all you did was tell me to run. I would have figured that out."

"You would have married him if I hadn't been there."

Maybe. It's not like I had a lot of time to get to know anyone, or that I even have a say in it. But if a good-looking prince had asked Father for my hand, wouldn't he have chosen him over some old man?

Pairing me with Lord Varrens seems like a last-ditch effort. "What do you care?"

"I don't."

"You wouldn't be in this cell if you hadn't stopped to warn me. Advice I didn't need, by the way."

"What I meant was, I don't care about *you*. Maybe Lothar can fake interest in a stinking paladin for a night, but he's always been the better actor. I'll give him that."

I push away from the wall, a burst of anger overcoming my fear, and move to face him. "Lothar was the only one who treated me like a person, and even if it was all a sham, at least he had the decency to fake it. Unlike everybody else who was there last night, treating me like a piece of property. And you can wipe that smug grin off your face, because I don't owe you *anything*."

"Please. Lothar would have killed you if not for me. Even with my help, I'm surprised you're still breathing."

I glare at him through the bars. "If this door wasn't in the way, I would slap you."

"There's that St. George charm. A slap in the face in exchange for saving your life? Sounds about right."

"You're the one who put me in danger in the first place. My dancing partner wasn't trying to kill me before you stabbed him in the chest."

"You have *no idea* what he planned to do to you. To use you for."

I swallow, wondering if I should believe him. Not that I think Lothar was there for any good reason, but still. "And what exactly were you doing there? Shouldn't a dragon prince have better things to do than go around crashing my sister's party?"

"Shouldn't a paladin have better things to do than cry in a dungeon?" He raises an eyebrow and takes a step closer. Torchlight catches the shock of dyed red hair at his forehead, while shadows from the bars in the window line his face, obscuring his sharp features and cocky smile. His skin looks pale and sallow, though maybe that's just the lighting. Around his neck is an iron dragon ring, glowing a faint red, enchanted with Celeste's magic—with St. George magic—keeping his powers bound and unusable. I've never seen one on a dragon up close. Blotchy red patches creep up his neck from under the ring. They look itchy and swollen, and there are lines of blood where he must have scratched at them. "It's not polite to stare," he whispers, his eyes a vivid green.

My cheeks get hot, and I glance down at my feet. "It looks painful, that's all."

"Well, you could always take it off. You could let me go, and then we'd be even."

Yeah, right. "Why did you tell me to run? And why didn't you change forms, like Lothar? You could have escaped."

"Oh, *could I?*" He sneers at me, his lip curling in disgust. "Thanks for the tip. I'll be sure to remember that for next time."

"There's not going to be a next time. You're going to rot in this dungeon until—" Until my sister and the other paladins kill him, once they feel he's outlived his usefulness. I clear my throat. "Until you're sentenced to die for your crimes."

He laughs. "You think I'm going to die here? This isn't the first time I've been caught, and it won't be the last."

"Right. And you're wearing that dragon ring because it brings out your eyes."

He grins. "Doesn't it?"

I grit my teeth in annoyance. I think about how Torrin and Celeste would be shocked to know I was down here, talking to a dragon. The whole barracks would be. They'd probably also tell me I shouldn't be here. He's dangerous, and I'm weak and powerless. A dud paladin with no business getting anywhere near a dragon, even one behind bars and bound by an enchanted iron ring around his neck.

I clench my fists, hot anger suddenly burning in my chest. Celeste and Torrin might be my closest friends, but sometimes it feels like they don't know the first thing about me.

Tears prickle and threaten to fall again, but I hold them back. I look Amelrik in the eyes, bright and green and striking, and ask in a voice that demands an answer, "Why did you help me last night? You say you saved my life, but you're a dragon and I'm a paladin."

He shrugs and looks away. "I didn't want Lothar to have the satisfaction of killing you."

"Oh." I can't help sounding disappointed. I don't know what I was expecting him to say. Did I really think he'd have some profound reason for helping me? That maybe, just once, someone saw me for who I really am, even for only a moment, and decided I was worth something? Even if that someone was a dragon. "Is that all?"

"Well, that *and*"—he sighs, putting a hand over his heart—"I've always had a soft spot for virgins." Then he snickers.

I gape at him.

The door to the dungeon clangs open, and Celeste calls out, "Vee!" her voice echoing down the stairs and through the hallway. She rushes over, putting a protective hand on my shoulder and angling herself between me and Amelrik. "You shouldn't be here." Then, to Amelrik, "Back away from the door, beast! I said *get back*!"

Amelrik holds his hands up and takes a step backward.

As soon as he does, Celeste whirls on me. "Virginia St. George, I can't believe you! Running off like that, and then I find you here, of all places, with a *dragon*."

"I'm *fine*," I tell her. "I can take care of myself."

"He's dangerous! You know that."

"He's locked up."

It's like she doesn't even hear me. "And you, with no . . ." She pauses, glancing over at Amelrik and then changing her mind about what she was going to say, probably something about how useless I'd be if he somehow escaped. "You know better. He might be bound in that cell, but that doesn't mean he's not deadly. Words can be a weapon, too."

"And you think I'm so stupid I'd just do whatever he said?"

"He's a liar," Celeste says, her voice hushed. "You can't believe a word from him." She sighs, putting her fingers to her temples. "But don't worry—we'll be taking care of him soon enough. Now come on, Vee. Father's so mad he's about to lock *you* up in one of these cells."

She tugs my arm, and I follow her, even though I think I'd rather be locked up in here than getting married against my will. But before I go, I glance over my shoulder one last time at Amelrik. He's standing at the door again, peering at me through the bars. His mouth turns down, just a little. Not angry or scared, but . . . well, for someone who claims not to care what happens to me, he looks awfully concerned. Our eyes meet, and something passes between us, some kind of understanding, and then Celeste is hauling me up the stairs, out of view.

5

FAMOUS LAST WORDS

Celeste is packing supplies for her dragon-hunting trip when I find her the next afternoon. She's leaving tomorrow morning with a group of other paladins to track down Lothar. When I see her standing in her room, inspecting her sword, I get this bad feeling, like ice water being poured down my back.

I'm never going to see her again.

The thought pops into my head, unbidden. I don't know where it came from. I shake my head to clear it and tell myself it's not true. Celeste can take care of herself, both with her sword and her magic. It's just my nerves getting the better of me.

I clear my throat to get her attention, even though I'm sure she knows I'm here, lurking in her doorway. The best dragon hunter in the five kingdoms doesn't *not* know her unstealthy little sister is standing right behind her.

She sheathes her sword and turns around, her dark blue cape whirling behind her. "Did you hear?" she says. "We've got a lead. It's only a matter of time before we track him down now."

The thought of getting anywhere near Lothar again sends prickles of dread running through my chest, but it's obvious Celeste can't wait to set out on the hunt.

"How'd you find him?" I ask, stalling, because I don't want to ask her what I really came here for. My voice comes out like a croak, and I clear my throat again.

Her expression turns grim. "The prisoner talked. After some . . . prompting."

She means Amelrik, and even though he's a dragon, and a jerk, I get a sinking feeling in my stomach. "You . . ."—I stop myself from saying "tortured"—"you interrogated him?"

Celeste nods. "He gave up the information about Lothar pretty easily. Not surprising, after what we saw between them the other night."

"But you believe him? You told me not to trust a word he said." Funny how her advice only applies to me.

"Vee, he wants us to kill Lothar. He made that clear at the party. And anyway, the Hawthorne and Elder clans have a pretty unstable history, from what I know. Tensions run high between them."

"So, what will happen to him now?"

Celeste tilts her head a little, shooting me an *Are you crazy?* look. "We'll hunt him down and slit him open from tail to gizzard."

"Not Lothar. Amelrik." Do dragons really have *gizzards*?

"Oh, we're far from done with him. He's got an awful lot to answer for."

So they're not going to kill him. At least, not yet. I realize I was holding my breath and let it out slowly. I still have questions of my own for him—questions I intend to get the answers to, whether Celeste wants me talking to him or not. She just doesn't need to know about it, that's all.

"I came here to ask you something," I tell her, finally getting to the reason I came to see her in the first place. "I . . ." I brace myself, taking in a deep breath. I want to say this in the calmest, most rational way possible, but instead I just start blurting it all out. "I need you to teach me magic! I know I'm not the ideal candidate or anything, and I *know* what I said, about being a dud and not having the power. Not *wanting* it. But . . ." I squeeze my eyes shut. This is the worst part. "You were right."

The words leave a bad taste in my mouth, as if admitting she was right this once means she was right about everything, ever. That every time I've ever disagreed with her—and, believe me, there have been plenty of times—I must have been in the wrong.

Celeste doesn't look like she's about to spout off an "I told you so," though. She mostly just looks confused. "You want me to teach you magic?" She raises a skeptical eyebrow.

Who else am I going to get to do it? After I practically begged Torrin to marry me and he turned me down, then saved my life, I'm not about to go crawling back to him, asking him to help me become a real paladin so I don't have to marry some nasty old man. Plus, he's not a St. George. He doesn't know the family power. And I'm not about to ask Father for help—not that he would—so that leaves Celeste.

"You said this is my chance. Do you want me to get married to Lord Older-Than-Dirt, or whatever his name is?"

"Varrens," she corrects me, as if it matters. Then she lets out a slow breath. "I'm leaving in the morning."

"In the *morning*. It's only noon."

She hesitates, thinking it over. She looks almost like she might give in, then shakes her head. "You told me yourself you don't even want the magic."

"And you told me it was my only way out of this marriage."

"I'm supposed to teach you something you haven't learned in seventeen years? In less than one day?"

My heart sinks. When she says it like that, it does sound pretty impossible. And it's not like I haven't been saying how impossible it is all along. Me and magic? Not going to happen. If it was, it would have happened a long time ago. But that doesn't mean I'm ready to give up and just accept that I'm going to be some walking skeleton's baby factory. "It's my last chance. And if anyone can teach me, it's you. My kind, smart, loving sister, who would never turn her back on me, and—"

"Flattery, Vee? Really? How vain do you think I am?"

"Not vain enough, apparently." I sigh. "I just want to try. One last time. And I'm going to do it whether you help me or not."

"Did I say I wouldn't?"

"You didn't exactly jump at the chance."

"Yes, well, your kind, smart, loving sister, who's also the best paladin in the world—you left that part out—*is* going to help you. I'm leaving in the morning. It might be a day trip, or it might be weeks. I might not be back in time for the wedding. So this really is our last chance. If I've got one day to teach you magic, then you're going to learn it in one day, damn it. Even if it takes all night."

"You don't mind? I mean, there's a chance"—a pretty big chance—"that I'm not going to succeed."

She rolls her eyes at me. "Then call it a wedding present. You either learn it or you don't, but at least you'll know you tried. And, besides, what's the harm in it?"

"Famous last words," I mutter.

"What?"

"Nothing. You're right. What could it hurt?" Worst case, I'm a failure at magic and I don't learn anything. Which isn't any different than how things are now. "We've got nothing to lose."

She claps me on the back, a little too hard, almost knocking the wind out of me. "That's the spirit!"

"Right." It's just my entire future that's on the line here. Just my happiness, my safety, and my uterus.

No big deal.

Celeste scowls at the dragon ring sitting on the dais in the Ceremonial Room. A cold, lifeless circle of iron, just like it's been for the past twelve hours. It's after midnight, and I'm exhausted and sweaty and ready to throw that stupid ring across the room.

"Again," she commands, her voice stern and her face impassive, not showing any of the disappointment I know she must be feeling.

I know I certainly am. "Celeste, it's not—"

"Keep trying," she snaps.

My arms are shaking from fatigue, but I hold my hands over the ring again. I shut my eyes and will the magic to work this time. I picture a spark igniting inside me, my St. George magic flowing through my veins and pouring into this stupid ring. I imagine it binding a dragon's powers and rendering them useless.

I *imagine* all that, but I don't actually *feel* anything. Well, unless feeling like I might collapse counts, but as far as magic goes, I've got nothing.

"You have to want it," Celeste says.

"You've been telling me that all day. It's not helping."

"And you haven't been listening."

I sigh and press my palms against my eyes, trying to remember why I ever thought this was a good idea. It's just making me feel worse about my situation, and Celeste telling me that I'm a failure because I don't want it enough? It's like saying I'm choosing to be old-man bait. Or worse, like I'm not guilty enough for what happened to Mother.

"*Again,*" Celeste says, even sterner this time, though she must be getting tired, too.

"It's late," I tell her. "You have to get up early tomorrow, for the hunt. And this is obviously not working."

"I'm not giving up, and neither should you."

I shake my head and slouch down on one of the wooden benches, my body sore and stiff. This rock-hard bench isn't exactly the most comfortable place I've ever sat, but right now it feels infinitely better than staying on my feet. "I've tried. I really have. But we've been at this all day, and now all night, and I don't have it in me to keep pretending anything's going to happen."

"You just have to—"

"What? Want it more?" I glare at her. "It doesn't matter how much I want it. I don't feel anything. I just . . . I don't have magic, okay?"

Celeste sits down next to me. I think she's going to lecture me some more, but she stays silent for a minute, then says, "Do you know why that dragon's locked up in our dungeon? Do you know why I didn't want you even talking to him?"

"Maybe because he's a *dragon*?" It all sounds pretty self-explanatory to me.

"Right, but it's more than that. He's also a liar. A con artist. The kind of criminal whose weapons are words and trickery. You can't trust a single thing he says."

"And you think I'm so stupid that I'd . . . what? Let him go if he asked me nicely enough?" I roll my eyes at her. "There's nothing he could ever say to make that happen."

"He's responsible for the deaths of hundreds of paladins. He's infiltrated cities up and down the countryside—ones with stronger forces than ours. He charms his way in and wins their trust, and then, once he knows their weaknesses, the purple dragons invade. They've taken out several paladin settlements."

I swallow, suddenly feeling sick. "They *what*? How long has this been going on?"

Celeste looks away. "A couple years." She clears her throat. "Almost three."

I gape at her. "And you never told me?"

"We didn't want to scare you."

We. So it wasn't just my sister who thought she needed to protect me. Is that why Torrin knew just how dangerous Amelrik was? Because he'd known about his crimes for years? "But you said Amelrik's from

Hawthorne clan. The purple dragons are from Elder. Are you saying he's working with them?" That doesn't make sense. I mean, it would explain how he knew Lothar, but not why he wanted to kill him. "I thought you said those two clans weren't on good terms."

"I did. Their history is . . . complicated." She looks away as she says it, and I know she's leaving something out, either because she thinks I won't understand or because she thinks it'll scare me. Either reason kind of pisses me off. "And anyway," she goes on, "it hasn't happened for a while. Nearly six months now."

"I could have handled it. I *can* handle it."

"You never leave the barracks. Not since . . ."

"Since I pretty much killed our mother? Yeah, I noticed."

"Vee, you didn't kill her. It wasn't your fault."

It's not my fault that I couldn't save our mother from a dragon, but it *is* my fault that I don't have magic, because I don't want it badly enough? "Yeah, right."

"I mean it. There was nothing you could have done, except get yourself killed, too. You have to stop beating yourself up about it, because it's not healthy, living like this. Never leaving the barracks. But if this is the only place you feel safe, then I didn't want you thinking dragons were going to show up at any moment and murder us all in our beds."

"Then why are you telling me now?"

"Because if you know just how dangerous that criminal is, then maybe you can picture what it would be like if he got out. If he was after you, and the only thing separating you from certain death was your magic, then maybe you could do it. I thought if the danger felt real, then maybe the magic would, too."

"The danger felt real when Mother died. When that dragon transformed out of nowhere and ripped her to shreds. I couldn't do anything then. What makes you think I can do it now?"

"That was a long time ago. And it doesn't matter what happened in the past. We have to keep trying. There's not always going to be someone around to protect you. The only way you're ever really going to feel safe is if you can rely on yourself."

She says it like she thinks I don't already know that. "Fine. Let's try this again." I heave myself up from the bench, stretching my arms and yawning.

"Close your eyes," Celeste says as I approach the dais. "Imagine that Amelrik's escaped. That he's hunting you through these halls, invading the one place you thought was safe. He's stronger and faster than you, and his senses are sharper. And *he's* got magic. He's going to transform into the monster he really is. One swipe of his claw could gut you. One fiery breath could roast you alive."

A shiver runs down my spine. I try to stay focused on the scenario Celeste is laying out for me, but instead of imagining what it would feel like to be sliced open, I can't help replaying Amelrik's words from earlier.

I don't care about you. Maybe Lothar can fake interest in a stinking paladin for a night, but he's always been the better actor.

And, of course, my favorite: *I've always had a soft spot for virgins.*

I remember the smirk on his face as he said that, and rage boils inside me. Amelrik doesn't know the first thing about me. Well, except for the virgin thing, but that's not any of his business. I didn't ask him to save me, if that's even what he did, and I certainly don't owe him anything.

I'm tired of needing people to save me. Whether it's Celeste or Torrin, or now even a freaking *dragon*. I'm tired of them all thinking I'm helpless.

You would have married him if I hadn't been there.

My hands clench around the dragon ring. I grit my teeth so hard I feel like they're going to break. I squeeze the iron collar like it's Amelrik's scrawny neck.

There's a flash of red. A spark that arcs between my hands, then fizzles out and disappears. I wouldn't even be sure I really saw it—maybe thinking about Amelrik made me just that pissed that I was actually seeing red—but a hint of sulfur lingers in the air.

Magic.

I drop the ring and jump back, as if it bit me. It lands on the dais with a clatter, looking like an ordinary piece of iron. Not enchanted. But . . .

"I felt it." I gulp in air like I don't remember how to breathe. Every nerve in my body is alive and on fire and not sure how to feel.

It was just a spark, but it was magic. Real magic.

Celeste's mouth is hanging open. Despite all her pep talks, she obviously can't believe it. Then she shrieks with joy and grabs me in a hug.

"I did it," I say, hardly able to believe it myself. I'm not a dud. All the St. George genes didn't pass me by. And if I did it once, maybe I can do it again.

And maybe I won't have to get married in two weeks.

6

YOU'RE NO PALADIN

The next evening, I march down to the dungeon and straight to Amelrik's cell. I yawn, still tired from staying up until almost sunrise, even though I slept until late afternoon. A fact that got me a stern talking-to from Father, since apparently I was supposed to have lunch with Lord Varrens.

I told him me missing my hot lunch date was probably for the best, since I didn't think I could sit so close to my future husband without ripping his clothes off right then and there. And think how scandalous *that* would be. Then Father turned an ugly shade of purply-red and started shouting at me to go to my room.

I *wanted* to tell him about my success last night, even if it was just a spark. But just a spark isn't a spell. It doesn't automatically make me paladin material, and, anyway, it only happened once. No matter how many times I pictured Amelrik's stupid face telling me how he saved my life, I couldn't re-create my success.

Which is why I'm here in the dungeon, getting fresh material. That, and there's something thrilling about defying my sister's orders not to talk to him again.

Celeste would kill me if she knew where I was. But she left at the crack of dawn with a group of paladins to go hunt down Lothar. She's miles away by now. And even if they catch him right away and come home early . . . Well, she'll be too tired from staying up all night and too happy about hanging his head on the wall to be mad at me. At least, not too mad. And Amelrik might be dangerous, but he's collared and behind bars. What's he going to do to me?

"You really are one to talk," I say, recalling my conversation with him, my voice echoing off the dungeon walls. "You're surprised *I'm* alive? You barely survived that encounter with Lothar. And you got captured by paladins. Great job on that. I've been thinking, and I'm pretty sure the reason you didn't transform is because you're a coward. In human form, you could blend into the crowd. As a dragon, you would have been an easy target, for Lothar and for us."

I pause, but there's no response.

"Did you hear me? I said you're a *coward*. At least Lothar tried to fight—all you did was run."

Still nothing. I stand in front of Amelrik's cell, not getting too close, but unable to see much inside except shadows. Is there even anyone in there?

And then I'm thinking about the scenario Celeste was concocting last night. About Amelrik getting free and roaming the halls, coming after me . . .

Maybe coming down here was stupider than I thought. I glance at his cell door, making sure it's closed and locked. Every little sound has me on edge, even just my shoe scuffing against the stone floor, and for a moment I convince myself that he's somehow gotten free and is right behind me, all claws and teeth, ready to grab me from the shadows and rip me apart.

I clench my fists and get ahold of myself. Even if he did somehow escape, he'd still have the dragon ring on. And if he wanted me dead, he could have let Lothar kill me the other night. I refuse to let my imagination get the better of me, and I move closer to the cell door.

A hand snatches at the bars from the other side, scaring me half to death. I scream and jump back, ready to run. And then I notice the hand is covered in blood.

Amelrik groans as he slowly pulls himself to his feet. He has a black eye and a bloody lip, but it looks like those are the least of his injuries.

"Virgin," he whispers, and there's a catch in his throat, like he's so relieved to see someone, even me, that he might cry.

"It's Virginia," I mutter, glancing away.

"You're here to torture me with words now, is that it?"

"I-I shouldn't have— I have to go."

"No, *stay*." The word comes out desperate, urgent.

The skin around the dragon ring has turned an even deeper red, almost purple, while the ring itself glows like an ember. Every breath has him wincing, though he tries to hide it, and I wonder what other injuries he must have, hidden from my view. His pain makes me uncomfortable, and part of me wants to run and not have to be here, and part of me wishes there was something I could do to help him.

Guilt snakes through my chest. Both for feeling any sympathy for him—he's a *dragon*, after all, and a wanted criminal—and for coming down here to antagonize him.

"It's okay," he says, his voice strained. "You don't have to look at me."

My guilt flares up another notch, and I force myself to meet his gaze. "I know what you did, to get in here. To deserve this."

A short burst of laughter escapes him, then quickly turns into a cough that leaves blood flecked across his lips. "And don't all dragons 'deserve' this in your eyes?"

"You're responsible for the deaths of hundreds of paladins." And even if the dragon ring blocks him from using his magic, he'll still heal faster than a normal person would. His suffering won't make up for what he's done—not that it ever could.

"Am I up to the hundreds now? I've lost count."

"That's it. I'm leaving." I turn to go.

"Wait!" He pauses, racked by coughing. When he speaks again, his voice is hoarse. "Your family's killed just as many of my kind. Why does that make me the criminal? I've never so much as had blood on my hands." He looks down at them, dried blood filling the lines in his palms, and laughs. "Unless this counts."

He's losing it. I feel a twinge of pity, a little warm spot in my chest I know shouldn't be there. But I can't help it.

When he looks up at me, his expression withers, his mouth a thin line. *"Don't,"* he says, his voice suddenly cold, his green eyes flashing in anger. His lip curls in a sneer. "Don't you dare look at me like that. I don't need your *pity*. If that's how you're going to be, then you can just go."

I arch my eyebrows at him. "I don't need your permission to stay or to leave. I'm not the prisoner here. And I don't pity dragons. A dragon killed my mother. He ripped her to shreds right in front of me. So don't think I could ever pity you, even for a moment." Even if maybe I was, just a little.

His mouth hangs partway open, as if he's about to say something, but then he keeps quiet. I can see his teeth. Maybe it's my imagination, but they look slightly sharper than human teeth should. He starts to speak, then has another coughing fit instead. He moves his hand up to cover his mouth, and when he draws it back, I can see blood. His eyes water, and he holds very still, as if the slightest movement will cause him excruciating pain. When he can finally speak again he says, "Have they killed him yet?" His voice is little more than a rasp.

I just stare at him, conflicting thoughts fighting in my head. "That doesn't sound good," I whisper.

"It's *nothing*. And it's nothing compared to what Lothar's going to get. Just tell me if they've killed him."

"I don't know."

"Then you're useless to me."

"Why do you want him dead?"

He flinches, as if my question hurt more than his injuries. "You smell worse today," he says, wrinkling his nose. "You stink like magic. It's making me sick."

"I'm going to take that as a compliment. I'm a paladin, after all, and you're a—"

He scoffs. "You're no paladin. Not really. If you were, they wouldn't have been marrying you off."

I glare at him. "Oh, yeah? And what about you? Getting my sister to fight your enemies for you? Funny that you wouldn't transform the other night, not even to get away, to save your life. Maybe you're not *really* even a dragon."

Something snaps in him—I can see it in his eyes—and then he lunges at the door. I jump back just as he slams against it, his hands grabbing the bars. Then his injuries catch up with him, and he cries out in agony.

My blood freezes in my veins at the sound. It feels like my heart stops, and I wonder why I'm still here, why I haven't left yet.

He wraps his arms around himself and bites his bloody lip.

"Amelrik?" I whisper, after my nerves have calmed down and I feel brave enough to speak.

"If I were in my true form, this would be nothing. *Nothing*. I'd heal up like *that*."

"But you're not," I remind him, even though it's obvious.

"You shouldn't be talking to me," he says, shaking his head. "You shouldn't be anywhere near me."

"Yeah, well, the last thing I need is yet another person telling me what to do."

"If this door wasn't here, if this ring wasn't around my neck . . ."

"But they are."

"And when they're not . . . you stay away from me, Virginia St. George." He swallows and looks me in the eyes, dead serious. "You stay as far away from me as possible."

7

FLUENT IN BEING HUMAN

I run back to the Ceremonial Room where the iron dragon ring still lies on the dais, Amelrik's words fresh in my head.

You stay away from me.

I grip the ring with both hands and squeeze my eyes shut, trying to conjure up my feelings from last night, the ones that made me angry enough to find my spark. He said I stink, that I'm useless, that I'm not even a paladin. All these things should piss me off. And they do, but . . .

My thoughts flick back to the other thing he said. About when he's free of that cell and of that ring around his neck. A dark shiver prickles up my spine and settles heavy in my chest. What did he mean? There's no way he could escape, and even if he did . . .

He was coughing up blood. He could barely stand. Maybe what he said was the pain talking, just the ramblings of a mad dragon with nothing to lose.

I force myself to take a deep breath and focus my thoughts. The dragon ring feels solid and reassuring in my hands. He was just trying to intimidate me, that's all. He's not going to get free. I saw him attack that door—and I heard his screams afterward. Maybe he's a liar, but his screams were real. There's no way he could get out, or get that ring off. Only a St. George can remove it, and that's not going to happen.

Celeste's warning creeps into my thoughts. *He's also a liar. A con artist. The kind of criminal whose weapons are words and trickery.* But I push it away, making a mental note not to tell her where I was tonight. Not that I was going to anyway.

He said I should stay away from him.

A draft wafts through the room, blowing past my ankles. I toss the dragon ring back down on the dais and go upstairs. I head to the Hathaways' set of rooms and knock on Torrin's door.

There's a look of surprise on his face when he answers. Then his eyes dart away guiltily. "Vee . . . I thought . . . I thought you were still mad."

"Oh, I *am*. Don't think this visit means I've forgiven you."

He swallows. "Well, I heard. About your . . ." He bites his lip, struggling to come up with the right words.

"Betrothal?"

"Yeah."

"Don't worry. I'm sure my future husband will keel over our first time together. Before anything, you know, *happens*. Then I'll have fulfilled my family duty."

"Uh . . . *right*." He wrinkles his nose. "Until your father makes another arrangement."

"I'll be in mourning. He won't be able to arrange anything for at least another six months."

"Well, as long as you have it all figured out."

I ignore his sarcasm and push my way into his room. There's a dried dragon claw lying haphazardly on a bookshelf in the corner. The scales are black, but when the light catches them, they shimmer with different colors. I must have seen this thing a thousand times, but I never noticed how beautiful it was. Then I wince, thinking of Amelrik. I imagine how gruesome it would be to walk into a dragon's lair and find a human hand, as if it was a trophy from an animal.

I shake my head, dismissing that thought. Dragons aren't animals, but they're not human, either. They're monsters. I know what they're capable of—I'm the last person who should feel any sympathy for them.

"I'm not here to talk about my upcoming nuptials," I tell Torrin, and I catch a flash of relief on his face. "Last night, I made a spark." I clench my hands, making the shape of an imaginary dragon ring. "It was magic. *Real* magic. From *me*."

"Wow." He blinks at me, too stunned to really say anything. "You're sure?"

"Yes, I'm sure." I glare at him. "How about a little faith?"

"Sorry. I didn't mean it like that. It's just . . . After all this time."

"Believe me, I know."

"But that means you don't have to get married *at all*." He grins. "Forget waiting for some old man to keel over. You can start training with the rest of us! I'll help you catch up."

I shake my head and lean against the wall, staring out his window, which overlooks the entrance to the barracks. The sky is clear, thousands of stars shining down from the darkness. "It was just a spark. Not a spell. And it was just once." I hold up a finger, emphasizing how singular it was. "So, not nearly enough to get me out of this marriage."

He runs a hand through his hair, which is getting too long. "I'm sorry, for the other night. I really am."

"You're sorry for what, exactly?" For saving me from dragon fire, but not from a horrible marriage? For looking at other girls all night at the party and never even thinking of looking at *me* that way?

"Don't be like that. You *know* what I'm sorry for. I shouldn't have said that."

Oh, right, *that*. "You mean when you said I could leave the barracks any time I wanted? That it's *my fault* I can't?"

"That's not what I said and you know it."

"Close enough." It's what he meant. I start to clench my teeth, but then force my jaw to relax. I'm here for information, not to berate him, even if he kind of deserves it. "I have some questions about the prisoner."

"The dragon? I heard you've been talking to him. I couldn't believe it."

"Where'd you hear that?"

"Mina. Celeste told her."

"And she told *you*?" I scowl, not liking that any of them have been gossiping about me. I mean, I guess the gossip could be worse. Maybe I should be thankful the only news spreading about me is that I was crazy enough to talk to a dragon. Not that I was almost duped by one at the party or that my father's arranged for me to marry one of his old-man friends. Someone who probably owes him a favor.

Torrin shrugs and sweeps his hair out of his face. "It doesn't matter who told me—it's true, isn't it? You shouldn't be talking to him. I don't even know why you would. You *hate* dragons. And now everyone thinks you've lost it, because of this marriage, and—"

"I don't care what anyone thinks." Well, I do, but only because I need to know whose wedding invitations to "forget" to write.

"Me neither. But, you have to admit, it really doesn't sound like you."

"And what *does* sound like me? Hiding in my room all day? Waiting for other people to decide my life for me?"

"Prince Amelrik is dangerous."

Prince. There it is again. He didn't seem much like a prince to me, but the only other prince I've ever met was Lothar, and I'm not sure that counts. "Celeste said he infiltrated other cities."

"He did. He's good at acting human. Most dragons can't stay in human form for very long—not without going crazy. It's one of the first lessons we got in paladin training. Usually there are signs. They have to go off into the woods every night. They eat alone. And there's just something . . . *off* about them, like they don't really get how to be human. Like someone who speaks a language but will never be fluent. But he's different."

"You're telling me Amelrik's fluent in being human."

"In *acting* human, but, yeah. That's exactly what I'm saying. It's how he's fooled so many people."

"Has he ever killed anyone himself?"

Torrin purses his lips and gives me a worried look. "He tricked hundreds of people, knowing they would be brutally murdered."

He said he never had blood on his hands. "I just don't understand."

"What? Why a dragon would kill paladins? Vee, you know what they're capable of."

"No, I mean, if Amelrik's such a ruthless killer, why did he save my life at the party?"

Torrin snorts. "He didn't save your life—*I* did. He's the one who almost got you killed."

"He told me to run. He risked his own life to tell me that, even knowing who I was. It just doesn't add up."

"Maybe spending all that time in human form really has made him crazy. I don't know. Can you ever really know what goes on inside a dragon's head?"

Or anyone's, I think, but I keep it to myself. "Why was he at the party at all? Better yet, why were there *two* dragons at the party? And why did Lothar want to dance with me?"

Torrin joins me at the window and stares outside. He's silent for a minute, then lets out a deep breath. "A paladin could be useful to a dragon."

"Exactly. A paladin could. Not *me*. Besides, what did he think he was going to do? Marry me?" I wrap my arms around myself and pace in front of Torrin's bed. He has a brown and green patchwork quilt his mother made him when we were kids. I remember wishing my mother would make me one, too, but she wasn't a seamstress like Mrs.

Hathaway, and I was too afraid to ask. Now of course I wish I had. It would have been one more keepsake to remember her by. I could have wrapped myself up in it and pretended it was her arms around me.

"Vee."

"No, really. It's one thing to dance with me, and yeah, I know my father was hoping for a quick marriage, but did Lothar seriously think he could get away with it? That he'd just put on the charm and I'd fall for it? And I know what you're going to say, that I *was* falling for it, but—"

"*Vee.*"

The urgency in his voice silences me. I stop pacing. Torrin's still staring out the window, only now his face is pale, his shoulders rigid. My voice is little more than a whisper. "What is it?"

"It's the hunting party," he says, his voice filled with dread. "They've returned. But your sister isn't with them."

8

A FATE WORSE THAN DEATH

She got attacked by dragons and was carried off. We believe her to be dead.

The words ring in my ears as I stand in the courtyard with my father and Torrin, listening to the hunting party recount what happened. Justinian, acting as their leader in Celeste's place, keeps his head bowed as he hands my father the burnt, bloody scrap of Celeste's dark blue cloak. All that's left of her.

Tears stream down my cheeks. I'm vaguely aware of Torrin squeezing my hand and the other paladins staring at me and looking guilty. Like it's their fault they couldn't protect her. But nobody ever needed to protect Celeste—she took care of herself *and* everybody else. What they don't know was that it was me. If she hadn't stayed up all night trying to teach me magic, she wouldn't have been off her guard. Celeste is the best—she would *never* have been dragged off.

No, Celeste *was* the best. Before dragons got her, catching her away from the safety of the group, leaving only this burnt-up, bloody piece of cloth behind, and . . .

I squeeze my eyes shut, not wanting to picture the gruesome remains. Not Celeste's and not my mother's.

"We're so sorry," Justinian says, speaking for the whole group. His gray-blue eyes meet my father's, then mine, while the other four paladins bow their heads. A tear slips down Ravenna's face, though she stays silent, as solemn and stoic as the others.

"Celeste," my father says, his voice sounding numb. "You can't be . . ." He looks over at me in disbelief, as if maybe, just maybe, they got the wrong daughter.

I've only seen my father cry once, and that was when my mother died. But now, hard sobs rack his shoulders. He throws any St. George stoicism to the wind and screams, clutching the scrap of Celeste's cloak to his chest. He falls to his knees, repeating, "Celeste. My Celeste. How could this have happened?"

There's blood on the piece of cloak, but maybe it's not her blood. Celeste would have fought, after all. Even if they took her in the end, she would have fought. And she must have, if they resorted to fire. The cloak is burnt around the edges. And I hope Celeste was burnt up by dragon's fire. I hope she was already dead when they dragged her off, saving her from a much worse fate. From the fate that happened to our mother.

That was my fault, and so is this, because I can't wield the family magic. If I could, Celeste wouldn't have needed to stay up late, futilely trying to teach me. And maybe I got a spark—maybe her efforts weren't completely wasted on me—but was it really worth *this*?

I would marry a thousand bony old men if it would bring Celeste back.

Torrin slips his strong arms around me and holds me to his chest when I start to sob. And I hate that I enjoy it—that for a moment I feel safe and loved and like nothing could ever hurt me—because I shouldn't enjoy anything. Not after what happened to Celeste, and especially not when she died because she tried to help me. Because she tried to help me find a way to feel strong and safe on my own.

But I also hate that I enjoy it, because Torrin's not mine. He's just my friend, and while I could see us having a life together, he made it clear he doesn't feel the same way. And I know I'll think about this moment later with longing and regret, wishing I could feel his arms around me again, holding me together when I want to fall apart.

I feel a surge of anger and push away from him. It isn't fair—none of this is. It's not fair that Celeste had to die, or that I can't do magic. That Torrin will never be more than my friend.

"Vee, wait," he says, putting a hand on my arm to stop me.

But I don't stop. I let my anger take over, drying up my tears and making me feel so *alive*. I run back inside the barracks, my feet pounding down the stairs to the dungeon. I run right to Amelrik's cell and kick his door as hard as I can. The impact hurts my foot, but I don't care.

"You monster!" I scream at him, hardly recognizing my own voice. "You're all murderers! All of you!"

Amelrik appears before me, a bewildered look on his bruised-up face, his green eyes staring back at me with curiosity. I lunge at the barred window, slipping my arm inside and clawing at him. My nails slash into his skin just as I feel two strong arms grab me from behind and pull me away.

"What the hell are you doing?!" Torrin says as I struggle to get away from him.

But I ignore Torrin, keeping my eyes on Amelrik. There are a couple of thin red cuts across his cheek where my nails bit into him, adding to his injuries. "Did you know you were sending her to her death?! Was that your plan all along?"

Amelrik's eyes widen. Then he closes them, looking pained. "So Lothar's not dead."

"That's what you care about?! You killed my sister!" As soon as the words leave my mouth, the fight goes out of me and my vision blurs, wobbly with tears. "You killed her! It's your fault she's dead. *Yours.*"

Torrin eases his grip, but he still keeps one arm around me, as if he's afraid I'll try and do something crazy again, like attack a dragon. "It's okay," he whispers, holding me close to him. And then he adds, as if he knows exactly what's on my mind, "It wasn't your fault."

I break down and sob, leaning my head against his shoulder. Every part of me hurts, like my insides have been scraped raw. My sister is gone. I'll never hear her voice or feel all warm when she smiles at me. I'll never watch her put on her armor and look like a goddess of the battlefield as she rides off on a hunt.

Then Amelrik's hushed voice cuts through my thoughts. "Which clan were they from?"

"Shut up," Torrin snarls. "Haven't you done enough?"

But Amelrik acts like he didn't hear him and only addresses me. "Virgin," he says, "listen to me. This is very important. What clan were they from?"

I shake my head, not knowing the answer and not caring.

"Come on, Vee," Torrin says. "Let's get out of here. You can stay with my family tonight—you shouldn't be alone."

I nod, too tired to speak, and let him steer me toward the door.

"Wait!" Amelrik calls. Then his breath catches and he winces, his face going pale. But he clenches his jaw against the pain and says, "You're not *listening* to me. The dragonkin. What *color* were they?"

I rack my brain, trying to remember what Justinian said about the mission. About Celeste. All I remember was feeling the overwhelming loss of my sister. But then his words float back to me. "Purple," I say. "I think they were purple."

"That's right," Torrin says, confirming my answer. He glares at Amelrik. "That *thing* sent them to find purple dragons, and that's exactly what they did."

Amelrik scowls, as if he suddenly got a bad taste in his mouth, but his shoulders sag in relief. "Your sister isn't dead."

A jolt sparks across my nerves. For a moment, I'm not sure I heard him right. *"What?"*

"I know them. If they were purple, then she's alive."

My heart pounds, my blood loud in my ears. I stare at him for a moment, until there's an ache in my chest, and I realize I'm holding my breath. "Why would it matter if they were purple?"

Torrin slips his hand into mine. "Don't listen to him. He's just messing with your mind. It's what he *does*."

"She's a St. George," Amelrik says. "She's too valuable to them."

"Valuable," I repeat, the word tasting strange in my mouth.

"There's a reason Lothar was at your party."

"And how would you know?" I don't know what color Amelrik is in dragon form, but Lothar was from Elder clan, Amelrik from Hawthorne. I think back to what Celeste said, about their clans having an unstable history. But she also implied Amelrik might have been working with the Elder clan. Even though it seemed like he hated them. None of it adds up, and I don't know what to believe.

"I . . ." Amelrik stares down at his feet, something like shame coloring his face. "I just know," he says quietly, not looking at me.

"Right," I mutter. I don't dare let myself believe him, even though there's concern in his eyes that looks genuine, and a conviction in his voice that sounds truthful. But no dragon would carry off a paladin of Celeste's caliber and let her live. And they would have *had* to kill her—she would never have let them take her alive. So even though I want to believe Amelrik with every fiber of my being, I know it can't be true. Whether he's lying to manipulate me or not, I can't let myself buy into it. Besides, he's a professional liar. He might not have actual blood on his hands, but he's responsible for enough deaths, and now Celeste's, too.

"Let's go," I tell Torrin, glaring at Amelrik and turning my back on him. I let Torrin lead me out of the dungeon and up the stairs, and I don't look back.

Not even when I hear Amelrik's voice say, "I'm telling you, she's not dead. At least, *not yet.*"

I hate the little spark of hope that flares to life in my chest at Amelrik's words. A seed of doubt wriggles its way into my thoughts, and I want so badly to believe that my sister is still alive. Even though I can't imagine what that would mean. There was blood on the scrap of her cloak. And it was *burnt.*

But none of that is really proof that she's dead, only that she was attacked, right?

"Don't think about it," Torrin says, his voice hushed, as he leads me upstairs toward his family's rooms. "He said that to mess with us. To get into your head."

I nod, biting my lip. He's probably right. "It's just . . . What if he's telling the truth?"

Torrin pauses in the hallway. I half expect him to gape at me like I'm insane, like I couldn't possibly be the girl he's known all his life, but he doesn't. Instead he looks thoughtful, his forehead wrinkling as he stops to consider that. "He can't *really* know," Torrin says, speaking slowly, sounding like he's trying to convince himself as much as me. "He wasn't there."

"Neither were we. And Justinian and the others, they didn't see her. They think they know what happened, but they brought back a piece of her cloak, not . . ." I swallow, my throat tightening at the thought of what they could have brought back. "It's a cloak. It could have gotten ripped when the dragons attacked. It doesn't mean she's dead."

"Maybe, but the others wouldn't have come home unless they were sure. They wouldn't have just jumped to conclusions."

"They would have searched for her first. And if that scrap of her cloak was all they found—"

"Vee, listen to yourself. Just because they didn't find a body, it doesn't mean anything good, all right?"

"I know." Tears well up in my eyes, and there's a horrible, raw ache in my chest. "But Amelrik could be telling the truth. He said if they were purple, then she's not dead. Maybe he really does know."

Torrin tilts his head in sympathy. His own voice wavers a little as he says, "A paladin getting dragged back *alive* to a dragon's lair is a fate worse than death. Celeste was my friend, and if those dragons took her, I hope she really is dead. For her own sake. And you can hate me for saying that, but it's the truth."

I nod. The tears spill down my cheeks now as I start to cry for real. Because he's right. If a dragon did manage to take Celeste alive, it would only be to cause her more pain before finally ending it. Or maybe to take its time eating her.

A shudder runs through my whole body, and I feel like I'm going to be sick.

If Amelrik was trying to tell me what I wanted to hear, he chose wrong.

And anyway, it doesn't matter what he thinks he knows. I know my sister, and she would have fought to the end. There's no way they could have taken her alive.

Unless . . . Unless taking her alive was their goal all along. Because she was *valuable*, whatever that means. If Amelrik was telling the truth, then there's a chance she's not dead. There's a chance she's undergoing an even worse fate right now, and we're just standing here, not doing anything about it.

9

HURT IS ALL YOU'RE GOING TO GET

Mina Blackarrow and Ravenna Port storm into the library three days later, quickly scanning the room. Mina's beady eyes narrow even further when she spots me.

Both of them are wearing black velvet funeral dresses, and I know exactly why they're here.

Mina marches over and slams her hands down on the wooden table where I'm sitting. "How could you?"

I tighten my grip on the book I'm reading, not wanting to let her see how much she's startled me, and don't look up.

Ravenna sniffs and dabs at her eyes with a blue handkerchief. "She was your own *sister*."

"No," I say, "she *is* my sister. She's still alive."

Ravenna lets out a little gasp and puts a hand to her mouth. She and Mina exchange a look. A pitying one.

"You missed her funeral," Mina whispers. "She would have wanted you to be there."

A hint of guilt creeps through my chest. Celeste would want me to be at her funeral—I know that. But I also know that attending would have been like giving up on her, like admitting she's never coming back, and I couldn't do that. Not when there's still a chance to save her.

"I know it's *difficult* for you," Mina says, implying that I find too many things difficult. "It was hard for us, too. We might not have been her flesh and blood, but we were her sisters in battle." She pauses, shuts her eyes, and then lets out a deep sigh. "Not going to your sister's funeral isn't something you can ever take back."

I slide my fingers along the smooth, worn edge of the table, hoping I'm making the right decisions. "I know. And *when* she's dead, *then* I'll go to her funeral. When she's not being held captive by vicious dragons who want who-knows-what with her and could be torturing her even as we speak, then I'll stop trying to figure out a way to save her."

Both girls stare at me. Mina's face looks suddenly pale, and Ravenna just shakes her head, tears sliding down her cheeks.

"She really has lost it," Ravenna whispers.

"I'm sitting right here," I mutter. "I can *hear* you."

"Celeste is dead, Vee," Mina says soberly, looking me in the eyes. "There's no saving her. And if there was . . ." She scowls at the book on the table, her lip curling in disgust. "If there was, then *this* wouldn't be the way. And you certainly wouldn't be the one to do it. *If* there was a way to save her, it would be dangerous—a paladin's job, not yours. And if you'd been there, you'd know that she's . . ." Her voice gets tight and she squeezes her eyes shut and swallows. "You'd know she's not coming back."

"This book says dragons have held paladins captive before. Did you even see the attack?"

"No, but—"

"Did you find her body?"

"There was blood. *So much.* You've never been out in the field, so you don't—"

"I know I wasn't there. I *know* I'm not a paladin like the rest of you. But I also know that you didn't see it happen. You didn't find any proof that my sister's not alive."

"We brought back her cloak. There was a lot of blood. And burn marks on the ground. And even if we didn't find her, getting carried off by dragons is the same as being dead. No, worse. If she wasn't dead when they took her, then she is now."

"You're just grasping at straws, Virginia," Ravenna says. She puts a hand over mine, trying to comfort me. "We all wish that this didn't happen, but pretending there's a way to get her back?" She shakes her head. "You're just going to make things worse for yourself. You have to let go."

Mina gives me a look of mixed pity and exasperation. Like the last thing she should have to do on the day of Celeste's funeral is try and explain to me why my sister's never coming back. "It's not like she's the first we've lost. Those scaly bastards have taken others. I've seen my best friends—like sisters and brothers to me—get mangled, maimed, eaten, burnt, and occasionally dragged off. And maybe I didn't see the bodies of the ones that got taken, but I never saw them alive again, either. And if that means they're not dead . . ." She shudders. "I don't care what your stupid book says. You don't know what you're talking about."

"Maybe I don't, but Amel—" I snap my mouth shut, stopping myself from mentioning him.

But apparently I wasn't quick enough, because Mina pauses, and then understanding blazes in her eyes. "Amelrik?" she breathes. "Is *that* what you were about to say?"

I swallow and then meet her gaze, even though the anger on her face makes my cheeks burn. "He said—"

"No." She holds up a hand. "Don't even tell me what lies he put in your head. He's a *dragon*. Dragons lie, Vee. And he's also our prisoner. He'd tell you whatever you wanted to hear and give you false hope, just to watch you squirm."

Ravenna wipes a few fresh tears from her eyes. "How could you believe a word he said? And after what happened to your mother?"

I bite my lip, fighting a flicker of doubt. "He wasn't lying."

Mina snorts. "And I suppose he told you that? As if you can believe anything he says. I know for a fact that Celeste didn't want you talking to him."

"I didn't believe him at first. I *wanted* to, but I didn't. But something about the way he said it . . . I couldn't just ignore it, so I started researching." I tap the dusty pages of the book. "There are instances of this happening before, of dragons capturing paladins and keeping them as pets."

Ravenna's eyes widen. Mina grits her teeth and looks ready to chew me out for even suggesting that, but then Ravenna leans in and whispers something to her. Probably something about how she should go easy on me because I'm obviously not in my right mind.

Mina takes a deep breath. "And when your new best friend told you Celeste was still alive, what reason did he give?"

I open my mouth to answer, then consider not telling her. She's not going to believe me, anyway. But getting Celeste back *is* going to be dangerous. And if I can't convince the other paladins to go after her, then there'll be *no one* to save her. And then I really should have gone to her funeral, because all this will be for nothing. "He said she was too valuable to them. Because she's a St. George."

"Why?"

"I don't— He didn't say."

"Of course not." Mina shakes her head, but any anger drains out of her, and she just looks tired. And sad. "He's playing you, Vee. I don't know what he wants with you, but you'd better stay away from him. It's what Celeste wanted. And I know we've had our differences, but"—she pauses, steeling herself for what she's about to say—"I don't want you to get hurt. And if you're talking to a dragon, then hurt is all you're going to get. I think you know that. So, promise us, all right? Promise us you won't ever speak to him again. For Celeste's sake."

I brace myself as I approach my father's study. This is how desperate I am. Because if there's one thing my encounter with Mina and Ravenna just taught me, it's that nobody's going to listen to me. But they'd listen to him. If it was my father, Lord St. George, saying the paladins needed to go on a rescue mission for Celeste, half a dozen of them would already be packing. Nobody would dare tell him they thought he was just crazy and grieving.

And okay, nobody told me that to my face, but I could tell it was what Mina and Ravenna were thinking. I get it—I'm not a paladin, and I feel guilty for what happened to Celeste. And I sort of got my information from a dragon prisoner who's known for lying. Maybe I wouldn't believe me, either. But I *know* in my heart that Celeste is alive. And if it was the other way around—if I was the one captured by dragons—I know she wouldn't give up on me.

I knock on the door, my stomach doing flip-flops, my mind racing, trying to come up with reasons why I *shouldn't* be doing this. My father and I don't exactly get along. I can't think of any reason why he should believe me, except that, besides me, he's the one who most wants Celeste back. And I have to talk to him before he hears the rumor that I'm crazy, which Mina and Ravenna will have no doubt spread to half the barracks by now.

"Come in," he calls, though his voice is soft, broken.

I hesitate, almost turning around and running, but then I force myself to go in. It doesn't matter what happens to me here. Not when Celeste's life is on the line.

"Virginia," my father says, sounding surprised to see me. He's sitting behind his heavy wooden desk, the scrap of Celeste's cloak in front of him. He quickly pulls it out of sight when I come in, like he doesn't want me to see how sad he is, as if that isn't obvious anyway. His eyes are bloodshot, and there are dark circles under them. He looks like he's aged ten years in the past few days.

"Father." I duck my head, acknowledging him. I can't remember the last time I was willingly in this room.

We stare awkwardly at each other for a moment. Then he says, "What brings you here?"

"I . . ." I bite my lip, knowing anything I say is going to sound crazy, but also that this is my only chance to convince him. "It's about Celeste."

The corners of his mouth turn down, his entire body sagging a little. "It was a beautiful ceremony," he says, nodding, and I realize he has no idea I wasn't there.

"I have to tell you something, and it might not make a lot of sense. But you have to listen to me."

His eyes dart toward mine, but he stays silent.

I swallow and go on. "I believe Celeste is still alive."

He winces, as if I'd slapped him. "We had her funeral today."

"I know, but nobody saw for sure that she was . . . not living. And there are all these accounts in the history books of dragons keeping paladin prisoners *alive*." I might be exaggerating there, just a little. I mean, it's true, there were reports that said that, but I could count them all on one hand. "We don't know she's dead."

There. I said it.

He blinks at me. Then his expression hardens. "Virginia," he growls. "You don't know what you're saying."

I wish people would stop telling me that. Not having magic powers and not being able to leave the barracks doesn't make me an idiot. "But I *know*, deep down, that it's true. That she's alive. Don't tell me you don't feel it, too."

"I . . ." He puts a hand over his heart, considering what I've said. "Of course I wish your sister was still—" He chokes up, covering his eyes and pausing to get ahold of himself. "I wish she was still with us. But a few stories in some history books isn't proof of anything."

"You could send a party after her. You *could*," I add, when he raises his eyebrows at me like I've just said something completely insane.

"Send a group of our best warriors to their deaths, is that what you mean?" He folds his hands in front of him and stares down his nose at me.

"You don't know that they wouldn't come back. And Celeste—"

"I *do* know. A hunting party can't take on an entire kingdom of dragons, just as one dragon couldn't bring down the entire barracks. Celeste is gone. It's better if you realize that, Virginia. We must grieve for her. But we must also be strong enough not to endanger the lives of others, no matter how much we wish she was still here."

I taste bitter tears in the back of my throat. He has a point, even if I don't want to admit it. "But I *know* she's out there. We can't just leave her. And if her friends knew she was alive, they'd want to save her, too. You know they would!"

"Enough!" He gets to his feet, towering over me. He rubs his forehead with his palms. "Even if we knew for sure she was alive, it would be foolish for anyone to go after her. And to send anyone on this whim of yours . . ." He shakes his head.

"It's not a whim. It's—" But I can't tell him the truth, that the reason I believe so strongly in this isn't just because of what I feel deep down, but because a *dragon* told me there was hope. Even just thinking it to myself sounds completely stupid. And if I said it out loud, to my father, he'd probably disown me. "I'll make you a deal," I tell him.

That gets his attention. He gives me a curious look. "I didn't know you were in any position to be bargaining with me."

"I'll marry Lord Varrens." The words scrape my throat, not wanting to come out. "I'll marry anyone you want—I'll even move far away, if that's what it takes. And in return, just send someone after her. *Anyone.* A group, a scout. *Please.*"

He presses his fingers together, his lip twisting in a scowl, and sits back down. "You're telling me you're going to do what you are already obligated to do, a matter you have *no choice* in, and all I have to do in return is essentially murder some of the finest paladins of your generation? Brave young men and women who can do what you can't, who know their duties and serve them well, and who would never even think of suggesting something so insolent?"

"I'll marry him willingly," I whisper, ignoring the sting of everything he just said, or at least trying to. "I'll be the obedient little bride you want me to be. No more snide comments or talking about how much I wish it wasn't happening."

He holds out his hands, palms up. Not in surrender, but in a gesture that says he doesn't know why I'm even saying this. "We all feel the loss of her," he says quietly. "So that's why I'm going to forget you said any of this. You're going to march out of here and go back to your room, where you'll remain until the wedding. Which will be tomorrow morning."

"*What?* But I won't be seventeen for another week!"

"Lord Varrens is eager to start your new life together." He looks away as he says it, and I get the impression that this wasn't Lord Varrens' idea, but that my father just can't wait to get rid of me.

"You're going to make me get married the day after my sister's funeral?"

"It will be a quiet ceremony, but a joyous occasion." He says that with so little enthusiasm that it's obvious not even he believes it. "And you will do as you're told. You will obey me in this, just as you will obey your husband after you take your vows."

I feel sick to my stomach. "You can't mean that."

"Of course I can. The ceremony will take place tomorrow, right after the dragon's execution at dawn."

My blood runs cold. "Execution?"

"It's his fault Celeste is dead. He must pay for his crimes."

"And me," I whisper. "Must I pay for my crimes, too? I know you blame me for Mother's death, and now Celeste is gone. Is that why you're pawning me off on someone else so quickly, before I'm even of age? Do you really hate me that much?"

He winces at the word "hate," but I notice he doesn't exactly deny it. "This is a matter of duty. Your sister knew her place in paladin society. It's time you did the same."

"Celeste wanted to question the prisoner. He has information that could be useful to us. Shouldn't we keep him alive, at least a little longer?"

"Questioning him is what got her killed." His voice tightens. His hands clench around the scrap of her cloak. "Now, if you'll excuse me, Virginia, I think you'd better take your leave. You have a wedding to prepare for, after all."

10

ALL BRIDES LOOK GORGEOUS ON THEIR WEDDING DAY

Torrin's mother comes to my room later and helps me try on my dress. There wasn't time to make a new one from scratch, but she's sewn some beads onto the white one I wore to the party. She's also covered up the chocolate stain on the front with a bunch of intricate white roses made of ribbon. Father must have had her working on this for days already.

Mrs. Hathaway puts her hands on my shoulders and smiles at me in the full-length mirror she brought with her. "Don't you look beautiful, my dear? A shame your mother couldn't see you like this."

I stare at myself in the mirror. The beads make the dress sparkle. The cut of the neck emphasizes the curve of my shoulders. And the train she's added to the back makes it look like a real wedding dress. It's beautiful—anyone could see that—but the girl in the mirror looks so unhappy that I don't know how anyone could ever associate the word "beautiful" with her. Brides are supposed to be smiling. They're supposed to look like they're starting their lives, not ending them.

And I know I'm not really beautiful. My chest isn't big enough and my waist isn't small enough and my face is too plain. If I was beautiful, guys would look at me the way they always look at Celeste or Mina or any of the other girls. They would ask me to dance at parties. And maybe their lack of interest has more to do with me not living up to my family name, but still. If I was beautiful, I would know it by now.

"All brides look gorgeous on their wedding day," Mrs. Hathaway adds, as if she can tell what I must be thinking. "Lord Varrens is very lucky to have you."

"But I'm not lucky to have him." The words come out small and bitter. I don't know how I can go through with this tomorrow. Father's going to have to stand next to me and move my head up and down when the priest asks if "I do."

Mrs. Hathaway sighs and pulls me to her in a hug. "You'll make the most of it. It's what we do. My marriage to Torrin's father was arranged, you know. I was as nervous as you are, but we made it work, and then we grew to love each other."

"Mr. Hathaway wasn't a hundred years old."

"Well, no, but . . ." She struggles to come up with a bright side to all this. "At least you won't have to leave the barracks. And he'll be kind to you. It could be worse."

I know I'm supposed to be grateful for that, but is it so wrong for me to want more in a husband? It's great that he's probably not going to be mean or beat me or anything. He's just going to force himself on me and make me bear his children—that's all. "I was supposed to marry someone I love." My voice shakes, on the verge of tears. I always *thought* that was what was supposed to happen, anyway. Even if it doesn't make sense for a dud like me.

"It will be all right." Mrs. Hathaway pats my back. "You'll see. And if you have any questions, about your wedding night—"

"I don't." It's going to be awful. I don't need to go over the details.

She raises her eyebrows. "If you're sure. I know I was terrified. My mother wouldn't talk about it, and all I knew was what little information me and the other girls had managed to put together. So if you change your mind, you let me know."

"Thanks, Mrs. Hathaway. For everything. But I think I'd like to be alone right now."

"Let me help you out of your dress, and then I'll let you be."

I nod, because I don't trust myself to speak.

"You know, I always thought that someday you and our Torrin would . . . Well, never you mind." She waves her hands and starts unbuttoning the dress. "Things rarely work out how we thought."

She can say that again.

It's almost dawn when I approach Amelrik's cell—nearly time for his execution.

He's awake, though his eyes are bloodshot, and I wonder if he's been up all night, like me. We stare at each other through the barred window. The lines from where I scratched him are still visible, though just barely. His black eye has turned yellow and mostly faded, though the skin near the dragon ring around his neck looks worse than ever.

"You're still here," I tell him.

"Sorry to inconvenience you."

"I mean, you didn't escape."

"Not yet. I thought you'd want one last chance to tell me I deserve this." He laughs. Not like he's making a joke, but like he knows these are his last moments alive. The laughter turns into a cough, and he winces, but it doesn't look like he's in as much pain as he was the other day. Or maybe that's just wishful thinking. But there's no blood on his lips, and I know dragons heal faster than humans, even without access to their magic.

I reach a hand into my pocket, feeling the cold iron of the key I stole. "Do you really believe my sister's alive?"

"Do you really believe I sent her to her death?"

I scowl at him. I don't know what to believe anymore. He's killed hundreds of people—a lot of them paladins—but he saved my life. He could have gotten away, but he saved me, and now he's going to die because of it. "You wanted Lothar dead—I believe that much. You thought Celeste could kill him for you, so . . ." I shut my eyes, hating what I'm about to say. "No, I don't think you sent her to her death. Not on purpose."

"Your sister's still alive. It's not something I believe—it's something I *know*."

"How? Your clan and his are enemies, aren't they?"

He bristles at that, his expression turning grim. "It's a long story. Too long." His eyes dart toward the hallway, though no one's coming for him yet.

"But you know where she is? You know where they would have taken her?"

He studies my face. "You'd never make it."

Not on my own. I clutch the key, still in my pocket, letting the metal dig into my hand. I can't believe what I'm about to do. "Why did you save me?"

"I told you. I have a soft spot for virgins. It is still Virgin, isn't it? I keep hearing something about a wedding."

"It's still *Virginia*. And I want the truth."

"You wouldn't like the answer." He moves closer to the door, his hands on the bars. "Are you sure you—" He stops, tilting his head and going very still, listening to something. "They're coming." There's real fear in his voice, despite all his talk before of getting out of here.

His hearing must be a lot better than mine, because I don't even hear footsteps on the stairs yet. The key digs into my skin. It wasn't hard to steal it. No one was guarding it, because no one in the barracks would be stupid enough to release the most wanted dragon in the five kingdoms. No one except me, apparently.

I don't even want to think about what Celeste would say if she was here. Or how much Father would hate me if he knew—more than he already does, I mean. And I wince as I picture the look on Torrin's face if he could see me now.

But, you have to admit, it really doesn't sound like you.

Torrin's words echo back to me. He thinks he knows me so well. But if just talking to a dragon doesn't sound like me, letting one out of prison practically makes me a different person.

But I saw myself in the mirror last night, when I was trying on my wedding dress. I looked like a different person then, too—I just didn't like what I saw. And what I'm doing now might be the stupidest thing I've ever done, or it might be the bravest, but either way, I like this version of myself a whole lot better.

My hands tremble as I hold up the key. Amelrik's eyes widen when he sees it. I try to keep my voice steady and in control, but it shakes a little, making it obvious how nervous I am. "You're not going to die today, and I'm sure as hell not going to get married. I'm going to open this door, and you're going to take me to my sister. We're going to rescue her."

Amelrik opens his mouth to speak, then swallows a mouthful of air instead. When he finally does say something, his face is pained. "I told you to stay away from me. If I ever got free. You don't know what you're doing."

"The next person who tells me that is getting *punched in the face.*" I make a fist. "You saved my life, and now I'm saving yours. You need St. George magic to get that dragon ring off your neck." The skin around the ring is still red and blotchy, looking more and more painful each time I see it. "Take me to my sister, and I'll take the ring off." He might know that I'm not a real paladin, because they're marrying me off, but he doesn't know I don't have the family power. After all, he even smelled magic on me the other day, when I made that spark. And once we find Celeste, I'll tell her how he helped me. I'll convince her to remove it. Which means I'm only sort of lying to him.

He looks like he has something to say to that, but the footsteps of the paladins coming to take him away are approaching—even I can hear them now—and we're running out of time. "You certainly waited until the last minute."

"Yeah, but I'm here now." I glance over my shoulder, then back at him. "Do we have a deal or not?"

"Deal," he says. "Just get me out of here."

11

TOO LATE TO TURN BACK NOW

I fumble with the key to Amelrik's cell. It sticks in the lock, and I have a momentary jolt of fear as I think maybe I grabbed the wrong one. I take it out to try again, but I'm so nervous, and my hands are so slippery, that I accidentally drop it.

Amelrik sucks in a breath, his face strained. He stares at me intensely, as if, you know, his life depends on me not screwing this up. Which isn't exactly helping my nerves.

It also doesn't help that the footsteps on the stairs are accompanied by voices. And of course I recognize them, because I know everyone in the barracks. But why did it have to be Torrin and Mina?

And why did they have to be talking about *me*?

"You should have told your girlfriend to show up for her own sister's funeral," Mina says. "Celeste would have wanted her there."

"She's *not* my girlfriend." Torrin says that a little too quickly.

"You spend enough time with her."

"Not like that. I would *never* . . . Vee's like my sister. She's getting married today, anyway."

"Lucky you. You'll finally be free from having to hang around with her."

My ears get hot, and I can feel my whole face turning red.

"Hurry," Amelrik whispers.

I nod, hating that he's witnessing this, and pick up the key. I tell myself it doesn't matter what they think of me, even if I don't actually believe it. But whatever their opinion—whatever Torrin, my supposed best friend, thinks about me—it's going to get a lot worse if they find me here.

"Aw, it's not like that," Torrin says, though he takes his sweet time about it.

I shove the key into the lock and pray that it turns this time. I can't have grabbed the wrong one. I was careful, and, either way, there's no time for mistakes. It's one thing to let a dragon go, but it's another to get caught failing at it.

"Still," Mina says, her voice getting louder as they get closer, "now that she's out of the picture, half the girls in the barracks will be practically throwing themselves at you."

Wow. She doesn't have to say that like *she's* going to be throwing herself at him. Or like she already is.

The key finally turns in the lock, and the door swings open, freeing Amelrik. My heart races, knowing Torrin and Mina are going to be here any second. There's no way we can fight our way out, and I don't think either of them would be very sympathetic if I told them I was just stealing their dragon prisoner to go find Celeste, who they think is dead. I can picture the pitying way they'd tilt their heads, wondering if I'd completely lost it.

Maybe I have. But it's too late to turn back now.

Amelrik's eyes dart over to the hallway. "Come on," I whisper, so quietly I'm almost mouthing the words. I motion for him to follow me, and we duck into the next cell down, which is empty and unlocked. I ease the door closed behind us just before Torrin and Mina arrive.

"Come on, dragon!" Mina calls as she approaches. "It's time for you to—" Her voice cuts out, a little strangled cry escaping her.

"What's wrong?" Torrin must not have seen yet.

"He's . . . he's *gone*."

"He can't be gone." There's movement, and then the sound of the cell door swinging open, followed by Torrin's panicked voice. "He was here! How could this have happened?!"

"Don't look at me like that! It's not my fault."

"You were the one who put him back in his cell last time, after questioning. Are you sure you—"

"Am I sure? Am I *sure* that I locked up a *dragon*?"

There's a pause, then Torrin says, "Well, are you?"

Mina scoffs. "Come on, he's got to be here." Her footsteps move toward us.

We press ourselves against the wall, staying out of sight of the window.

Torrin follows her. "You really think he's just going to be hiding in a different cell?"

Mina stops on the other side of the door, so, so close to us. "Listen, Hathaway, everyone knows your girlfriend's been talking to him. And she's . . ."

"What, Mina?"

"I can't believe I have to say it. Vee's completely unstable."

I go tense, and it takes effort to keep my breathing steady. Not that I couldn't guess she thought that about me, but hearing her say it out loud to Torrin makes my blood run cold.

Amelrik's right next to me. Close enough that I can feel his shoulder against mine, and the warmth of his body heat. Can he tell how much their conversation is freaking me out?

"Oh, come on," Torrin says. "Vee's a little weird sometimes, but she's not crazy."

Weird? He thinks I'm weird? I mean, I guess I know I am, but *he's* not supposed to know that. Or, at least, he's not supposed to say it. Especially not to Mina Blackarrow, of all people.

"Did she tell you she thinks Celeste's still alive? You know where she heard that? From the dragon."

"I know—I was there."

"He's been filling her head with lies, and she's been willingly talking to him. She was never the same after her mother died, and now dragons murdered her sister, too, and she has to marry that awful old man. I don't know why I have to spell this out for you. She's nuts."

Amelrik shifts his weight a little. I wonder what he makes of all this—does he think I'm crazy, too?—but it's dark in here, and I can't see his face.

"She's not." Torrin's voice shakes. He's pissed at Mina now, despite their flirting earlier, and the way he was so eager to correct her about us not being a couple. "And even if she's had some bad things happen lately, it's *Vee*. She hates dragons. She's absolutely terrified of them. She's the last person who would ever let one go."

Shut up, Torrin. Shut up, shut up, shut up.

"He's not here," Mina says. "I've looked in all the cells. We'd better go report this."

"Did you hear me? I said she wouldn't do this."

"I heard you."

"And?"

Mina sighs. "And, like I said, we'd better go report it."

We wait until they're gone, and then I lead Amelrik out of the dungeon, around the back hallway, and up the staircase to my room. It's the last place I *ever* thought a dragon would be, and certainly not because I brought one here.

But it's also the last place anyone would look for him, and with Torrin and Mina starting up a search, it's not safe to leave the barracks right now. When I decided to bust Amelrik out of jail, I thought I'd have more time. I didn't plan for anyone to find out he was gone until we were well away from the barracks.

Amelrik stands in the middle of my room, his shoulders stiff, not touching anything. He was limping on the way up here, and I wonder how bad his injuries are and how much he's healed over the past few days. He frowns at my wedding dress, which is on a wooden dummy in one corner. He looks like he'd rather be anywhere but here. "You're bringing a boy to your room on your wedding day?" He raises an eyebrow at me. "Is that your plan to get out of your marriage, *Virgin*?"

I can feel my face heating up, and now there's not even the dim lighting of the dungeon to hide behind. "That's not— I just saved your life, you know."

"So you can use me for your own purposes. You made that clear."

"Not like *that*. And if losing my virginity or getting caught with some guy in my room was all it took to get out of this marriage, don't you think I would have done it by now?"

He tilts his head, not believing me.

"My father wouldn't let a little thing like 'the loss of my virtue' or whatever get in the way. He blames me for what happened to my mother. He doesn't want me around—especially now that Celeste's gone." I let my hands fall to my sides, trying to look like it doesn't bother me. Or at least not too much.

Amelrik's staring at me, a concerned expression on his face.

Great, apparently even a dragon feels sorry for me. "Don't look at me like that."

"Like what?"

"Like you *care*." Which he doesn't. "I didn't tell you that so you'd think I . . . Look, my point was that I'm not stupid, okay? If there was an easy way out of this marriage, I would have taken it."

"So instead you're running away with a dragon."

"I'm doing that to save Celeste. I don't know what's going to happen when I get back." Maybe Lord Varrens won't want me after all this, or maybe he'll have died of old age by then.

"*If* you get back," Amelrik mutters. He moves away from the wedding dress and over to my bookshelf.

"Those are books," I tell him. "They have words inside that tell stories or give us information."

He looks at me like I'm incredibly, unbelievably stupid. "I know what books are."

"Oh." Oops. "I just thought . . ."

"You just thought what? That dragons don't have books? Even if we didn't, I've lived among humans off and on for years. And despite how uncivilized most of you are, this isn't the first time I've come across a bookshelf."

"So, you can read?"

He scoffs. "Can I *read*?"

I swallow. "English, I mean. I'm sure you can read dragon language." Though I hadn't thought about it before now.

His eyes widen, and he blinks at me. "Dragon language? Are you serious?"

I have no idea what I've said wrong—at least, not this time—but he's obviously offended. I should probably shut up instead of risking sticking my foot in my mouth again, but I don't. "Well, you can, can't you?" Maybe they don't have a written version, but he said they have books.

"There's more than one 'dragon language.' But yes, I can read Vairlin, my native tongue. And Drost, and some Marish, though I'm kind of getting rusty at it. And I've been speaking 'human language,' as you probably call it, my entire life. I can read it, and—this is really going to shake up your whole worldview—I can even *write*." He mimes scribbling with a pen.

"Okay. So you can read. And write. I didn't know." Maybe he's lived with humans for years, but it's not like I've been living with dragons or anything. "But if you've been speaking English your whole life, why do you have an accent?"

He sighs and flips through a couple of books on my shelf, though none of them seem to interest him. "I don't. *You're* the one with the accent. Everyone outside of the Valley, humans and dragons alike, talk like their mouths are full of marbles."

That's so not what I sound like. At least, I don't think.

There's suddenly a loud knock on the door, and Torrin shouts, "Vee?"

Me and Amelrik both freeze. I share a look with him. Then I come to my senses and motion for him to hide.

He mouths the word *Where?*

"Vee?" Torrin says again. "Are you there? I'm coming in!"

"No! Wait, I'm . . . I'm naked! I mean, I'm changing!"

"Well, that'll scare him off," Amelrik whispers.

I shove him toward the bed, accidentally nudging him in the ribs. Or maybe more like punching him, if I'm being honest. He gasps. His face goes pale, and his eyes water.

So, maybe not that healed, then.

"I really need to talk to you!" Torrin shouts. "It's urgent!"

"Just a second!" I'd meant for Amelrik to hide under the bed, but since he's standing in the middle of my room, looking like it's all he can do just to breathe, that's not exactly going to happen. *"Get down,"* I hiss, pressing on his shoulder.

He seems worried, but he doesn't have a lot of options—none, really—so he sinks down to the floor. I grab my bedspread and throw it over him.

"I won't look," Torrin says, opening the door. "I promise." He comes in with a hand over his eyes. "I swear, Vee, I can't see anything."

I glance over at Amelrik, who looks like a wadded-up blanket and blends in really well with the pile of dirty laundry next to him. If you weren't looking too close, you might not even notice that the wadded-up blanket is breathing. "I'd still feel better if you were facing the door." Though he must really not be able to see anything, or else he'd know I'm fully clothed.

Torrin turns around, letting his hand fall away from his face. "You're not going to like this, but you need to know. So I'm just going to say it."

I rustle some clothes on the floor, trying to make it sound like I'm actually getting dressed. "So say it already."

"The dragon's loose. Me and Mina went to haul him up to his execution, and he was just *gone*. I don't know how it happened. Mina swears she locked him in after the last interrogation session."

"You mean *torture*. Call it what it is."

"We don't know when he escaped. She swears she locked the door, and Justinian's trying to figure out who might have seen Amelrik in his cell since then. But that doesn't change the fact that a dangerous prisoner—a *dragon*—is loose in the barracks. I'm sorry, Vee. I know this must really be freaking you out, and today is, well . . . It's hard enough for you as it is. If you want me to stay—"

"*No.*"

He's quiet a second. "Are you mad at me for something?"

"Am I *still mad*, you mean?"

"I already apologized for what I said."

As if that makes up for it. "It's not that."

"Okay. Is this about the wedding? Because, Vee, you know I— Are you dressed yet?"

I've stopped making getting-dressed sounds. "I'm completely naked. You really shouldn't be here, alone with me, on my wedding day."

He knows I'm lying. At least, I'm pretty sure he does, because he sighs, exasperated, and turns around to face me. "Don't be mad."

"You don't even know what I'm mad about." I take a step to the right, hoping to block his view of Amelrik. Or at least the blanket he's hiding under. Listening to all this.

"You wanted me to marry you." Torrin moves closer and looks me right in the eyes.

I glance away. "'Want' is a strong word."

"I hate that this is happening to you. And I do love you . . . just not like that. Plus, I'm in training."

"Right. I know. You don't have to say it. You don't have to come here, today especially, and rub it in."

"I'm not trying to. But don't resent me for it. You're practically family. I don't want to lose you."

And I'm supposed to . . . what? Reassure him that everything's okay, no hard feelings, and even though he's going to be busy finishing his paladin training, and I'm going to be busy making sons for my new husband, we'll still see each other all the time? He probably *will* have girls throwing themselves at him, like Mina said. Does he seriously want me to hang around and watch that happen, while I've got a baby on each hip or something?

Not that *that's* going to happen, because I'm getting out of here. But he doesn't need to know that part.

"Vee?" he says, when I don't answer him.

"I have to get ready for my wedding. Unless Father wants to call it off on account of a dangerous dragon being on the loose?"

"I haven't heard anything about postponing it. Are you sure you'll be okay here, by yourself? I know how you feel about dragons."

I wish he'd stop saying that. "You can't protect me all the time, Torrin."

"Yeah, but it's like you didn't hear me. Maybe it hasn't sunk in yet. The dragon could be *anywhere*. He could be in the barracks, in your home. Where you *live*."

"Or maybe he left. Maybe he was smart and got as far away from this place as possible."

"He'd need a St. George to remove that dragon ring. And it's not like he knows you don't—"

I speak quickly, interrupting him before he can give away my secret. "He doesn't know where my room is. And sticking around here in the hopes of getting that dragon ring off is a big risk. Don't you think he'd rather be alive?"

Torrin stares at me. "No, I don't. The rings drive them *mad*. It's horrible. He'll go crazy if he has to stay like that."

I almost glance over at Amelrik. Almost, but I catch myself in time.

"He's got to be pretty desperate, and you've been talking to him. I can't understand why. But Mina thought . . ."

I snort. "I don't care what Mina Blackarrow thinks. And even though we never sent out invitations to this wedding, you can tell her she's *not* invited."

He scratches his ear, not meeting my gaze. "She thinks you might have had something to do with the prisoner escaping. I told her that wasn't possible."

"It's not." Guilt tightens my chest.

"Did he seem crazy to you? The last time you spoke?"

"He's a *dragon*. How should I know?"

"Did he ask you to do anything for him?"

"You mean, did he ask me to let him out?"

"No. I know you wouldn't. But maybe he asked you to do something seemingly innocent that was somehow part of his plan."

I shake my head. "He didn't ask me for anything. And even if he did, I don't know how you can think I'd be that stupid."

His shoulders relax a little, and he lets out a deep breath. "I know you wouldn't be. You'd never do anything like that."

"Right."

"I mean, I never thought you'd willingly talk to him, either."

"I was curious about something, that's all. It's not like we were friends."

He makes a face at even the idea of that. "If he mentioned anything that might be helpful—"

"What? Like his hopes and dreams about escaping and not getting *tortured* anymore?"

Torrin scowls. "We did what we had to. We needed information. It's not like he didn't deserve every moment of it, and since when do you sympathize with dragons?"

"I *don't*. I'm just saying it's obvious that he'd want to get out of here." The whole barracks has decided his fate, just like they've decided mine, whether either of us likes it or not. So maybe I do sympathize, at least a little, but that's not why I'm helping him escape. "If you're done insulting me, I have a wedding to prepare for."

"Vee, I didn't mean to . . . You're sure you're okay alone?"

Does it matter? He would let me be alone for the rest of my life, unloved and stuck with a man four times my age who I hardly know, who only wants me so I can bear his children—probably more girls he won't be happy with. And I get that Torrin doesn't like me like that. I can't expect him to ruin his life to save mine.

I just wish he seemed more broken up about it.

"I'll be fine," I tell him.

Torrin looks skeptical about that, and I almost think he's going to argue some more. But then he gives in and says, "Don't leave this room. Not until someone comes to get you for the wedding. And put something in front of the door."

"Yeah, sure."

"I mean it, Vee." He sounds so serious, like he really is worried about me, even if he's worried about the wrong thing. "Amelrik might come looking for you. The last thing I want is for you to be alone here with him, unable to protect yourself."

12

THE BEST KIND OF TRICKERY

I pull the blanket off of Amelrik. He pushes himself to his feet, wincing a little but obviously recovered from me sort of punching him in his not-fully-healed ribs. He stares at me. I stare back, wishing he hadn't heard that conversation.

"I didn't want to marry him." The words taste like a lie, no matter how much I want to pretend they're true. "It's not like I— I don't *like* him that way. But he's my best friend, and I didn't have a lot of prospects."

Amelrik snorts.

"What?"

"Nothing."

"No. You don't get to judge me like that and not say anything."

"Some friend." He shrugs. "No wonder you jumped at Lothar like you did."

"I didn't—" I clench my fists, swallowing the denial. "Lothar was the only suitor even close to my age." Or with any decent hygiene. If "suitor" is even the right word. I'm still not sure what he was doing there—what either of them was doing there—but trying to marry me probably wasn't it. "And Torrin *is* my friend."

"Did I say he wasn't?"

"You implied it. But it's none of your business."

"You made it my business when you decided to run away with me on your wedding day."

"Don't say it like that. That's not what's happening here. You don't know anything about it."

"I might not know the details, but you can't say I don't know *any-thing* about it. I've had to listen to two conversations about it today alone. Well, about you and him. And there really doesn't seem to be a 'you and him,' if you know what I mean."

"Don't. It's bad enough that Torrin came in here and said that." As if I didn't already know. As if he hadn't made that perfectly clear before. "I don't need you to—" I narrow my eyes at him. "What do you mean, today alone?"

"You think this was the only time some paladins have come into the dungeon, gossiping?" He sits down on my bed—a dragon, *on my bed*—and gingerly presses his fingers to his ribs.

I hadn't thought about it. "You mean Mina and Torrin?"

"Lots of people."

"And they were talking about me?" I can believe that they were—of course they were—but I can't believe I'm finding out like this. "Whatever they said, it doesn't mean you know me or what's going on in my life."

"I know what I've—" He stops in midsentence, suddenly catching sight of the mirror on my nightstand. It's a hand mirror, the kind that looks sort of like a hairbrush, except with glass instead of bristles. He snatches it up and stares at himself.

"Hey!" I yank it away from him and hold it close to my chest. "That was my mother's!" My stomach twists. A dragon killed my mother, and now I let one touch something of hers. I let one *into my room*.

I sink down next to him on the bed. I hate how petty and selfish I'm being, but I also hate feeling like I'm dishonoring her.

Amelrik's expression is so pained, I could swear he looks worse off than when I punched him in the ribs. He presses his hands to his face.

Okay. Now I'm pretty sure there's a dragon *crying* in my room. The most dangerous criminal in the five kingdoms. "Sorry. It's just . . . I think the only other person who's touched it besides me is Celeste."

Amelrik nods.

"Are you crying because I was so grabby? Or because of how you look?"

"I'm not crying." He lets his hands drop long enough to prove his point, then puts them back, taking in a deep breath.

And all right, I guess he's not technically crying. But he's obviously not okay, either. "You don't look that bad. I mean, the bruises on your face are at that rotten-fruit stage, where they're all yellow and brown. Which doesn't look great, but you'll heal. And . . ." I almost mention the scratches on his face and how they're not even that visible, but since I'm the one who gave them to him, I decide not to. "That red bit of your hair is growing out, and I can see the roots, but it looks fine like that. I think you could even let it grow out all the way, and—"

"*No.*"

"Okay. Fine." I want to ask him why it matters, because obviously it does, but I don't want him to think I care. Plus, it's probably some dragon custom that everybody knows about except me, and then he'll look at me like I'm the stupidest person alive again. "I didn't say you had to. Just that if you did, it still wouldn't look bad."

"This isn't about how I look. Not my face, I mean."

And then I know what he must have seen in the mirror that bothered him so much, even before he gestures to his neck. To the dragon ring.

It looks really bad. I knew that already, but seeing it up close is even worse. Swollen, blotchy, red patches creep up and down his neck, reaching under his skin with twisting fingers. There are still marks where he must have scratched, though they're open and oozing now, instead of healing like the rest of him.

I have no idea what to say. I'm sure if I open my mouth, it'll be the wrong thing. Not that it matters, though, right? He's a dragon, and he deserves this. Except those thoughts don't sit right with me. I don't know if he deserves it or not, and it's hard to sit next to someone who's so obviously upset and do nothing.

He's also a liar. A con artist.

You can't trust a single thing he says.

Celeste's words come back to me, and I can't help wondering how true they are. Amelrik never asked me for anything, just like I told Torrin. He didn't ask me to free him, and I believed the fear in his eyes when he thought he was about to be executed. But now here we are. He's free, just like he said he would be.

And wouldn't that be the best kind of trickery? If the person being tricked never even knew it had happened? If they thought the whole thing was their idea?

A chill runs down my spine. Everything he's ever said to me could have been a carefully orchestrated lie. One that *everyone* warned me about, and I didn't listen.

And yet, if he's telling the truth, then this is my only chance to get Celeste back. There's also no way I'm staying here and getting married to Lord Varrens. I'm running away today, with or without Amelrik.

I glance over at him. He's staring at his hands now, inspecting the blood that's stained the lines of his palms. "Don't worry, Virgin," he says, not looking up. "I haven't gone mad."

Not yet, he means. "So it's true. What Torrin said."

"You really don't know anything. No wonder they're marrying you off."

"I know that a dragon killed my mother. Right in front of me, in the marketplace. We *knew* him. We thought he was human. That's what you do, right? That's *your* specialty—pretending to be human and getting people to trust you. But one day he transformed and ripped her to shreds. So maybe all dragons are mad to begin with, even without the rings."

Amelrik studies my face. His eyes are still bloodshot, and the red makes the green of his irises that much more vivid. "I never asked you to trust me. I never asked anyone to."

"But everyone that has . . . they ended up dead, didn't they?"

He looks away, which is as good an answer as any. "I did what I had to. Just like I'm doing now. Just like we both are."

"I'll take the ring off as soon as we find Celeste."

"And then there'll be another St. George free in the world." He makes a disgusted sound. "She's the one who put this ring on me. She's the one who did this." He gestures to his chest, to whatever's wrong with his ribs. "And your *best friend* did this." He points to the bruises on his face, then to his right leg, the one he was limping on. "Some company you keep. And now, in order to get this ring off, you'd make me help her."

"She's my sister. She's all I have. Whatever she did to you . . ." I swallow. "It was her job. It's what she had to do." Even if it was awful.

He scoffs. "They wanted to know how to find Lothar. I *wanted* them to kill him. I was counting on it." He mutters that last part, then shakes his head. "I would have told them without the beating."

"But you're a liar. You've built up a reputation for conning paladins and getting them killed."

"Good thing you're not one of them, then, eh?"

"The truth comes from pain." It's a paladin saying.

Amelrik's eyes blaze. The reddish light of the dragon ring glows brighter. He scoots away from me, then jumps up from the bed, like he can't stand to be next to me for even one more second. "And how much truth did my mother have left when you St. Georges were done with her? How much?! Your mother might be dead, but at least you knew who she was. You knew that she—" He swallows down the words, not finishing whatever he was about to say. "There are worse ways to die than being ripped apart. There's the slow, lingering kind of death, the kind that eats away at you, bit by bit, until not even a shadow remains of who you used to be. Only lies come from pain—not the truth."

"I didn't know. About your mother. I'm sorry."

"Don't be. You didn't have anything to do with it."

"How do you know?" Not that I want him to think I go around torturing people's mothers. Or anyone, really.

"You probably weren't even born yet. And it didn't happen here."

"Still. That's horrible."

"Just promise me something. Don't let me die with this ring on. And if something happens, if I . . ." He presses his forehead to the wall for a second, then looks back up at me, his eyes meeting mine. "If I go insane, if I start to lose it, promise you'll kill me."

"*What?*"

"Just promise me. Because I'd rather be executed today than live knowing what I might do if I end up like her."

"Okay." My voice shakes, and it doesn't sound much like a promise.

"Okay, what?"

I feel sick as I say the words. "If you go crazy, I'll—I'll kill you. And I won't let you die with that ring on." Two promises I know I can't keep.

But Amelrik nods, seeming satisfied, and I just hope it doesn't come to that.

13

JUST BECAUSE I WAS SUPPOSED TO DIE TODAY DOESN'T MEAN IT'S OKAY TO GET ME KILLED

I take Amelrik up to the wall that surrounds the city. We don't even have to leave the barracks to get there, and then it's just a matter of creeping a little ways over to the spot closest to the river. They haven't stopped the search for him yet, but I'm supposed to be at the altar in half an hour. I should be putting on my dress right now—no, I should already have it on—and we don't have time to wait.

From up here, I can see the forest stretching off to the east. There are mountains in the distance. Some of them are farther away than others, obscured by more and more layers of mist. I take a deep breath, savoring the view, because who knows if I'll ever see it again.

Plus, looking out at the mountains is way less scary than looking down at the river rushing below us—kind of really far below us, actually—like Amelrik's doing.

"You must be used to this."

He frowns. "Used to what? Jumping to my death?"

"Yeah. Well, no, but you must get to see everything from up high all the time. This must be nothing to a dragon. Just another ho-hum breathtaking view from above."

"Right. Ho-hum." He gazes out over the trees and sighs, and the longing in his voice is unmistakable.

He probably wishes he was flying right now, and here I am, rubbing it in. I wonder what he looks like, in dragon form, and what it would be like to fly. Maybe if I had wings, leaving the safety of the barracks would be easier. If I could just take off, go wherever I wanted, and then zoom right back as soon as anything bad happened . . .

The thought of that kind of freedom makes my stomach drop. It's exciting and terrifying all at the same time. But the idea of leaving the barracks at all—wings or no wings—is overwhelming, and when I look down at the river, my vision blurs and I feel like I'm going to throw up. A wave of dizziness hits me. I lose track of which way is up, and my legs start to buckle.

Amelrik grabs my arm to steady me.

"Let go," I snap, trying to jerk away out of instinct.

He keeps his hold on me. "Are you afraid of heights?"

"I come up here all the time. I just . . ." *I just can't handle the thought of leaving.* It's not even like I want to stay here. Two dragons infiltrated Celeste's party only a week ago, and now one escaped from prison. And, okay, I'm the one that busted him out, but still. Any illusions of safety the barracks held are broken. Torrin will never love me the way I want him to, Celeste is missing, and my father can't get rid of me fast enough. If I stay, I'll have to marry Lord Varrens. I'll have to let him climb on top of me and do whatever he wants to me, and I'll have to bear his children. If I don't leave the barracks *right now,* that'll be my life. Forever.

I'd rather face whatever unknown dangers wait beyond the city walls. Or at least I tell myself that, and logically, I know it's true. But my body doesn't respond to logic, and my chest gets tight.

I'm going to suffocate. I can't get enough air.

And Torrin thinks this is a choice. That I could just decide to be normal and leave if I really wanted to.

"Hey," Amelrik says. "You're still on the wall. It's okay."

I nod, trying to calm down enough to breathe properly again.

"Though this is kind of a stupid escape plan if you're afraid of heights."

"It's *not* that. And shut up—this plan is saving your life."

"Not if you freak out to death before you take this ring off."

"I'm not going to freak out to death. That's not even a thing." Or at least I'm not going to let it be a thing for me. "It's just that something really bad happened the last time I left the barracks." There. I said it.

Instantly, I wish I could take it back, even though it's not like I even told him that much. But I'm so tired of everybody knowing that about me. Judging me for it. Is it so bad if I want to keep just one person in the dark?

Amelrik gives me a questioning look, but I don't elaborate, and he doesn't push it.

Probably because he doesn't actually care that much, but it's still a relief not to have to explain myself.

My chest isn't tight anymore, and I can breathe okay again. Amelrik's still got his hand on my arm. I glance down at it, then up at him. He realizes I don't need his help anymore—er, not that I ever actually needed it—and quickly lets go, taking a step away from me, as if to emphasize the fact that he didn't enjoy having to touch me.

He tests out his right leg, the one with the limp, putting more weight on it, then stretching it out. He peers down at the water again. "You know, just because I was supposed to die today doesn't mean it's okay to get me killed."

"It's fine. Celeste and her friends used to jump in from here."

"Used to?"

"Well, until Mother found out, and then she nearly flayed them alive. But no one ever got hurt. Of course, that was in the summer . . ." When the water was a lot calmer.

Amelrik eyes me with suspicion. "It's spring."

"And what? I should have waited a couple months to rescue you?" I can't control what season it is. Or how fast the water's moving . . . Maybe this *is* a bad idea.

"We should jump together." He reaches for me.

"What?! No!" Panic flares in my chest, and I pull away, as if he was actually about to drag me down. Away from the barracks. Before I was ready.

But I'll never be ready.

"Then you have to jump first," Amelrik says. "Because if I go, and you chicken out—"

A shout from the courtyard interrupts him. "It's the dragon! And he's got the St. George girl!"

The St. George girl? Really? I glance down to see who it was and recognize Liza, one of the scullery maids who serves in the barracks. I see her, like, almost every day. She *knows* my name.

Amelrik says something in a guttural language I don't know—though it's not hard to guess that it's some kind of expletive—and grabs my arm. "Hold your breath!"

"No, wait! I'm not ready to—"

But it's too late.

He leaps off the wall, toward the river, dragging me with him.

14

DO I LOOK LIKE A WILD ANIMAL TO YOU?

The first thing I know about the water is that it's *cold*. So cold it seeps into every part of me, making my bones ache.

The second thing is that it's moving way too fast, and this was a terrible, horrible idea.

The river drags us along with it, pulling Amelrik away, so he no longer has hold of me. Water rushes over my head, getting in my mouth, and then it sucks me under. I haven't been swimming in years, and even if I had, this is way beyond my skill level.

I fight against the water, but it's so much stronger than I am. The cold slows me down, too, making it hard to keep moving. I struggle to the surface—or maybe the river pushes me up—just long enough to gulp in new air, and then I'm under again.

This time, the water holds me down. I can't get back to the top, and won't everyone feel stupid if I actually die the first step I take after leaving the barracks? But my lungs scream for air, and now I'm not just fighting the water, but against myself, because every instinct I have is telling me to breathe.

I don't know how much more I can take, and then I feel an arm around me. It's warm, despite how cold the water is, but that thought barely registers. All I care about is that someone pulls me to the surface. As soon as the air hits my face, I gasp for breath.

The world makes a lot more sense now that I'm actually breathing, and I realize Amelrik's the one with his arm around me, dragging me sideways through the turbulent water.

We don't so much get to shore as we do crash into it, and then we crawl onto dry land.

"What the hell was that?!" I'm shaking. From the cold, from almost drowning, from the fact that that stupid leap was the biggest step I've taken in years. Both literally and figuratively. And it wasn't even my choice.

Amelrik's on his hands and knees. His face is pale, except for the blood dripping from a gash on his forehead. He coughs up some water and glares at me. "You're welcome."

"You had no right to do that!" I want to hit him, but instead I draw my knees up and wrap my arms around them.

He flops down on the ground, breathing hard, still trying to catch his breath. He looks pained each time his chest moves. "Why? Because that's twice I've saved your life now?"

"You jumped! And you dragged me down with you! Who told you to do that?!"

"And I was supposed to leave you on the wall? I don't think so."

"I was going to do it. I was going to jump on my own." I want so badly for that to be true, even though I'm not sure I believe it. And now here I am, outside of the barracks for the first time in years. The sky's way too big. The trees are too tall. The whole world looms over me, heavy and encroaching, like it's just waiting for its chance to crush me.

Amelrik sits up, watching me like I'm crazy. Blood from his forehead runs across his face. He wipes it from his eyes with the back of his hand. "We need to get going. The river gave us a head start, but they'll be coming for us."

I nod, knowing he's right, but I don't move.

He gets to his feet, his movements stiff, and I wonder what it cost him to fight against the river like that. To save me when he could have easily let me drown.

"Thanks," I whisper, staring at my knees when I say it.

"Don't. I didn't do it for you." But he doesn't look at me when he says that, either. "Come on. Let's go."

My arms and legs don't want to move. It's more than just the cold from the river. This is it. Amelrik might have made the leap for me when he dragged me off the wall with him, but now I have to get up and take that first real step. I have to leave everything I know behind and head off into the unknown with a *dragon*.

He never asked me to trust him, but what choice do I have?

Amelrik holds out a hand to help me up, since I'm taking so long.

I think about refusing, to prove I can do this on my own, but in the end I decide I have to pick my battles, and this isn't one of them. His skin is warm, even though mine's freezing. Part of me doesn't want to let go of him—because he's warm, because even though he's a dragon, he's *someone*, and I don't know if I can do this alone—but the last thing I'm going to do right now is cling to him. He saved my life because he needs my help. It's the same reason I saved his, and it doesn't mean either of us actually cares about the other.

I let go of him and take that first step.

By sunset, I'm miserable.

Like, totally and completely.

And I can definitely say that this has been the longest day of my life, and not just because I didn't sleep last night.

We travel all day, though at least we're not going too fast. I kind of thought Amelrik would be the type to outpace me the whole way, but he's limping too much for that. His limp gets more pronounced as the day wears on. Jumping in the river probably didn't help. Neither did not eating, and I, for one, am *starving*. And exhausted. And I accidentally stuck my hand in tree sap earlier, and it won't come off. Now it has a thin layer of dirt stuck to it, and that's not coming off, either.

"This is it," I tell Amelrik, stopping in a tiny clearing that looks like as good a place as any to spend the night. And if we don't rest soon—or, like, right now—he's going to have to drag me, because I don't think I can keep this up. "Right here. The perfect camping spot."

"What makes it perfect?"

"It's where I'm standing, and I'm too tired to go another step."

I think for a second that he's going to argue, but then he just looks relieved to have an excuse to stop for the night.

We didn't bring any supplies—there wasn't anything *to* bring, since I was stuck in my room—so there's no camp to set up. Our idea of making camp is pretty much just slumping to the ground. Which is cold, by the way. Not nearly as cold as the river was, but it's not what I'd call comfortable, either. I sit with my back against a tree, even though I'm pretty sure it means a spider is going to crawl into my hair or something. And while that will totally creep me out if it happens, I'm an adventurer now. And worrying about spiders getting in my hair doesn't sound like something a badass adventurer would do.

Or any kind of badass, really.

My stomach growls. My head hurts from not eating and from exerting myself so much today. "So, I know you can probably still see well enough in the dark and everything, but don't feel like you have to wait that long. Because I'm really hungry now."

"What?"

"There's no way you're not starving, too."

"Yeah, but I don't know why you'd think I'd have any food. I've spent the past week in a *dungeon*."

"Right, right. I don't expect you to have any food—I expect you to *go get* food. You know, hunting and stuff?"

"What?"

"Stop saying what."

"I will when you start making sense."

I pick at the sap stuck to my hand. "Neither of us brought anything to eat, and you're a wild animal. Wild animals hunt for their food. So . . . get to it."

He makes a noise that's half scoff, half laugh. "I'm a what?"

"A wild animal."

"Do I look like a wild animal to you?" He gestures to himself, fully clothed and all that, which I have to admit is not very wild-animal-like.

"Not right now. But you are a dragon, so go catch a sheep or something."

"A sheep. Here, in the woods. With what? My bare hands?"

Okay, so maybe I didn't think this through.

"Just take this iron ring off my neck, and I'll gladly go look for a sheep for you."

"That's not happening. But you've still got more experience than me. You know, going on adventures. How do you usually eat?"

"At the table. My 'adventures' don't usually involve roughing it in the wilderness."

"Well, that's just great."

"And I'm not a wild animal."

Now he tells me. I mean, I guess I sort of knew that—he is a prince, after all, as hard to imagine as that is—but I just assumed that he'd know what to do. "If we can't eat tonight, can you at least make a fire? It's getting cold." At the barracks, it would still be warm out, even after dark. It's only twilight now, though it's fading fast, and I'm already feeling the chill. Goose bumps prickle along my arms.

"No fire. It might give us away, if anyone's still looking for us."

If? Of course people are looking for us. They think I got hauled off by a wanted criminal, right? They wouldn't just give up. Not that I want anyone to find us, but I at least want them to *care* about finding us. About finding me.

"Okay, so no food and no getting warm."

"It's not cold."

"Easy for you to say." I remember how warm his skin felt, even while in the freezing river. So maybe dragons don't really get chilly or anything, even in human form.

"Just go to sleep. We'll find food in the morning. Or we'll be dead, because we didn't cover enough ground. Well, I'll be dead. You'll be dragged back home."

Where I'd have an awful lot of explaining to do. But I don't think anyone's going to find us. He's just being paranoid, which I guess I would be too if getting found meant my death. It's not like we could have gone any farther tonight, anyway. We're both exhausted, and I can't see in the dark. Picking my way through these woods was hard enough in daylight.

Amelrik lies down on the ground. The dragon ring chokes him a little bit, and he has to shift around until he finds an okay position.

I stay huddled next to my tree. It's almost completely dark now, and no matter what he says, it *is* getting cold. I wonder how far I am from the barracks, from home—because even if there's nothing for me there, that's still what it is—and suddenly I feel so utterly alone. It hits me fast, sharp as a sword, and then I'm glad it's so dark out, because tears spring to my eyes.

I've never spent a night outside of the barracks. Even before my mother died and I refused to leave them. I've always been surrounded by people I know, by familiar rooms and hallways. There are no rooms here. There's nothing even remotely familiar.

Hot tears slide down my cheeks—at least they're warm—and I wipe them away with the back of my hand and get a whiff of pine sap. I probably just smeared dirt across my face.

I can't take the silence, the feeling that I'm in a void. I hope my voice doesn't give away that I've been crying. I also hope Amelrik's not asleep already. "So, you're really a prince?"

"Why, Virgin? Do I not seem regal enough to you?" His words are bitter, defensive.

"You're not what I expected. I mean, for a prince to be like. Not that I've ever met one before—well, not before you and Lothar—and I certainly don't know what I expect a *dragon* prince to be like. But . . . no. Not really."

"My father is the king of Hawthorne clan. My mother, the queen. That makes me a prince, last time I checked."

"Your mother? I thought your mother was . . ." I try to think of a tactful way to say it, but I hate when people dance around the subject. Euphemisms don't make it any easier. "You said she died."

There's a pause. Kind of a long pause, and I think maybe I offended him, after all. But then he says, "She was still a queen."

"So, are you, like, going to inherit the throne?"

"What I'm going to do is *sleep*. I suggest you do the same."

Which I take to mean no, he's not going to inherit. That or he thinks I'm being too nosy. But I don't care if I am—I'm alone with him, out in the woods, and I think I have a right to know who I'm traveling with. "How do you know Lothar? Because the two of you obviously have some kind of history, but your clans are enemies, right?"

He sighs, loudly, making it clear he's annoyed. "I lived with Elder clan for nearly six years as part of a political hostage exchange. It kept the peace, more or less. For a while."

"You were a *hostage?*"

"A political hostage. I wasn't kept in chains or anything. I am royalty, after all. I lived with the Elder king's family, as a guest."

"And Lothar lived with your family?"

He laughs. "Oh, no. Not him. The prince of Elder clan was far too valuable to be traded away. Not him, and not his sisters. It was a cousin, someone royal who wouldn't be missed too much if anything happened to him. But my father had no problem trading *me.*"

"That sucks. You had to have been pretty young, right?"

"I was fourteen. It was the right choice."

"But still. I know what that's like. My father traded me away, too. And . . . it just sucks, whether it's the right choice or not."

There's another long silence, and then he whispers, almost so quietly I don't hear, "Yes, it does."

I close my eyes, not feeling nearly so alone now. I start to drift off, but before I can actually fall asleep, a thought wakes me up. I open my eyes again, even though it's too dark to see.

Amelrik said he lived with Elder clan. Past tense. I doubt that they would have made some kind of permanent peace, and I admit I don't know a whole lot about this kind of thing, but I really don't think they would have just let him go.

But he's here, my prisoner, not theirs.

So what happened?

I start to ask as much, but his breathing is slow and steady, and I realize he's already asleep.

15

KILLING DRAGONS IS SORT OF HIS JOB

I wake up feeling warm and safe, and it takes me a second to remember that I'm not in my bed. Well, the ground isn't exactly comfortable, or anything like my bed, so it's not a difficult conclusion to make. But there's a moment where I don't remember anything that happened yesterday, and then it all comes flooding back.

Breaking a dragon out of jail. Leaving home with him.

Curling up with him last night to stay warm.

Wait, *what?*

Amelrik's arm is draped over me. I'm lying with my back to him, his body pressed against mine, and I can feel his breath on my neck.

Okay, I vaguely remember deciding that sleeping sitting up against a tree was overrated sometime last night, after I kept waking up with a crick in my neck. I remember lying down beside Amelrik. But this clearing is small enough that it would have been impossible *not* to lie down next to him. So that part's not my fault. But he was asleep, and I was so cold, and maybe I parked myself a little closer to him than necessary.

But not *this* close. And I didn't force him to put his arm around me or anything.

Still, maybe I can slip away without waking him up, and then nobody has to know this happened. I'll just act totally normal, and Amelrik will never know.

"Get away from him, Vee."

Torrin's voice startles the hell out of me. Not just because I had no idea anyone else was here, but because of the hostility in it.

Amelrik's definitely awake now. He mutters something unintelligible—or maybe just not in English—and jerks away from me.

So much for no one finding out. I can't tell if he's as embarrassed as I am to have woken up huddled together like that, but I guess he has bigger problems, like Torrin holding a sword to his chest.

I sit up, knocking pine needles off of myself. Torrin is *not* happy. That's clear from everything about him, from the way his shoulders are bunched up to the betrayed look on his face. Oh, and, you know, the fact that he's about to kill Amelrik. But killing dragons is sort of his job, so maybe that doesn't count.

"This isn't what it looks like," I tell him. Even though I'm not exactly sure what it looks like.

"I spent all night tracking you." He says that to me, though he keeps his eyes on Amelrik. "The others gave up, but not me. Oh, no. I was so worried about you! I left you alone in your room when I knew there was a dragon on the loose. And if something had happened to you, I don't know how I'd . . . I thought he kidnapped you! And then I find you like *this*! With him." Torrin practically spits the words.

"For the record," Amelrik says, "she kidnapped *me*."

"Shut up." Torrin puts more pressure on his sword, showing he means business. "I ought to cut out your heart right now."

"Don't!" I scramble to my feet, wishing I could put myself between them, but it's too late for that. Way too late.

Torrin gives me a look full of disgust. And pity. "What were you thinking, Vee? Letting a dragon out of prison? Helping him escape? I don't know what lies he told you, but I know this isn't you. You wouldn't do something like this. Not unless—"

"Unless what? Unless someone tricked me into it?"

"You hate dragons."

But I don't hate this one. The thought flashes through my head, and I realize it's true. "I can think for myself. I don't need you or Father"—or even Celeste—"doing it for me. Just because I'm doing something you don't like doesn't mean it wasn't my choice."

"He told you Celeste is still alive. And you wanted to believe it so badly, you'd do anything he said. I wanted to believe, too, but it's a lie he told to manipulate you. Go on, dragon." Torrin slides the tip of his sword up to Amelrik's neck, angling it just below the dragon ring. "Tell her the truth so we can go home."

Go home? Is he serious? I didn't leave the barracks for the first time in four and a half years and tromp through the wilderness until I was ready to collapse yesterday just to turn around and go home.

Amelrik's eyes find mine, searching for something. "She doesn't want to leave with you, paladin."

Torrin grimaces at that and pushes on the sword point until blood trickles down Amelrik's neck. "The truth. Now."

"Torrin, stop!"

Amelrik gives him a defiant look. "What does it matter? You're going to kill me no matter what I say."

"Torrin!" I try to shove him back a step, away from Amelrik, but Torrin's a lot stronger than I am, and he resists. "Let him go—I *need* him!"

That gets his attention. He actually looks over at me.

"To find Celeste, I mean."

"Celeste is dead. And if you go after her, you're going to get yourself killed, too."

"At least it'll be my choice! Father had my whole life laid out for me. If I go back, I'm going to have to get married. And maybe that doesn't sound so horrible to you, but it's not okay with me. Having someone I don't care about, that I *despise*, force himself on me every night?!"

Torrin winces at the words "force himself."

"To have to spend the rest of my life with someone like that?" Or, in Lord Varrens' case, the rest of his. "Trapped and unhappy and . . ." *Unloved.* "What part of that sounds even remotely okay to you?"

Torrin steps back from Amelrik, lowering his sword. "I know it's horrible, Vee. You think I don't know that? That I actually want that for you? But you're not a paladin, and there's nothing to . . . I don't know what you expect."

I fold my arms across my chest and turn away, refusing to look at him. "I have to find Celeste. If there's even a chance that she—"

"He's lying to you!"

I glance over at Amelrik. He meets my gaze and holds it, like he has nothing to hide. "I can't go home. Not yet."

"I should kill him. You know that." Torrin points his sword in Amelrik's direction.

Amelrik's on his feet now, and he takes a step back, putting more distance between them. And I'm pretty sure he also hisses at him. Which, under other circumstances, I might find funny.

I stand in front of Torrin's sword. "No."

"We'll go home, and I'll say he kidnapped you. We won't tell anyone what you did. It'll be okay. And maybe I can talk to your father, convince him to wait a little while for the wedding. You've been through some trauma, and—"

"I said *no.* I'm not an idiot. I know you and the whole barracks think that I am, that you need to protect me all the time, but that stops *now.* I don't need your help—I just need you to leave us alone." Ugh.

The words sound so cruel, and they taste bitter in my mouth. But I can't let him kill Amelrik, and I can't let him drag me back home.

Torrin opens his mouth, then closes it, too shocked to speak. Hurt twitches across his face. "What is he to you? That you would choose him, a *dragon*, over me?"

"I'm not choosing anyone." I stare at my feet, hating myself for hurting him. For not making him understand. But maybe I can't, because *I* don't even understand. Freeing Amelrik, leaving the barracks . . . It's about finding Celeste, but it's about something more than that, too.

"Like hell you're not. Is this really what you want, Vee? You're going to get yourself killed, and I'm just supposed to stand here and let that happen?! It's like I don't even know you! I should take you back home, but you know what? I'm not sure I could lie about what you've done. Not when you're acting so crazy. And your father's been through enough already."

"What's that supposed to mean?"

"It means it would be less shameful for him to think a dragon kidnapped you than to know the truth."

His words are like a slap in the face, harsh and stinging. My mouth slips open, and then I glare at him. "I think you'd better leave now."

"You don't know what you're doing."

"Well, we'll see about that."

16

I DON'T TRUST ANYONE

"This is seriously supposed to work?" I'm standing in the middle of a stream. A fish slips past me, lightning fast, swimming with the current. I don't know how Amelrik thinks we're going to catch any of these things.

He's standing a little farther downstream. He glances over his shoulder at me. "You've got a better idea?"

Nope. And my stomach is growling for, like, the millionth time today, so I guess we're catching fish. Or at least attempting to. With our bare hands. "This isn't doing much to dispel the idea that you're a wild animal, you know."

"If it makes you feel any better, I've never done this before." His hands dive under the water as he lunges at a fish. He doesn't catch it, though he does manage to splash himself in the face.

"It doesn't." In fact, it makes me feel like we're going to starve to death. Another fish races by, and I make a grab for it. I touch some scales—which are really slippery—but that's as close as I get. "If you've never done this before, how do you know it will work?"

"I"—he tries for another one, only succeeding in splashing a bunch of water around—"don't."

Well, if I don't get to eat, at least I get to watch him make a fool of himself.

I have my pant legs hiked up to my knees, though the bottom edges are already wet. The cold from the water seeps into my feet and my shins, making my bones ache and my flesh go numb. I think about how cold I was last night, and about how warm I was when I woke up. You know, with Amelrik's arm wrapped around me and his body pressed against mine.

I didn't have much chance to process it, what with Torrin trying to kill him and take me back home. But we're alone now, just us and these stupid, overly slippery fish. And Amelrik's facing the other direction. So if I stop to think about what happened, and maybe even that it felt pretty good, he won't see it on my face.

Not that I'm saying it felt good to be that close to him. I mean, it did, but I'm not *officially* saying that. And, to be fair, I only felt that way when I wasn't awake enough to really know what the situation was. I've never slept in the same bed—or, in this case, on the same dirt—as a boy before. Not that Amelrik counts as "a boy." I mean, he *is*, technically, but he's also a dragon, and I don't think of him that way.

But my point is, it felt nice to be held so tight, to feel wanted, and that could have happened with anybody. Plus, whatever feelings it gave me, it wasn't real. Amelrik doesn't care about me. Maybe he doesn't hate me, but I'm just a way to get that dragon ring off of him. There is no *wanting*.

Just because I can't picture this ever happening with any of the guys at the barracks—who would never be caught dead sleeping so close to me, let alone actually touching me—doesn't mean it means something.

And spending what was supposed to be my wedding night curled up in Amelrik's arms doesn't mean anything, either.

I will absolutely not bring this up or ask him about it in any way. We'll just never mention it, and pretend that nothing happened, because nothing did.

End of story.

I clear my throat. Part of my brain is telling me to stop, even as the words leave my mouth, but that part apparently gets outvoted. "So, about how we woke up this morning."

I say that right as Amelrik lunges at a fish. His foot slips, and he falls in the stream, getting completely soaked.

I laugh. I can't help it.

He picks himself up, dripping wet, and glares at me. "I was asleep. I didn't . . . I didn't know what I was doing. It wasn't on purpose."

"So, it was an accident."

"Right. Yes. Exactly." He seems relieved that we cleared that up.

We're quiet for a minute. I make a few grabs at some fish, but they get away. It doesn't help that I can't concentrate. There's another question floating around in my thoughts, and I know I shouldn't ask it, but how am I supposed to catch anything if I can't focus properly? It's probably better to just ask and get it over with.

"Do you sleep with a lot of girls, then?"

Amelrik almost slips again, but this time manages to catch himself. His shoulders stiffen. "Do I *what?*"

"It's just that, you must sleep with a lot of girls for, um, wrapping yourself around me to be second nature or whatever."

His face turns a little red. "I told you, it was an accident."

"I know, that's what I'm saying. I've never . . . I've never spent the night with anyone, and *I* didn't accidentally do anything like that. It just seems like something you'd do if you were used to sleeping with another person, that's all." I shrug, kind of wishing I hadn't said anything, but also really wanting to know the answer.

"That's not— That's none of your business."

"So, a *lot* of girls is what I'm hearing."

"Why would you assume it was a lot? Why not just one?"

"You got people to trust you. That was, like, your job or something. I assume that it, uh, included seducing people."

A pained expression crosses his face. Then he scowls and turns away.

I think I've offended him again. But he can't just say it's none of my business and expect me to *not* assume things. I mean, he's not giving me much to go on. And it's not like he doesn't know my history, which happens to be blank, but still. He knows I tried to get Torrin to marry me, which is pretty mortifying, to say the least.

Amelrik's standing in the stream, poised to try and catch something, but halfheartedly, like he's just going through the motions.

My stomach growls again, and I slip my hands into the water. I'm not convinced that this is going to work, but it beats standing here in awkward silence.

After a while, Amelrik gives up on pretending to fish and turns to face me. He looks like he has something to say. I figure he's going to tell me again how his, er, love life?—sex life?—is really none of my business. But before he can say anything, a fish swims right into my hands, and I shriek with joy. I clasp my fingers around it, and even though it's really slippery, I manage to keep my hold on it and pull it out of the water.

"I did it!" Excitement bubbles up in my chest. I caught one. And if I can catch one, I can catch another. We're not going to starve to death. At least, not today, and not because of me.

I smile real big at Amelrik, happier than I've been in . . . I don't even know how long.

He smiles back, looking just as excited as I am, all offenses and breaches of privacy forgotten, at least for the moment.

I'm sitting by Amelrik later, watching the fire. It's dark out, and cold, and the heat from the flames feels really good. My stomach is full from all the fish we ate today. And while it's still weird to be away from home, it doesn't seem as scary as it did before. Even though we're farther away from the barracks, and anything familiar, and, let's face it, everything I've ever known.

Okay, so maybe it is still scary. But not *as* much.

At least we have the fire, now that we know no one's looking for us. That's one good thing about Torrin showing up, I guess. And there's more space here than where we slept last night. Room to have a fire and to sleep on opposite sides of it. So there's, like, no chance of waking up in Amelrik's arms again.

Which is a huge relief. I'm not disappointed at all. Nooope.

Amelrik's sitting with his knees pulled up to his chest, his arms folded on top of them. He glances over at me.

And catches me maybe kind of staring at him. I look away, hoping he didn't notice.

"So," he says. "About what you said earlier. About me, uh, seducing people. Not that it's any of your business, because it's not, but I want you to know I didn't do that."

A branch in the fire crackles, sending a stray spark into the air. "You tricked people, though, didn't you? You made them think you were someone you weren't, to earn their trust, all so you could hurt them." Just like the dragon who killed my mother. I feel a rush of shame. Was I really thinking about waking up in his arms? That I'd be disappointed if it didn't happen again? He's no better than my mother's killer.

"Okay, yeah. All right. I've done things I'm not proud of. But not . . . never like *that*."

"Oh, so all the girls you slept with knew what you were?"

"That's not—"

"Because there's no way you would have told them the truth." He couldn't have. "And maybe you think it doesn't count as seduction, but you still got them to trust you more than they should have. So you can say you didn't do it, but—"

"I didn't, okay? There weren't any."

"Weren't any what?"

"There weren't . . . I mean, I didn't . . ." He clears his throat. "I've never, um, you know."

"What?"

"Slept with anyone."

"You know that 'sleeping with someone' is a euphemism for sex, right?" Because there's no way that's what he meant.

"Yeah, I do. And I haven't."

"Oh." That's definitely not something I thought we'd have in common. "You've really never done it with anyone? Like, *ever*?"

"I think I'd remember."

"Right, but . . . Not even with other dragons?"

He clenches his jaw, a bitter expression crossing his face. "I didn't tell you so you could ask stupid questions."

"But *you*? A virgin? That's just— Wait, is this some kind of dragon custom I don't know about?"

"No."

"Are you betrothed?"

"No."

"Are you—"

"This isn't a guessing game for your amusement."

"I'm just trying to figure it out."

"*Figure it out?* There's nothing to figure out. I shouldn't have even told you. I just didn't want you to think that about me."

"But there has to be a reason. Did you take a vow of celibacy?"

"No. And what part of 'this isn't a game' didn't you understand?"

"Is there . . . Is there something wrong with—"

"There's nothing wrong with me!" He shouts the words, his voice breaking a little. He's obviously mad, but there's something else there, too. Sadness, and pain. Like I didn't just piss him off—I actually hurt him.

A pang of guilt spreads through my chest.

He presses his forehead to his arms. And right now, it's hard to see him as a spy who got people killed. I know what he is and what he's done, and yet, how can the person who did those things be the same one who's sitting next to me now? Looking so upset, so *human*?

The silence between us is really awkward. Maybe I should just call it quits and go to bed, before I accidentally say something even stupider and make this worse, but I don't want to leave things like this. "So, what kinds of books do you like to read?"

He lifts his head, giving me a really incredulous look.

I keep going. "I just read this one series, about this princess who solves really gruesome murder mysteries."

"I read that one, too."

"You did?" I don't know why, but I didn't expect to have read any of the same books as him. "Which one's your favorite?"

He answers right away, not having to think about it. "Book three."

I laugh. In book three, a prince and his family come to the castle. He's a possible suitor, and the king and queen really want Princess Genevieve to make a good impression. But then a string of murders takes place, and she has to solve them while keeping everyone from finding out what's going on. It's pretty hilarious.

I think that one might be my favorite, too, but I don't want to sound like I'm copying him. "What about book five? When she meets Orlando?" Orlando's a bandit who's also been known to solve a mystery or two.

"It's no book three, but it has its moments."

"She's marrying him in book seven."

He snorts. "Yeah, right."

"She *is*. Book six ends with him proposing." Actually, it ends with both him and a prince—who she's always kind of had a thing for—proposing.

"What about Liam?"

That's the prince. "What about him? Too little too late, that's what I say. He might be a more suitable match, but everyone knows Genevieve's heart is with Orlando. Besides, Liam doesn't solve mysteries. He'd just get in the way."

"She's a princess. She can't marry an outlaw."

"She can, too. They could solve mysteries on the road together."

"Do you *want* the series to end? The whole point is that she's a princess, and she has to deal with court drama and being part of high society and all that, while also solving murders. I don't see how it can keep going if she leaves everything for him. But book seven comes out pretty soon, so I guess we'll see."

"You mean *you'll* see when she marries Orlando and they live happily ever after. And if that is the end of the series—I'm not saying I want it to be, but if it is—there are worse ways it could happen, you know?"

"I don't really care who she marries, as long as there are more books."

"Not me. Orlando, or else."

He smirks at that.

I yawn, stretching my arms over my head. I'm tired, and it's probably time to sleep, but that means moving to the other side of the fire, where I'll be alone. And it's not that I can't be alone, but I kind of don't want to be. If I just lay down right here, would he move to the other side, or would he stay? And do I even want him to?

Part of me does. Just like how part of me felt really safe and good waking up in his arms this morning. But that part of me is wrong, because I know what he is. A dragon, a liar, an infiltrator. How can I take comfort in being beside him, knowing any of that?

Amelrik's voice startles me out of my thoughts. "I don't trust anyone." He glances over at me, then away again. "I can't."

"What?"

"You wanted to know what the reason was. Why I haven't . . ." He swallows. "I've never been close enough with anyone to trust them that much. To let anything happen."

"Oh."

"Being that intimate with someone . . . It's a big deal. People act like it's not, but it is. I mean, it is for me." His eyes search mine, and he looks really nervous. "I can't imagine letting anybody get that close."

I want to ask him about it. Like, really bad. Because that can't just be it. If he doesn't trust people, there has to be a reason, right? And does he mean he can't imagine it happening now, or, like, ever? But it seems like it was hard enough for him to say as much as he did, and I don't want to push it and upset him again. No matter how curious I am.

So I just say, "Okay," and try really hard to leave it at that.

He watches me for a minute, waiting for the other shoe to drop. When it doesn't, he exhales, looking really relieved.

17

TWO USES

"How much farther is it? I mean, how much longer before we get to where they've got Celeste?" It's the next day, and me and Amelrik are walking through the woods.

"At the pace we've been going? Two more days."

Two days. It's not that long, but to Celeste, it might be an eternity. "And then?"

"And then you take this iron ring off my neck."

"Uh, no. Not until after we rescue her. That was the deal." And he doesn't have much choice, since I can't actually take it off.

"You expect me to walk into Elder clan like this? As your prisoner? How am I supposed to help you when I might as well be wearing a big sign that says 'captive'?"

I hadn't thought about it like that. Actually, I hadn't really thought about *how* we'd rescue Celeste—I figured we'd know once we got there. "You said you lived with them for a long time. But you don't live with them now. And obviously you and Lothar don't get along."

"That's nothing new."

"What I'm getting at is are you sure you can just walk in there, even with the ring off? Because if you're not a political hostage anymore, then something must have happ—"

I don't finish that sentence because the ground suddenly falls out from under me. I reach out, grabbing on to Amelrik for support, and end up dragging him with me.

We land really hard at the bottom of a huge pit.

My arm hurts bad enough that I'm afraid to look. When I do, I see a long gash that runs almost the length of my forearm. There's some dirt in it, making it sting. Besides that, I think I might end up with some bruises—one of my legs feels banged up, and so does one shoulder.

Amelrik brushes the dirt off of himself. "Are you okay?"

Not really, but I don't want to admit it. "I'm fine."

He ignores what I said and inspects the gash on my arm. "You should wash that out, once we get out of here."

I look up at the dirt walls surrounding us. They're way too tall for us to just climb out. "And how are we supposed to do that?"

Amelrik studies the walls, considering them for a moment. "It's not that far."

"Maybe not for you."

"I just mean it's doable. I'll boost you up, and then you help me. We'll—"

There are men's voices in the distance. Coming toward us. I can't make out most of what they're saying, but I catch the word "trap."

Amelrik's eyes get wide. He sniffs the air. "Hunters."

"Oh, good. Maybe they can get us out."

He grabs my arms, which makes the gash hurt worse.

"*Ow!* Hey!"

"You have to take this ring off of me!" His breathing is unsteady, and he looks really freaked out.

"What?"

"The dragon ring! They can't find me with it on. If they do, they'll *know*."

"This is a trap for game. We're not animals. They have to let us go. Don't they?"

He's shaking his head. His eyes dart up to the top of the hole, then back to me, frantic. "We don't have time to get out of here, and if they see me like this, I'm dead."

"I . . ."

The voices are getting closer.

He looks into my eyes, pleading with me. "You promised you wouldn't let me die like this!"

"I don't . . ." *I don't have the power to take it off.* I didn't think I'd need to before we found Celeste. He's waiting for me to say something, to *do* something. Maybe I should tell him the truth, but how can I? And even if I could take off the dragon ring, could I really trust him that much?

Maybe he's wrong. Maybe the hunters won't care what he is.

But then there are footsteps above us, and it's too late. I see the hope in Amelrik's eyes shatter. I've let him down, and I didn't even tell him why.

Three bearded faces peer over the top of the hole. "Well, well, well," one of them says. "What do we have here?"

Another one squints down at us. "Looks like a dragon. All collared up and ready for us. I never thought we'd catch one of those—certainly not with such a simple trap. Must be our lucky day."

"Thanks for the help," I tell the hunters, once they've hauled us out of the pit, "but we really have to be going."

They've got their weapons pointed at us, and none of them moves to let us leave.

Not that I really thought that they would.

All three of them look us over, like they're deciding what we're worth.

"What clan are you from, dragon?" the red-headed one asks. His name is Bern, and he seems to be their leader.

Amelrik stays silent and doesn't answer.

One of the other hunters lunges forward. His fist collides with Amelrik's jaw, making a loud *crack*. "He asked you a question!"

Amelrik spits blood in his face.

The hunter looks like he's going to hit him again, but Bern stops him. "No matter, Gavin, no matter. It'll be a surprise when we get to the village."

I feel like everyone knows what they're talking about except me. "What will be a surprise?"

"Why, the color of his head. I don't suppose you know the answer, paladin? I'm hoping for red. Or maybe blue. Blue would look best in the lodge. But no, don't tell us. We'll find out soon enough."

I don't know why they're assuming I'm a paladin—though who else would be traveling through the woods with a collared dragon?—but I decide to go with it. "That's right—I am a paladin." My voice shakes a little, though, which isn't exactly selling it. "And that's *my* dragon."

"Is that so?" Bern laughs, and the other two join in.

"That's right. He belongs to me."

"You know, on second thought, you don't look much like a paladin. No sword, no armor."

"Well, I am. I'm a St. George, and I put that dragon ring around his neck. That means he's mine."

"That might be so, Miss St. George, but you can only bind dragons, and we ain't no dragons. The way I see it, we've got the steel, and you've got nothing."

Okay, so he might be right about that. I glance over at Amelrik, who's giving me this exasperated look, like I'm just making things worse.

"I got separated from my group. My hunting party. Me and my dragon did, I mean. But they're really close, and they'll be here any second."

"Uh-huh." All three of them share a look, and they laugh again.

"It's true. And anyway, like I said, he's mine. You can't have him."

"My sword says that I can. His head's going on the trophy wall. And Sam here"—he points to the third hunter, the blond one—"is going to eat his heart. Supposed to be good for virility," he adds.

Sam nods. "My wife wants another baby."

I can't believe this. "That's the stupidest thing I've ever heard."

Bern makes a *hmph* noise. "Can't expect you to understand. And what were you going to do with him? Kill him and leave him for the crows?" He clucks his tongue. "You paladins are so wasteful."

I make a face. I can feel Amelrik's gaze on me, but I can't look at him. He thinks I let this happen. That I could have prevented it.

"Now, a paladin, on the other hand," Bern goes on, "is a different story. There's only one use for those. Well, two, since you're a woman."

My stomach twists. I really, *really* wish I'd listened to Amelrik. Oh, and that I had magic. Obviously. *"What?"*

"After we get you both back to the village, you'll undo that ring for us. If you really are a St. George, there's another hunting party we might make a trade with. They've been talking about going on a dragon hunt. Could be they'll want a paladin to take along."

I swallow, not liking the sound of any of that.

"And of course, if it turns out you're lying about being a paladin, we won't be able to sell you. Well, not to them, anyway. But like I said, you got two uses, being a woman and all."

18

I'm Virginia freaking St. George

The hunters are marching us back to their village. We're following a dirt road, and they've got our hands tied behind our backs, with ropes attached, like leashes. Every time they pull on them, it feels like my arms are going to come out of the sockets. There's no way out of this, and they said their village isn't far. We should be there sometime this afternoon.

Amelrik's walking beside me. He leans in close and whispers, "Take the ring off."

The hunters are absorbed in some story Bern is telling about catching a wild boar. I don't think they're paying attention, but I keep my voice low anyway. "I know what I promised, but—"

"I can save us—just not with this ring around my neck."

"I can't."

He's quiet for a second. "You'd rather I died. After everything that's . . . You'd rather you were sold to hunters—who *will* make two uses out of you, do not doubt that—than give me my freedom."

"If you had your freedom, you'd just leave." A dragon could fight off these hunters, but he could also fly away and abandon me here.

"Is that what you think of me?"

Maybe. I don't know. But . . . I look over at him and shake my head. Maybe he wouldn't help me find Celeste if that ring wasn't around his neck, if he didn't need me to take it off, but I don't believe he'd leave me here with these men. "It doesn't matter what I think, because I . . . I can't."

"You won't, you mean." His voice sounds bitter, betrayed, and I hate all the things he must be thinking about me.

"No, I mean I *can't*. I lied to you. I needed your help, and I thought Celeste could do it, once we rescued her. I didn't think something like this would happen."

"What do you mean, you can't? You're a *St. George*."

"Yeah, but why do you think they were marrying me off? You said yourself that I'm no paladin. Well, I'm not. I don't even have magic."

"But . . . No. I smelled it on you before. I know I did."

"I was trying to learn so Father couldn't force me to get married. Celeste was helping me. She stayed up all night, and that's why she got captured. All this is my fault, and her helping turned out to be for nothing. I managed to make a spark, but only once, and that was it." My whole life, just one spark.

"But—"

My arms jerk behind me as the hunters pull on my leash. They do the same to Amelrik. I think maybe they've caught us talking, but then Bern announces they're stopping for lunch.

There's a clearing on the side of the road where someone's set up a couple little tables and some logs to sit on.

They tie our leashes to a tree beside the clearing, then crowd around one of the tables and pull out a loaf of bread, a chunk of cheese, some apples, and some jerky from their packs.

My stomach growls, and my mouth waters.

Gavin hears my stomach and laughs. "No point in feeding you. But I might give you a scrap or two if you *beg*." He looks right at me, and I know the offer—if you can call it that—doesn't apply to Amelrik.

"But do sit down," Bern says, in between tearing off a hunk of bread and stuffing cheese in his mouth. "Don't let it be said that I'm not a gracious host." He laughs, bits of food spraying out across their table.

Our leashes reach just past one of the logs. I entertain the idea of standing the whole time, to defy them and to look like I'm stronger than I am, but I'm too tired to put up a front. I sit down. The bark on the log is worn and not as uncomfortable as it looks, though it's still kind of lumpy.

Amelrik sits down next to me. "You couldn't have gotten that spark if you didn't have magic."

I glance at the hunters, to make sure they're not paying attention. We were facing away from them on the road, but here they could easily look over and notice us talking. They seem to be too busy eating to care what we're doing right now, though, so long as it's not escaping.

"It was a total fluke," I tell him. "And it was one spark—not even a spell. It was nothing."

"No, it wasn't. It was real. You think I don't know the stink of paladin magic? Of *St. George* magic?" He makes a face, like even the words taste bad. "Magic isn't just a spark. It's something that's in your blood. And if you have it, it's there."

"I've spent my whole life trying to do magic. What makes you think it would work now?"

"This is our only chance to get out of here, and you know what will happen to us if we don't."

"But—"

"They want to *eat my heart*." He tilts his head, emphasizing how awful and ridiculous that is. "They're barbarians. Worse than paladins, even."

"Wow, thanks."

"I can save us."

"But I can't."

"You have to try. Please, Virgin—Virginia. *Please.* You have magic—you just have to use it."

"I don't know how. And maybe I do have magic, somewhere, but it doesn't feel like it."

He considers that. "Maybe you don't—"

"Want it enough? That's what Celeste says."

He scoffs. "And you're risking your life for her?"

"She's my sister. You don't know her. I mean, you only know one side of her."

"Does your heart beat because you *want* it to? Would your lungs stop working because you didn't want air badly enough? Magic is like being alive. You don't have to want it. It's just there."

Nobody's ever talked about magic like that to me before. Like they don't blame me for not being able to make it work. "But I still don't know how to—"

"Hey!" Bern shouts. "No talking!" He eyes us suspiciously. "Lunch is over anyway. You two had best get up." He motions for Sam and Gavin to untie our leashes from the tree.

"*Try,*" Amelrik whispers, getting to his feet.

Easy for him to say. But we don't have much time, and he's right. This is our only chance of getting out of this mess—I can't just do nothing. I close my eyes and concentrate.

"What's wrong with her?" Bern asks. Then, to me, he says, "You, girl, you'd better get up if you know what's good for you."

Fear squirms in my stomach and spreads through my chest, but I try to ignore it. Whatever they do to me now, it won't be worse than what's going to happen if we don't get out of here.

"I said *get up!*"

"Don't touch her!" Amelrik shouts. I open my eyes in time to see him step forward and take the blow Bern meant for me.

"A dragon protecting a paladin? Now I've seen everything."

"Could be that she's not a paladin," Sam says. "Could be that she's just a liar."

I ignore them, shutting my eyes again and focusing on what I have to do. I try to think of magic like Amelrik said, as something that's just *there*. I made a spark before. The magic exists, even if I don't know how to use it.

Bern snorts. "Doesn't matter what she is—this isn't up for discussion. Someone get her up and let's get going. I've got to walk off all that cheese I just ate."

"Step aside, dragon," Gavin says. "I'll haul her off of there with the rope if I have to. Is that what you want?"

"Nobody hurts her." Amelrik's voice is low, almost a growl.

Goose bumps spread across my arms. *There's going to be a fight.*

I hardly have time to register that thought before someone hits him. Hard. And then again.

The sound makes me sick. He's doing this for me. No, he's doing this for both of us, but they're going to beat the hell out of him, because I can't take that ring off. The only thing that ever worked, that allowed me to make a spark, was thinking about how much I hated him. Or thought I did. And now there's no chance of that, because I *don't*. Because he's maybe even sort of my friend—kind of my only friend right now—and all I know is I don't want them to hurt him. I can't let them put his head on their wall, or eat his heart, or any other crazy stuff they're going to try. Maybe he's only doing this because he needs me, not because he cares, but I care what happens to *him*. And I might not know him all that well, but if there's even a chance of getting that ring off and getting out of here, I know he'll stand there and take whatever they give him until he literally can't anymore.

He said magic is in my blood. Maybe it is, and if I can't feel it, that's only because it's such a basic part of me. Like my heartbeat, like my breathing—always there, always happening, even when I don't notice it.

I broke a dragon out of jail. I caught fish with my bare hands. I'm not the helpless dud everyone at the barracks thinks I am. I'm *Virginia freaking St. George*, and I can do this.

I never learned how to undo the spell on a dragon ring, but I picture the iron shattering, the magic dissipating.

Amelrik cries out as another blow hits him. I open my eyes and see him double over and fall to the ground. The hunters start kicking him. In the ribs, in the stomach, in the face.

"Stop!" I scream, my voice shrill and terrified. And I feel something. A tingling in my hands. There's a flash of red, and the smell of sulfur, and a cracking sound as the dragon ring breaks apart. "Amelrik, now!"

The hunters notice the ring. One of them swears. They back off to find their swords and their axes.

Bern grabs me by the hair, yanking my head back. "You'll pay for that." Cold metal presses against my throat.

Great. I finally manage to cast a spell, and before I can even celebrate, this jerk is going to kill me.

The knife pricks my skin. I'm so sure I'm going to die. And then Amelrik tears Bern away from me with superhuman strength, the knife skittering to the ground. "I said *don't touch her!*"

I look at Amelrik, expecting to see a dragon. I'm not sure what I'm seeing.

He's transformed and broken out of his bonds—that much is clear—but his body is still human. No, his body is still *mostly* human. Leathery black wings with flashes of red underneath spread out from his back, having ripped through his shirt. His hands are still hands, but with hooked claws at the ends. His eyes are cat's eyes—yellow with black slits. Patches of black scales cover the outside of his forearms, like armor. They creep up the sides of his neck and along the very edges of his face.

I gasp. This is why he didn't change forms the night of the party, when Lothar was goading him. Even if I'd never seen a dragon before,

I'd know that he looks horribly wrong. Disfigured. Hideous. Words I never thought I'd think about him before this moment.

He deflects Gavin's sword with his scaled forearm, then takes the weapon from him, flinging it to the ground. Bern comes at him with an ax. Amelrik slashes at him with his claws. They come away bloody.

Bern drops the ax and presses his hands to his sides. "Retreat!" he shouts, and Gavin and Sam fall in with him, backing out of the clearing and hurrying off down the road.

Amelrik's yellow eyes meet mine. He sees the shock on my face— the revulsion that I wish wasn't there—and it's like I hit him. Like I hit him harder than any of those hunters ever could.

19

AN UNDERGROUND ABYSS

I hold in my questions as long as I can. I make it all the way to that night, when we're sitting by the fire, chewing on the last of the food the hunters left behind. Amelrik gobbled down most of it earlier, after he changed back into human form. We've hardly said a word to each other since then, and the silence has been so tense and awkward. I can't take it anymore. I open my mouth to speak.

"*No,*" Amelrik snaps.

"I didn't say anything."

"Whatever stupid question you were going to ask, the answer is no." He scribbles idly in the dirt with a stick, not looking at me.

"It's not a stupid question." And even if it is, I have to say *something*, because saying nothing is killing me. "Are you half dragon, half . . . human?"

He shoves the stick harder into the dirt. "You're not even sure what you think the other half is? That's a new level of offensive, even for you. And no, I'm not."

"So your parents are both dragons, you're just—"

"Don't."

"—different."

He flinches. "I hate that word."

There's a sliver of apple peel stuck between my teeth. I worry at it with my tongue. "Do your wings work?"

He stares at me, his green eyes bright and piercing. Maybe it's related to his transformation earlier, or maybe it's because the dragon ring is gone, but they seem more vivid. "Do I look like I want to talk about this?"

"I just mean, can you fly?"

"No."

"Oh. So, those red bits under your wings . . . is that why you dye your hair like that?" I gesture to the red streak in the front.

"I told you I lived with Elder clan for a long time. I started doing this to remember where I came from." He pauses, then corrects himself. "To remind *everybody else* where I came from. That I wasn't one of them."

Yeah, I don't think they needed any help with that. "Maybe, sometime, can I touch—"

"*No.*"

He was pretty quick with that one. I guess he doesn't want me touching any part of him. "I was just going to say your wings."

"I know what you were going to say."

"You can't blame me for being curious. Are there other dragons like you? Is this just something that happens? Is it . . . is it why your father sent you away?"

He drops the stick and clenches his fists. "Stop. Just . . . *stop.* I don't want to talk about it. Not with you, not with anyone!"

"But—"

"Not ever!" He gets up and storms off to the other side of the fire, away from me. Then a second later he storms back. "You don't know me. You don't get to ask me those questions and gawk at me and ask *to touch* me, like I'm some kind of sideshow attraction! Okay?!"

There's a bitter taste in the back of my throat, and my eyes are about to water. "Yeah. Okay."

"You saved my life, but I've saved yours three times now. I don't owe you anything. And I'm certainly not here with you because I want to be!"

"Then why are you here? The dragon ring is off—you don't need me anymore. Just tell me where to find Celeste, and I'll figure this out on my own." Somehow.

He sighs, his anger softening a little. "I'm still going with you."

"No, you're right. You don't owe me anything."

"You don't know the first thing about dragons. You'd never make it on your own."

"You're really going to still help me?" I give him a skeptical look. "Even though the ring is off and you don't want to be here?" And even though I can't stop asking him annoying questions?

"I made a promise. Unlike some people, I keep mine. Besides, I'm not leaving you alone to get yourself killed."

"You would do that? For me?"

He shrugs and looks away. "I've saved your life three times so far—what's one more?"

I don't know what I was expecting the entrance to Elder clan to look like, but I guess I thought it would be more intimidating. It's basically just the opening to a cave. A carved-out space in the rock that leads off into darkness. And okay, maybe a scary hole that leads off into an underground abyss full of dragons is intimidating enough. I've come to kind of trust Amelrik—maybe more than just kind of—but these dragons aren't him. They could be violent and cruel, impatient and hateful.

They could take one look at me and decide to kill or torture me. They could be all the things that he's not.

But Celeste is down there, waiting for me to rescue her, even if she doesn't know it yet. There's no question of whether or not I'm going in.

Amelrik breathes in deep, like he's savoring the essence of this place. "We're here," he says, and if I didn't know better, I'd think he sounded happy about that. Maybe he's just glad that this is finally going to be over. But then he takes my hand in his and smiles at me. "Once we're inside, follow my lead."

"That'll be easier if you actually tell me the plan." And also if he starts making sense.

"The plan is I do the talking and you play along."

"But—"

"You want to get your sister back, don't you? Stick close to me. And do *not* wander off."

"Is that why you're holding my hand?" Because he thinks I'm going to get distracted by the first shiny thing I see and disappear?

He quickly lets go of me. "You're right. It should be like this." He holds out his arm instead, all serious and formal, like he's about to escort me into a ball or something.

Whoa. "That's not what I meant. You don't have to hold on to me. I'm not a child."

"Do you want to look like an important guest of royalty, or like a common slave?"

"Gee, are those my only options?"

"You're making an entrance with a *prince*. Try to act like it. That means take my arm. And stand up straight."

His accent is getting thicker, and he's talking really fast, so that it takes me a couple seconds to figure out what he said. And meanwhile he's staring at me like I'm a complete moron. "I am standing up straight." Close enough, anyway.

He huffs in frustration, then looks me over and makes a face. "You should have had a bath."

"*I* should have had a bath?"

"Both of us. But it's too late now, and . . . just try not to embarrass me."

Embarrass him? What does he think I'm going to do?

I take his arm like he said. If I want to get Celeste back, that means trusting him. Even if walking into a dragon clan's lair is just about the scariest thing I've ever done, and any one of them could rip me apart with the slightest twitch of their claw.

"You're sure about this?" I ask him.

"As sure as I'm ever going to be."

Which isn't exactly the reassurance I was looking for. But he's already leading me inside, and I didn't come this far just to chicken out.

20

WHERE EXACTLY DO YOU THINK YOU ARE?

It's a big deal that Amelrik is here, in the tunnels of Elder clan. I can't see very well, since there's only the occasional torch on the wall for lighting, but I can hear just fine. All the dragons stop their conversations as we pass by and start muttering to each other. Only a few of them say anything in English—I know I hear the word "prince" a couple times—but even when I can't understand what they're saying, it's not hard to guess they're talking about him.

It's so dark I can barely even see the purple of their scales—they all just look kind of black. Some of the dragons perch on rocky overhangs, staring down at us, while others lounge in caverns or make their way through the tunnels, scales and claws scraping against stone as they go about their business. Their eyes reflect the light with flashes of green. I don't dare look at any of them for too long, and, despite what I said outside, I keep my arm tight around Amelrik's.

I can't believe I'm here. Underground. Surrounded by a whole clan of dragons.

I'm probably going to die today.

There's the sound of feet slapping against the floor—not a dragon's, but a human's—as someone comes running up to us. For just a second, my heart leaps, thinking it's Celeste. That nothing bad at all happened to her and she's free to leave with me.

But it's not her. Of course it's not.

This girl—who must really be a dragon—has long dark hair and looks like she's around Amelrik's age, possibly a little older. She's also *completely naked.*

She stops in front of Amelrik, staring at him with her hands in front of her mouth. "It's *you.* But it can't be. We thought . . ." Her voice breaks. She sounds like she's going to cry. "I thought I was never going to see you again! It's been so long, and they told us you were dead!"

He pulls away from me and hugs her tight. "I know what they told you. It wasn't true."

What? I have no idea what's going on. Oh, except that Amelrik's embracing some naked girl, and neither of them seems to think that's weird.

It's like he's forgotten I'm here, and I'm suddenly aware of how alone I am. If I looked away a little too long and he walked off without me, we might never find each other. If he even tried to look for me. He could easily decide not to, or some other dragon could find me first—which seems pretty likely—and then I'd just be gone.

When they're done hugging, the two of them step back and look each other over. Then just when I think I can't feel any more left out, they start talking excitedly in what I assume is their native language—what did he say it was? Vairlin?—and it's like I don't even exist.

I clear my throat. Loudly.

The naked girl glances over at me. She tilts her head in my direction and says something to Amelrik.

He laughs.

Great. What did she say about me that was so funny?

"Virginia, this is my cousin, Odilia."

Oh. His *cousin*. Not his girlfriend or anything. Unless dragons don't view cousins as off-limits. She could still be both. "Wait, what's your cousin doing with Elder clan? Did she get traded, too?"

"Wow." He blinks at me. "Where exactly do you think you are?"

"You know where I—"

"How many times do I have to tell you? This is *Hawthorne* clan. Haw. Thorne." He shares a look with Odilia and rolls his eyes, like *Can you believe how stupid she is?*

"We're *where*?!" I glance around at the tunnel walls, as if that's going to tell me anything.

He forces a smile, his teeth clenched. "Remember what we talked about?"

"If this is Hawthorne clan, then what are we doing here? What about Celeste?!"

"I'll explain it to you again *later*." Then, to Odilia, he says, "You'll have to excuse her. Humans get so confused once they lose sight of the sun."

Odilia nods knowingly, like that's actually a thing. Then she frowns and asks him something in Vairlin. They go off again, talking really fast, only this time they seem angry. I don't have to speak the language to know they're having an argument. Possibly about me. Odilia keeps waving her hands in my direction, and I think Amelrik might have said "St. George" once or twice, though it's hard to know for sure. He folds his arms across his chest, and the two of them stare each other down, neither one apparently wanting to yield.

"It's my choice," Amelrik finally says. His voice is quiet, but also unwavering, not inviting any doubt.

Odilia clucks her tongue. "I hope you know what you're doing, cousin." Her tone implies that she's pretty sure he has no idea what he's doing. She moves away from us, and then there's the sound of bones crunching and skin tearing as she changes forms, turning into a sleek black dragon with the same flashes of red under her wings as Amelrik.

Amelrik looks pissed. He takes my arm again and says, "Come on," before storming off down the hall.

"What did she say?" Because whatever it was, it obviously got to him.

He hunches his shoulders—now who's not standing up straight? "It was just . . . It was nothing."

Yeah, right. "Where are we really right now?"

"Hawthorne. I thought I made that clear."

He thinks he made that clear? Maybe he did, but only after he tricked me into coming here. "You lied to me." My voice sounds so small, even as it echoes against the walls.

"So did you."

"But . . ." But my lie wasn't as big as his. At least, not for me. "Is Celeste here?"

"It was Elder clan who captured her. You know that."

"I also thought I knew where we were! That I knew where you were taking me! Is Celeste even still alive?" My insides cinch up, and I hold my breath while I wait for his answer.

"I wouldn't lie about that."

How am I supposed to know what he would or wouldn't lie about? "We're supposed to be rescuing Celeste, so what are we doing here?"

"Don't worry. This is all part of the plan."

If he doesn't want me to worry, maybe he should stop giving me so many reasons to. "Why did you lie and say we were going to Elder clan? If this really is part of the plan, why didn't you tell me?"

"Because it's a delay, and you wouldn't have accepted that. You think we can just walk up to Elder clan and steal their St. George?"

"Their St. George? You make her sound like an object. She's my *sister*."

"They won't want to let her go. You're better off here. *For now,*" he adds, though it sounds like an afterthought. "I promise she'll be all right. And I told you to play along. Causing a scene in front of Odilia is one thing—"

"Wait, you think *I* caused a scene?"

"—but we're about to have an audience with my father. He might not be happy to see me. Whatever I say—whatever happens in there— it's extremely important that you back me up."

"So you just want me to go along with whatever you say, no matter what it is?"

"Our lives depend on it."

"Your father wouldn't kill you, would he?"

Amelrik looks away. "You don't know the situation. It's complicated. Odilia was right when she said I'm not supposed to be here."

She must have said that while they were arguing. "So explain it to me."

"There's no time. He'll have already heard about my return. Either we go talk to him now, or we run like hell. And we never get your sister back, and I . . ." A pained look crosses his face, and he stops himself from whatever he was about to say. "Please, Virginia. I need you to do this for me."

He's not telling me everything. But the dread in his voice when he talked about seeing his father was real. Then again, I believed him when he said this was Elder clan, so what do I know? "Answer one question for me, and I want the truth this time. What's the real reason you saved my life that night of the party?"

"You won't like it."

"I don't care." I just want to know if there's any hope of trusting him.

"It was the way everyone was treating you. Like there was something *wrong* with you, like you'd never be good enough."

"So you felt sorry for me." He's right—I don't like that answer.

"I thought we had something in common. That's why I told you to run."

"And what's wrong with that?"

"Don't patronize me."

"I'm not."

He makes a *hmph* noise, like he doesn't believe me. "You asked for the truth, and I gave it to you. Now come on—we're keeping my father waiting, and I'd like to get this over with."

21

GO WITH THIS

The king sits with his court, all in dragon form, at the end of a gigantic chamber. I thought I would be the terrified one, walking into a room full of dragons who could easily decide to kill me, but Amelrik's practically shaking as he leads me over to them.

"Remember," he whispers, "follow my lead."

I nod, not daring to speak. I feel like if I do, my voice will come out way too loud.

All the dragons look the same to me, but it's obvious which one is the king. He sits in the middle, with the others gathered around him, silently watching us approach. I can't read any of their expressions, but there's definitely tension in the room, and none of this seems particularly welcoming.

We stop right in front of him. Amelrik drops to his knees, then gets down on all fours and presses his forehead to the ground in some elaborate bow.

I'm still standing.

He lifts his head just enough to glare at me and clears his throat.

Oh, right. I get down on the floor, too, trying to copy what he's doing. I hate not being able to see what's going on, but it's not like knowing that a dragon is about to squash me or burn me to a crisp is going to make it not happen. Or make me magically fast enough to avoid it. Plus, you know, there's a whole room full of them.

Scratch that. A whole *lair* full. If they decided I wasn't leaving here alive, there'd be absolutely nothing I could do about it. And now I'm kind of glad I'm already on the floor, because my whole body feels like pudding.

There's the sickening sound of flesh and bone twisting and rearranging as the king changes forms to match his son. Then—and this is the *worst* thing I've ever heard—the rest of the court does the same. It's like the sound of my mother dying, a dozen times over, all at once.

The king stands before us. I'm wondering just how long we're going to have to stay like this when he says, "Rise."

Finally. I start to get to my feet, but I make the mistake of glancing up from my position on the floor. Like Odilia, the king isn't wearing *anything*. I guess there's no point, since their clothes would just rip apart every time they transformed. But seeing Amelrik's naked father—seeing *all* of him—was not something I needed to happen today. I quickly look down at the ground again, careful to keep my eyes averted even after I'm standing. Not that anybody seems to care—I guess they're used to not wearing clothes here. But still.

The king cups Amelrik's face in his hands, studying him, like he's afraid this isn't really happening. "Amelrik. My son." There's so much emotion in his voice. Relief and joy mixed with sadness and pain.

"Father." Amelrik lets out a deep breath, and it's like a huge weight lifts from him.

The rest of the court is absolutely silent, watching this play out.

The king takes a step back, letting go of Amelrik. There's no relief in his voice now—only horror—when he says, *"What have you done?"*

Amelrik flinches. "I've come home."

"Do you realize what they'd do if they knew you were here? And oh, if she saw you . . ." He makes a cutting motion with his arms. "I have no son! My son is dead!" He turns to one of the members of his court and says, "No one mentions this. *No one.* He was never here."

"No!" Amelrik's voice echoes through the chamber. He clenches his fists. "I'm not leaving. Not this time." He glances over at me, then back at his father. "You need me."

"I am your king! Do not presume to tell me what I—"

Amelrik interrupts him, shouting something in Vairlin. I have no idea what he says, but the king goes quiet, and a murmur runs through the court. All eyes are suddenly on me.

The king scowls at Amelrik, looking really pissed off. Actually, all the dragons look pretty pissed off. And none of them looks happy that I'm here. Or that I exist at all. The king sneers at me, a low growl emanating from his throat, and I think he's about two seconds away from changing back into a dragon and ripping me apart.

Amelrik steps in front of me and starts talking really fast. In their language, of course, because why should I know what's going on? I definitely hear the words "St. George" this time, though—as if it wasn't already clear he's talking about me.

The king asks him something. He doesn't sound very happy about any of this. They go back and forth for a while, until Amelrik grabs my hand and pulls me forward, so I'm standing next to him. He leans in close and whispers in my ear. "Tell them you will."

"I will what?"

"Just say it. Like you mean it."

I look around at all the dragons—the naked men and women staring intently at me. I have no idea what I'm promising right now, but they're all waiting for me to say it, and they look like they're going to kill me if I don't. "I . . ." My voice comes out a croak. I pause to clear it. The sound reverberates across the giant room, seeming crazy loud. "I *will.*"

The dragons gasp and speak to each other in surprised whispers, though at least they sound less angry.

Amelrik squeezes my hand. He looks pleased with me. Not just pleased, but like he's really glad that I'm here.

Warmth spreads through my chest, unbidden, and I can't help grinning at him.

The king shouts something—not angrily this time, but more like he's making an announcement.

Then Amelrik holds his arm up, bringing mine with it, so that they're both raised above our heads. "You heard your king! If anyone challenges her, they challenge their prince and all of Hawthorne clan! Virginia St. George belongs to me and me alone!"

Wait, I *what*?!

"Go with this," he whispers.

"Go with what? What are you—"

He kisses me.

I've never kissed anyone before, and I sure as hell haven't kissed a dragon. I try to pull away at first, out of instinct. He can't expect me to actually go along with *this*. But his arms are around me, holding me close, his warmth encompassing me. He presses his lips softly against mine, kissing me like he means it. My insides melt. A thrill runs from my stomach down to my toes. And suddenly pulling away is the last thing on my mind.

22

IF I HAD ANY STANDING AS A ST. GEORGE, I CERTAINLY DON'T ANYMORE

Amelrik acts like nothing happened. It's infuriating, to say the least.

We're in his old room, which is a small, oblong chamber in the Royal Branch of the cave system. There's a leather flap hanging from a fixture in the rock that serves as a door. A couple of servants in human form—naked, of course—are hurriedly lighting lamps and braziers and dusting off all the furniture. I imagine it's easier to do housework when you have thumbs, but the room is also small enough that a full-grown dragon wouldn't fit inside. I wonder if that's intentional.

Once everything's lit up, Amelrik dismisses them, telling them to bring us some roast beef and potatoes—I guess dragons don't eat that differently from us—along with some fresh clothes. I watch them leave, thinking that as soon as they're gone, he's going to explain himself. But instead he surveys the room, his expression full of awe. "It's exactly how I left it."

Meanwhile, my mind is reeling. I have no idea what's going on here or what just happened, other than that he kissed me. And that I liked it. Maybe a lot. Okay, definitely a lot, but I'm not ready to admit that. My first kiss was with a dragon, and if I had any standing as a St. George, I certainly don't anymore.

Amelrik's room is better lit than the rest of the caverns we've seen. There's a giant four-poster bed in the back with a wooden chest at the foot of it. Next to it is a desk with some parchment and ink and a stack of wax tablets. A marble chessboard stands off to one side. At least, I think it's chess, but all the pieces look like dragons instead of humans. It has its own table—also marble—and the chess pieces seem to be cut from *jewels*. One of the armies is emerald, the other sapphire.

One whole wall of the cavern has shelving carved into the stone. Every bit of available space on it is crammed with books. Amelrik runs his hands over their spines. He pulls one off the shelf and holds it out for me. "Here, if you like the *Princess Mysteries*, you'll like this, too."

I flip through it, but none of it's in English. "I can't read this."

"What? Oh, right." He sighs, disappointed with me, and takes it back.

"So, what was that about?"

His shoulders stiffen, so I know he knows what I mean. "What was *what* about?"

"Are we . . ." I'm almost too afraid to ask this. "Did we just get married?" *Please say no. Please say no.*

He raises his eyebrows. "You're joking, right?"

"I didn't hear an answer."

"I'm a prince!" He puts a hand to his chest. "I can't marry a human! Especially not one of paladin blood. And especially not in front of my father."

"What was that kiss about, then?"

"Last I checked, kissing someone doesn't mean you're married."

"No, I mean, why did you do it?" And why did he have to do it so well?

"I had to show them I was serious about you belonging to me. That's all."

If that's all, then why did it feel like he meant it? "I *don't* belong to you."

"Hey. Keep your voice down." He makes sure the door flap is closed, then motions for me to follow him deeper into the room. "Be careful what you say. Someone might hear you."

"But—"

"Look, I know I don't own you. But everybody else in this place? They *can't* know that. If they find out the truth, they'll kill you. And then me."

"So they have to think you *own* me? Right. And you keep saying humans are uncivilized."

"You can't just go wandering around unclaimed. It's dangerous. And they know you're a St. George, so you're *really* not supposed to be here. I'm responsible for you. Both for keeping you safe and for not letting you hurt anyone."

"They think I'm going to hurt someone?"

"With your magic."

"Magic I don't have."

"*Shh!* What the hell is wrong with you? Obviously I told them you did. I had to convince them we needed you. Elder clan has a St. George—we can't let them get an advantage over us."

"So you told them I can cast binding spells?"

"Better than your sister. And with you, we have the advantage. Celeste is a hostage, but I told them you were on our side, that you *want* to help us. Well, that you want to help me in particular."

"Oh, yeah? Because right now, I kind of want to murder you in par—"

He claps a hand over my mouth. "Watch it, Virgin. You're committing treason."

I lick his palm. He immediately lets go, making a face.

"You don't get to call me Virgin. Not when you're one, too. And, anyway, I was joking." Mostly.

"It's still treason. You're under enough suspicion as it is. The only reason either of us is here is because I convinced the court that I have control over you."

"And because they think I can do magic."

"You *can*."

"I cast one spell, and it's not even the one you told them I could do." I keep my voice low, because maybe he has a point about not letting anyone overhear these things. "And I was only able to cast that one because you were . . . It was special circumstances. I can't do it on command."

"You don't have to. Everyone just needs to think you can. And that you're choosing not to and honoring your vow."

"My vow. What, exactly, did I promise to do?"

He suddenly gets real interested in a book on the shelf.

"Amelrik?"

"It's, uh, not important. Oh, look. Here's one for you. Start with this." He hands me another book.

This one is a lot thinner, with drawings, clearly meant for children. I think it might be the alphabet. "I don't want to learn your language—I want to know what you said!"

He stares at me. "You hear what's wrong with that, right?"

"You know what I mean! *What* did I promise?"

"Just your, uh, undying loyalty and devotion to me and to Hawthorne clan."

"I did *what*?!"

A bell rings outside the entrance flap. Amelrik motions for me to be quiet and tells the servants to come in. It's a guy and a girl, the same ones who were here before. The guy's carrying a large silver tray with a cover over it, and the girl has a pile of folded-up clothing in her arms. Both of them are eyeing me warily.

While Amelrik tells them where to put everything, I sit down on his bed. Which is apparently *amazing*. The mattress is thick and full of down. The bedspread is velvet, and the sheets are a soft cotton. I flop backward and sink into the bedding. I don't know if I've ever been this comfortable.

After the servants leave, Amelrik sits next to me. "It's not a big deal. The vow you took, I mean."

"Says you. I don't go around pledging my undying devotion to just anyone."

"Yeah, but you made that pledge to me, and I know it's not real. You didn't mean what you promised—you didn't even know *what* you were promising—so it doesn't count."

I sit up, even though I kind of never want to move from this bed. "I pledged myself to you, and then you kissed me. So, what, they think we're lovers?"

"Er . . . More like that you're in love with me."

Great. I'm really coming out ahead in this scenario. "And this has to do with getting Celeste back? Because I'm not seeing the connection."

"You can't cast the binding spell, and I can't . . . We have to be smart about this, because that's all we have." He looks me over. "Well, all I have."

"Thanks."

"We'll go during the Feast of Eventide. Everyone will be busy eating and watching the entertainment, including the royal family. Your sister won't be allowed at the feast. She won't be completely unguarded, but it's our best chance."

I'm quiet a second, taking that in. "And when is the Feast of Eventide?"

"In a few weeks."

"A few *weeks*?!"

"This is what I was talking about. You're freaking out about the delay."

"But Celeste . . ."

"She's too valuable—they won't kill her. And we can't rescue her if we're dead, which is what we'll be if we don't go about this the right way."

"But . . . Wait, so this Feast of Eventide, it's just an Elder clan thing?"

"No. It's one of the biggest holidays of the year."

"So your clan's having a big celebration, too, right? Won't they notice if you don't show up?"

He scoffs. "My father has never allowed me to go. So, no, they won't."

"Seriously?"

"Everyone has to be in dragon form to attend. He doesn't feel that I meet the requirements."

Ouch. "So you've never even been?"

"Oh, no. I went to all of the feasts that were held at Elder clan while I was living with them. The Elder king doesn't share the same opinion about me as my own father. And anyway, I was a guest. It would have been rude for them to exclude me."

"I think it was rude for your father to exclude you."

"It's complicated." He looks down at his hands. "You don't understand."

"I'm pretty sure I do. Just because he's ashamed of you doesn't mean—"

Amelrik inhales sharply, his whole body going tense. "My father doesn't . . . He has good reason to feel how he does."

"But—"

"Come on. We should eat before our food gets too cold. And you are *not* eating on my bed."

"I wasn't going to. But really, Amelrik, don't you think it's wrong for him to—"

"No, I don't. And it's really none of your business, so *stay out of it.*"

23

DAUGHTERS SHOULD GET MORE CREDIT

It's later that evening. At least, I'm pretty sure it's evening, even though it's hard to tell, underground like this. We've eaten and bathed—*bathed*, with soap!—and changed into soft pajamas. I lie down on the bed again, and if I thought it was comfortable before, it's even better now that I'm clean and full.

Who knew that running away with a dragon prince would have such benefits?

I climb under the covers and start to drift off, only to be startled awake when Amelrik clears his throat.

I open my eyes. He's looming over me, looking pretty annoyed.

He folds his arms across his chest. "What do you think you're doing?"

"Sleeping."

"Not in my bed you're not."

"I'm your guest. Guests sleep in the bed."

"I am a *prince*. Princes sleep in the bed. What if someone comes in and finds you there, and me . . ." He glances around, not seeing anywhere else to sleep. ". . . not? Do you know how that would look?"

"No one will come in unless you tell them to, right?" I am *so* tired, and *so* comfortable—I can't imagine moving.

"Get up, Virginia. I'll give you a blanket and a pillow. You can sleep on the floor."

"The floor? The floor is made of *rock*. I just spent the last few nights on the ground, and now you're going to make me sleep on a rock?"

"I spent the last few nights on the ground, too, and before that, I spent a week in a dungeon. Plus, it's been *six years* since I slept in my own bed."

"Uh, you lived with Elder clan for that long, right? Your bed there must have felt like yours."

He makes a frustrated sound in the back of his throat. "That's not the point!"

He's getting pretty worked up about this. I slide over so I'm only taking up one side. "Here. There's room for both of us."

"That's not what I . . ." He takes a step back. "It's inappropriate."

"We slept closer than this on the ground that first night." Which, okay, maybe was kind of inappropriate, but he didn't have a problem with it then. "And everyone thinks we're lovers, anyway, right? So if they see us sharing a bed, they won't think anything of it. Or is there some rule against that?"

"Well, no, but . . ."

"Let me put it this way. I'm not moving. So you're either going to have to sleep on the floor, or you're going to have to sleep next to me."

"But that's . . . It's *my* bed, and you don't . . ." He sighs. "*Fine.* But scoot over more. And this is only for tonight. And only because I'm too tired to argue with you." He douses the lights, then comes back and climbs in, leaving as much space between us as possible.

And even though it was my suggestion, and even though there's plenty of room and we're not even touching or anything, I am suddenly *very* aware that he's a boy, and that he's in my bed. Er, I mean, that I'm in his, but still. Sleeping on the ground sort of next to him was one thing, but sleeping in a bed together feels . . . intimate. Especially after the way he kissed me earlier.

It hits me how ridiculous this situation is. A giddy nervousness builds up inside my chest, and then I can't help it—I start cracking up. Really loudly. My laughter shakes the bed.

"Virginia?" Amelrik sounds like he thinks I've lost it. A dragon, who's in the same bed as me, is concerned that I'm crazy.

I start laughing even harder—so hard that tears slide down my cheeks.

Amelrik turns toward me. I can't see him in the dark, but I can tell by his movements. "Are you okay?"

"It's just . . . the two of us . . . *here* . . ." I'm laughing so much, it's difficult to get the words out. I force myself to take a few deep breaths, trying to calm down enough to speak. I still feel giddy, like I could burst out laughing again at any moment, but for the most part I think I have it under control. I wipe the tears from my eyes. "I hadn't left the barracks in four and a half *years*. Because I was so afraid of dragons. And now here I am, in a dragons' lair, in bed with one."

I start laughing again, even though Amelrik is silent, like he doesn't find that at all hilarious. I think maybe I freaked him out when I said I was in bed with him—even though technically I am—but then he says, "Four and a half years?"

And suddenly it's not funny anymore. I forgot he didn't know that. He saw me get freaked out when we were leaving the barracks, but he didn't know how bad it was. He was the one person in my life who didn't, the only one who treated me like a normal person, and I just ruined it.

"The barracks used to be the only place where I felt safe. So I, um, just didn't leave."

"What happened four and a half years ago?"

I pretend I don't hear him. "And then you and Lothar infiltrated it. The one place in the whole world where I was sure there weren't any dragons, and you guys showed up." And if Amelrik hadn't exposed what Lothar really was, what would have happened to me? Would I be in Celeste's place right now? Or would they have killed me when they found out I was a dud? "My father was going to marry me off to one of his friends. Someone old enough to be my grandfather. And everyone at that auction was there because of my bloodline, but this guy didn't even have the decency to care about that!"

"The nerve."

"He just wanted me to be his baby factory and pump out sons. Like sons are so great. I mean," I add, "not that there shouldn't be sons or anything. I didn't mean you shouldn't exist. Just that daughters should get more credit. But what I'm trying to say is, I was so afraid of dragons that I couldn't even leave the barracks, but if I hadn't run off with one—with you—I'd be in Lord Varrens' bed right now. Maybe having to let him climb on top of me, and . . ." I shudder. This would have been our fourth night together, so it definitely would have happened by now. Probably several times. "If I'd married him, I could have stayed at the barracks forever, but I never would have felt safe again."

"It was your mother dying, wasn't it? The reason you didn't leave the barracks."

I hate that he guessed it so easily, but what else would it have been? "I watched her get ripped apart by a dragon. He was a vendor in the marketplace. We thought we knew him. And then, one day, he transformed and murdered her right in front of me. She wasn't from one of the Families. She didn't have magic. But I'm a St. George. I should have been able to save her. Celeste would have, if she'd been there instead. But I just watched it happen. My mother was screaming for help. I'd never heard anyone sound so terrified. And I just stood there, unable to move. It's my fault she died."

"No, it's not."

"My mother got brutally murdered because I can't use magic. Now Celeste's in trouble for the same reason. Everyone back at the barracks knows how useless I am. That's why they all treat me like that. Like I'm not good enough. It's not like I *decided* to never leave the barracks again. Torrin thinks I did. That I could have left any time I wanted, if I just stopped being so dramatic. They *all* thought that. I know they did, even if they didn't say it. But it wasn't a decision I made—it just sort of happened. Every time I thought about leaving, or any time I got too close to the entrance to town, I felt like I was going to die. I couldn't breathe, and I'd start shaking, and it was like I was standing there in the marketplace all over again, watching it happen. The only reason I jumped from that wall was because you dragged me. I was never going to do it on my own. And now you know how useless I am, too, and I . . . I wish you didn't."

He's quiet for a minute.

My heart's pounding. I shouldn't have told him any of that. Just because I'm always asking him stuff doesn't mean he needs to know that everybody hates me because I practically killed my own mother. I can't use magic, and I'm not a paladin. I'm a failure as a St. George, and the only thing I could have possibly been good for was getting married and making more St. Georges, to do what I couldn't. And what did I do? I ran away with a dragon prince instead. Like you do.

"What color was he?"

"That's what you have to say? I tell you all that, and you . . . You know what, never mind." I tug the blankets around my shoulder and turn away from him. There's an ache in my throat. I never should have said anything. I don't know what I was expecting. Even the people at home who care about me think that I'm a lost cause, so what's Amelrik, who hardly knows me, supposed to think?

"I wasn't trying to change the subject."

"I can't hear you—I'm asleep. I have another busy day of spilling all my embarrassing secrets tomorrow, and I need my rest."

"I'm trying to talk to you about something."

"And I'm trying to get you to leave me alone!" I flop over onto my other side and accidentally smash my forehead into his chin.

"Ow."

"That's what you get for creeping up on me and not staying on your side of my—of *your*—bed. And for being all 'oh, what color was he?' As if I care!"

"I wasn't creeping up on you! I was just trying to . . . He was light green, right?"

"Yeah, but—"

"Maybe around thirty?"

"I guess. Something like that."

"Then it wouldn't have mattered."

"What wouldn't?"

"Whether you had magic or not. The dragonkin from Rowan clan go through this, uh, hormonal shift around then. It makes them prone to violent outbursts, and they have to transform more often. It also makes them resistant to magic. The binding spell wouldn't have worked on him. You'd need a *really* experienced St. George for that. Even Celeste's magic wouldn't have been enough."

"What?" I whisper it. He's put this idea out there, this delicate, fragile idea that could change everything, and I feel like any sudden movements or loud noises might shatter it.

"He probably didn't even mean to hurt her. They're required to spend a few years living among humans, usually in their twenties. It's not supposed to coincide with the hormonal shift, but sometimes the shift happens early. Anyway, what I'm trying to say, Virginia, is that it wasn't your fault. There was nothing you could have done."

"You'd better not be making this up to make me feel better. Because if you are, you can expect a punch in the face. If I can find it in the dark. You know what? You can expect a *kick*." Punches are for when the lamps are lit.

"I swear I'm not making it up."

"But then . . . why didn't anybody tell me?" Why did they all act like I was to blame?

"Because paladins are ignorant. Knowing how to kill dragons doesn't mean they know how we live, or that they even care to know."

"It wasn't my fault." I try out the words to see how they feel on my tongue. And I know I believe them because relief washes over me. A knot in my stomach untwists, and my whole body feels lighter.

I could hug him. But, much like punching, it's too dark for that. And being in his bed together is inappropriate enough without adding hugging to the mix. But I don't know how else to say all the things that need to be said.

"It wasn't your fault," he repeats.

And I think how funny it is that I feel safer here with him, in a dragon's den, than I ever could have back home.

24

THE MOOD-ENHANCING QUALITY OF SPIT

"Close your eyes," Amelrik says.

It's two days later, and we're outside, climbing a steep hill. It's the kind of hill whose sole purpose in life is to make me aware of just how out of shape I am. Sweat drips down my forehead and down the sides of my nose, and I can hardly breathe. Amelrik's a lot faster than me, now that his injuries are healed, and he keeps bounding up ahead and then coming back down to wait.

When I told him it was my birthday, he got really excited and said he had the perfect thing for us to do. I'd planned to spend the whole day reading—I gathered up a bunch of books in English from his shelf— and maybe I would have stuck to that plan if I knew he intended to make me go outside and climb this hill with him. Nothing could be worth sweating this much.

"You want me to close my eyes? We're on a hill."

"We're on a cliff, actually. We're almost to the top."

"We're almost to the top of a *cliff*, and you want me to not be able to see?"

"It's not far, and it'll be better this way. It's not like I'm going to let you fall." He holds out his hand.

I'm still skeptical. But I figure I can open my eyes again if I really need to. I take his hand and let him guide me over the last ridge. I kind of cheat a little bit, though, because I peek down at the ground a couple times, just to make sure I'm not about to trip on anything.

We get to the top. A gust of wind whirls through my hair and cools the sweat on my face.

"Okay, *now*," Amelrik says.

I open my eyes and gasp.

We're higher up than I've ever been, overlooking a sparkling blue lake. The water's so blue, it looks like a painting. Forest stretches out for miles in every direction. I can see some buildings crowded together in the distance, which must be a town. Puffy white clouds dot the sky, highlighted by the sun. I know I can't really be that much closer to them, but it feels like I could reach out and touch one.

Across the lake, on the opposite cliff, dragons spread their wings and leap into the air, or fold them along their backs and dive down into the water. I've always thought of dragons as lumbering and, well, beast-like, but there's so much grace and skill in their movements that those words couldn't ever describe them.

It's the most beautiful thing I've ever seen. Not just the dragons, but the lake and the town and the trees and the sky. All of it. "It's amazing."

Amelrik grins. "I always liked it up here."

I watch another dragon take off, catching the wind with its wings. A fish leaps out of the water far below—just a quick flash of silver—and then disappears again.

Amelrik sits down on the ground, a little ways back from the ledge. I join him, really wishing we'd brought lunch with us. We're quiet for a while, just enjoying the view. Then Amelrik says, "What would you be doing for your birthday if you were back home? What do you usually do, I mean?"

Nothing like this. "Torrin would go to the bakery in town and get me these chocolate-chip pastries I love. They're best when they're warm, so he'd run back home as fast as he could, before they could cool off too much. That was after I stopped leaving the barracks."

Amelrik rolls his eyes. "Gee, how nice of him."

"What? It *was* nice."

"Oh, right, considering that he didn't even believe you about not being able to leave. And you only got to have them once a year?"

I look down at my knees. When he puts it like that, it doesn't sound so great. "It's not like anybody else was volunteering. And it was a long way to run just so I could have some warm pastries."

"Well, obviously I can't get you those. What else?"

"Me and Celeste would stay up late and look at the stars—"

"That, we can do."

"—and talk about boys."

"Or not."

"We don't have to do anything else. It's not like me and you are actually . . ." What? Lovers? Friends? But aren't we? Friends, I mean. Obviously we're not lovers, even though we slept in the same bed again last night. But that was only because there's really nowhere else to sleep—it's not because we *want* to be that close to each other. It's not like it's *comforting* that he's only an arm's length away, that at any time I could reach out and touch someone familiar and know I'm not alone in this strange, foreign place.

"Do you like theater?"

"Dragons have theater? Like, plays and stuff?"

"Your ignorance knows no bounds. Of course we do."

"Would any of it be in English?"

He opens his mouth to speak, then pauses to think that over. "I'll come up with something else."

I'm about to tell him again that he doesn't need to, even though it's nice of him to make the effort, when a dragon comes flying at us from somewhere over the lake. It swoops down low, like it's going to grab us with its claws. Fear floods my chest, and I'm sure that this is it—I'm going to die in the next few seconds.

Amelrik stays calm, like this is no big deal. "It's okay," he says. "It's just Odilia."

I want to ask how he can tell, but that seems rude.

The dragon keeps its claws to itself and doesn't gut us, landing behind us instead. It changes into human form, and then I see that it is indeed Odilia. Naked, of course.

"Just Odilia?!" She smacks him playfully on the back of the head before sitting down on his other side. "I saw you over here. We have a lot to catch up on."

"You saw me over here *with Virginia*. We're trying to figure out what to do for her birthday."

I think he's trying to tell her she's interrupting, but she doesn't take the hint. She leans forward and glances over at me, clearly not liking what she sees. She says something to him in Vairlin, and then he glares at her.

"What did she say?" I whisper.

"Nothing." But Amelrik's face gets kind of red, so I know it must have been something embarrassing.

Odilia laughs, pleased with herself. "Tell me what happened with Elder clan, cousin. Six months ago they told us you were dead. I cried for days, and your father shut himself away for a week, hardly speaking to anyone."

"He did?"

"He blamed himself for sending you there. When Raban died, he was sick with worry over what they would do to you."

"Who's Raban?" And why did Odilia have to come over here and start talking about things I don't understand?

"The hostage from Elder clan," Amelrik says. "He drowned in the lake. Lothar put on a big show of mourning him. Raban's death was an accident, but Lothar hated me so much, he riled everyone up about it, until there was nothing his father could do to make it right, except . . ." He swallows. "I thought he really was going to kill me. He was more of a father to me than mine ever was, and—"

"Amelrik!" Odilia snaps. "You don't mean that."

"—I could see how much it upset him, knowing what he had to do. He hoped it would blow over, that if he put it off long enough, people would forget. But Lothar saw to it that they didn't. So when the day came, the king took me out into the woods for my execution. His hands were shaking—he couldn't do it. He cut my bonds instead and told me to run."

Odilia considers that for a moment. "Still, I know what he made you do for them. Some father he was to you!"

"He made me feel like I was more than just a guest. Like I was part of his family."

She snorts. "That's why he exploited you and sent you off to live with humans? To trick them for his own gain? Who does that, especially to someone like you? You were a tool to him."

He clenches his fists. "You weren't there. You don't know."

"Anyone could see there's something wrong with that situation, cousin. Even your little whore here could tell you that."

Um, hello? Whores don't pledge their undying devotion. I don't think, anyway.

"That's enough, Odilia!"

"It makes me sick to think of anyone taking advantage of you." She looks at me when she says that.

"I can take care of myself. You don't have to—"

Two more dragons swoop over us, chasing each other. They circle around and dive into the water, then leap out of it into the air and come back, half landing, half crashing on the ground behind us. They shake the water off themselves, splashing us with freezing-cold droplets.

Odilia's laughing. When they change into human form, I see that they're two guys, around her age. Both are lean and well muscled—not that I'm, uh, paying attention to that or anything, and I'm certainly not looking at anything below the belt—and both of them are grinning at her.

"Osric! Godwin!" she scolds, but it's obvious she's not really mad. "What do you think you're doing?"

"Showing off," Amelrik mutters.

The boys don't seem to hear him. The slightly taller one—who I think is Osric—rakes a hand through his sandy-blond hair. "Trying to get you to come flying with us before anyone from another team tries to steal you away. We're practicing for the games."

"Well, I don't know," she says.

"Please, Odilia?" Godwin tilts his head and bats his eyes at her.

Osric elbows him in the ribs. "I won the race—I get to ask her."

"You already had your chance. I'm getting her to say yes."

Odilia's eating up all the attention. "Boys, you know I would, but I'm here with my cousin."

"He can come, too. We've got more spots open on our team. He'll have to leave his human behind, though."

She clears her throat. "My *cousin*. The one I told you about?"

"What are you . . . Oh. *Ohhhh*. Right. That cousin." Osric nods.

Godwin is still confused. "Which cousin? The dead one?"

Osric smacks his arm. "No, you idiot. Does he look dead to you?" He lowers his voice, but we can all hear anyway. "The crippled one."

"Oh."

They're not grinning anymore, and they both give Amelrik really solemn looks.

"It's okay, Odilia," Osric says. "We can hang out here with you. We'll practice later—we've got plenty of time before the games."

"Well . . ." Odilia glances at Amelrik.

"Just go," he says, waving her off. "You were the one who interrupted us in the first place."

"Really? You're the best." She reaches out and ruffles his hair as she gets up.

Osric and Godwin take running leaps off the edge of the cliff and transform in midair, so they're dragons by the time they hit the water. They just barely make it.

"You stupid boys!" Odilia shouts after them, but she's laughing again. She transforms first, then dives in, too.

Amelrik sighs. His excitement from earlier is gone, and now he just seems sad.

"Come closer," I tell him, even though we're already sitting right next to each other.

"What?"

"I need to tell you something."

"So tell me."

"It's a secret. I have to whisper it."

His forehead wrinkles, and at first I think he's not going to do it. But then curiosity gets the better of him, and he leans toward me.

I make like I'm going to whisper in his ear, and then at the last second I lick the side of his face instead. His skin is salty with sweat.

"Hey!" He wipes my spit off with his sleeve, but he's also grinning and trying not to laugh. "What was that for?"

"Human saliva is a little-known pick-me-up, but only when applied liberally and directly from the tongue."

"Is that so?"

"It worked, didn't it?"

He smiles at me. "That doesn't prove anything."

"It doesn't *not* prove it. And it's my birthday. I'm pretty sure you're not supposed to argue with someone on their birthday."

"Funny, I've never heard that before."

"Well, you didn't know about the mood-enhancing quality of spit, either, so obviously you still have a few things to learn."

25
NOT LIKE THE REST OF THEM

It's the next afternoon, and me and Amelrik are taking a walk through the woods, no hills this time. I made him promise that part before I'd come out here with him. He said he just wanted to take a walk, but he seems really nervous, and there's obviously something on his mind.

And I know it's stupid—really stupid—but part of me hopes that the thing on his mind is me, and that he's going to kiss me again. For reals this time, even though it certainly felt real enough before. It's stupid for several reasons. One, because I'm a St. George and he's a dragon and I shouldn't want that, and two, because of course he doesn't feel that way about me. Guys *never* feel that way about me, and I'm sure a dragon prince is no exception.

I mean, he's made it clear that he only kissed me because he had to. The only reason he's letting me sleep in his bed is to keep up appearances, and because I refused to leave. He went out of his way to make my birthday fun yesterday, but that's what you do on someone's birthday if you're their friend. And it's especially what you do when they know absolutely no one else and are far from home.

Amelrik stops at a clearing off the side of the trail. He looks around, pausing to listen—I guess to make sure we're alone. "Virginia . . . don't be mad, but this isn't just a walk."

"Uh-huh. I kind of figured that."

"There's something we need to talk about. No, there's something we need to *do*, and . . ." He scratches his ear, not quite looking at me. "You might not like this."

"I might, though." Especially if it's anything like last time.

"I figure it's not a good idea to do it back home."

"You mean, because of the bed situation?" Maybe sharing a bed won't be weird if we only kiss when we're out here.

"What does the bed have to do with anything?"

"Um." Crap. "Nothing?"

He raises an eyebrow at me. "I haven't even told you what I'm talking about."

"So tell me already. I don't have all day."

"You kind of do. But, anyway, what I'm saying is . . ." He lets out a deep breath. "We need to practice your magic."

"We *what*?" That is not what I signed up for. "I don't do magic, okay? And even if I did, I don't see how you'd figure into it."

"Because you need someone to practice on."

"You want me to practice on *you*?"

"No, I really don't. But there's no one else."

"Just get a dragon ring."

He scowls at me. "Dragons don't keep dragon rings around! And even if we did, it's not enough. There's no way anyone's *ever* putting one of those on me again, and we need to know if the spell's actually working. And that means you cast the binding spell on me, and I . . . I see if I can still transform."

"How is that different from having a dragon ring on?"

"It doesn't hurt the same way." He puts a hand to his neck, where the ring was, even though it's completely healed. "And it's only temporary."

The spell lasts different amounts of time, depending on how strong the caster is. Celeste's lasts for twelve hours, while mine would probably only last twelve seconds. "Okay, but you obviously don't really want to do this, and neither do I, so I don't see the point. And you said the Elder king is like a father to you. Can't you just talk to him?"

"Talk to him?"

"About Celeste. Ask him if he'll let her go."

"Are you serious? I'm supposed to be dead. He was supposed to have killed me."

"Yeah, but—"

"You want me, an escaped hostage with a death sentence still hanging over his head, to stroll up to the king and ask him nicely if he'll let your sister, a dangerous weapon, go free? Forget the fact that he'd be obligated to execute me on the spot, and that there's no way I'd *ever* get an audience with him. How would it look if he just handed over their St. George to another clan?"

"Like he was doing you a favor? A really big one?"

Amelrik sighs. "When we go to Elder clan, *no one* can know I'm there. And if we're going to rescue your sister, it wouldn't hurt to have magic. It might even save our lives."

"So you want me to do this because of Celeste? And it has nothing to do with you telling everyone in your clan that I'm a better paladin than her?"

"Well . . ."

"You said I didn't have to do magic!"

"You don't! Probably! At least for a while. But it might come up, and if it does and you can't do anything, we are *dead*. And as much as I really, really don't want to do this, I want to keep living even more. I assume you feel the same way."

"If you want to keep living, maybe you should stop pissing me off. And did we have to come all the way out here for this?"

"I don't want my room to stink."

"Won't the other dragons smell it on me? If I do manage to make, like, a spark or something?" If he thinks I'm going to actually cast a whole spell, he's going to be disappointed.

"We'll rinse off in the lake first before we go home."

"That's fine for you, but that lake is *cold*." I remember when Osric and Godwin shook water all over us yesterday, and that was bad enough.

"You can't go back inside the caves stinking of paladin magic. And you certainly aren't getting into my bed like that. In fact, you should probably take an actual bath first."

"Yes, Mother."

He presses his hands to his face. "Let's just get this over with."

We move to the far side of the clearing. Amelrik stands right in front of me, his head held high, like he's putting on a brave front as he faces his executioner. He takes a step back. Then another. Then he changes his mind and steps forward again. He wipes his palms on his pant legs and takes in a slow breath. "Okay. Okay. I'm ready. Do it now. I'm— No, no, wait. *Wait!*"

You'd think from the way he's saying that that I was actually *doing* something, instead of watching him have some kind of breakdown. "We don't have to do this."

"Yes, we do."

"But we don't have to do it *today*."

"If we put it off, I'm going to lose my nerve."

"Going to?"

He glares at me. "I wore that dragon ring for ten days, I think I can handle this."

"You know you don't actually have anything to worry about, right? There's no way I'm really going to manage the binding spell."

"Just hurry up before I change my mind."

"Chicken out, you mean. But . . . okay." I try to remember what he said before, about magic being a part of me, and how it's not something I choose to have—it's just there. I imagine the energy for the spell leaving me and binding him into human form. Which seems pretty unnecessary, all things considered. "This isn't working."

"Did you even try?"

"If I say yes, can we go back?"

"You cast a spell before. You can do it again."

"That one was a lot simpler, and it was an emergency. I don't really know how I did it."

"Great. That's exactly what you should tell my father if he ever asks about it. I'm sure he and everyone else who believed me about you will totally understand and there will be no hard feelings."

"Hey, I didn't ask you to lie to them. You told them what they wanted to hear. You said I was better than *Celeste*."

"I told them you were the better St. George. That much at least wasn't a lie."

I laugh in disbelief. "Yeah, right. As if that could ever be even remotely true."

Amelrik shakes his head. "Don't say that, Virginia. You're so much better than her, and you don't even know it."

"I've lived in her shadow my whole life. *That's* what I know."

"Your sister wouldn't have had anything to do with me, even if it was the only way to get you back. She would never have done all this to save you, if the circumstances were reversed."

"She . . ." Okay, she never would have teamed up with a dragon— not in a million years—and especially not the one she told me was so dangerous. "She wouldn't have given up on me. Not that easily."

"But she wouldn't have come here. She *couldn't* have, because I wouldn't have brought her. Your sister is the worst kind of paladin, because she believes all dragons are evil and that it's her job to murder every last one of us."

"That's not—"

"True? Yes, *it is*. She wants to hurt us as much as possible. That's what she uses her magic for. And that's not you."

"I'm supposed to be like her. My whole life, that's all anyone's ever wanted from me." Everyone except for Amelrik, that is.

"But what do you want? Maybe the reason you could never do magic before was because you're not like the rest of them. You don't want to hurt anybody, but that's exactly what you would've had to do if you could cast the binding spell. Maybe you were scared of dragons, and maybe . . . maybe you still hate us, but that doesn't mean you want to hurt us, either."

"I don't hate dragons." Not anymore. *And I don't hate you.*

"You have magic. We both know that much. And you're a better person than your sister, or any other paladin I've ever met, and maybe it feels like being able to use magic means you have to be like them, but you don't."

"You think I would have rather gotten married to some random old man than be a paladin? That it was a choice?"

"No. Not at all. I don't think you want either of those things, though. Magic isn't about wanting it enough, and it never will be. But it is about knowing *what* you want."

Too bad I don't know what that is. But I think I see his point. And the idea that I don't have to be a paladin, that I don't have to live up to Celeste, is, well, pretty freeing. "Okay, I'll try the spell. For reals this time."

"Right. For reals this time." He doesn't sound too happy about that.

I look into his eyes, trying to remember how it felt when I used my magic before. I think about the binding spell, imagining a dragon ring around his neck. But even just the thought of him suffering like that again makes my stomach clench, and I realize that isn't going to work.

But he needs me to be able to do this. We both do. So instead I think about how I would never let Celeste or Torrin—or anyone— torture him again. I think about how much I want to punch his father in the face for never letting him go to the Feast of Eventide and for acting like he's not good enough. I can't punch any dragons, but I can learn to cast this spell and maybe keep him safe.

My hands tingle worse than if they'd fallen asleep, and a bright flash of red bursts from my palms. The smell of sulfur fills the air. And Amelrik's right—this would have totally stunk up his room.

Not that I care, because *I just cast the binding spell.* A thrill runs down my spine. "I did it! Take that, um . . . *world!*"

Amelrik's face looks pale. I thought he'd be happy, but maybe he just doesn't like being bound again. He said it didn't hurt the same way as the dragon ring, not that it didn't hurt *at all.*

"I don't think it worked," he says.

"What?"

"I didn't feel anything."

"But I cast *something.*" I can still smell it. "Didn't I? Don't tell me that was just a really big spark."

"The point of this was to practice. You don't have to get it on your first try."

"Maybe it did work, though. Go ahead. Try and change forms."

"I don't need to. I know it didn't."

"You said the whole point of this was so we could know for sure. This was my first binding spell—it could just be really weak and that's why you don't think it worked. And it might only last a little while, so we don't have time to argue about it."

"But I—"

"No." I put my hands on my hips. "This is the first time I've ever even come close to casting this, and we are going to find out if I did it or not."

"Okay." He squeezes his eyes closed real quick, then opens them again. He starts to take his shirt off.

"Whoa. What are you doing? I said transform, not get naked."

"I'm *not.* It's just . . . my wings."

Oh, right. I remember last time how they ripped through his clothes.

He pulls his shirt over his head, and despite how much time we've spent together, and despite how little clothing everyone else wears around here, this is the first time I've seen him without it.

This is the first time I've seen how muscular his arms are, or gotten a good look at the way his neck meets his shoulders, or at how his collarbone sticks out, creating a hollow space behind it.

Erg. It's great that he actually got me to cast magic and all, but why couldn't he have brought me out here to kiss me?

There's the sound of flesh ripping and changing, though it's not as loud or as involved as with the other dragons. His eyes turn yellow. Dark scales spread down his neck and along his sides, stopping just above his hips. Dark wings jut out from his back.

"It didn't work," he says, his voice a whisper.

I take a step closer to him.

He practically stumbles backward to keep the distance between us, holding up a clawed hand to ward me off. *"Don't."*

"I won't . . . I won't touch you."

His eyes search mine, like he doesn't believe me, or like maybe he's afraid to.

This is the boy whose bed I share. Who sleeps next to me, barely an arm's length away. And now he's terrified to let me anywhere near him.

I just want to look. I want to do it without fear or revulsion, to make up for the shock he saw on my face last time. Because I bet everyone else in the world who's ever seen him like this had that same reaction, and I wish . . . I wish I'd been the exception. I wish I could take it back.

His eyes are so different—it's hard to see him as the same person. If he'd kissed me while he was like this, would I have still melted inside? Would I have been able to go along with it, or would I have freaked out?

I remember how safe I felt when I woke up with his arm around me. But now I imagine it with scales, and what I feel is a twinge of horror.

Amelrik changes back into human form, wrapping his arms around himself and turning away from me. He puts his shirt back on, and I study the sharpness of his shoulder blades, thinking about how only moments ago he had wings.

26

IT'S LIKE YOU WANT ME TO MURDER YOU

I wake up early one morning—or maybe I should say I'm *woken* up—because someone is moving around the room, picking things up and setting them back down again, and generally making a lot of noise. I open my eyes just enough to see that it's Amelrik, then decide to go back to sleep. And even though the lamps are lit, and even though I can't actually tell what time it is, I'm pretty sure that it's too early for either of us to be awake yet.

He must have noticed me stir, though, because as soon as I close my eyes, he practically jumps onto the bed. "Virginia?" He shakes my shoulder. "Hey, Virginia. Are you awake?"

I pretend to be asleep. I'm starting to suspect that he was making all that noise on purpose. You'd think that after living together for two weeks he'd know better than that. Virginia St. George does *not* get up early.

"Come on, Virginia. I know you're not asleep."

I keep my eyes closed. "If you know that, then why are you asking? It's like you *want* me to murder you."

"No, it's like I want you to wake up and see the present I got you."

"Present?" Why didn't he lead with that? And did I say Virginia St. George doesn't get up early? What I meant was, Virginia St. George doesn't get up early *without a good reason*. I sit up and rub the crud out of my eyes. "My birthday was over a week ago." Not that I'm complaining.

"Yeah, I know, but this wasn't out then." He hands me a book.

My heart leaps when I see the title: *Princess Mysteries #7—The Gentleman's Curse.* "Whoa! Where did you . . . How did you get this?"

"There's a town, not that far from here. The general store opens early, and they carry books."

If he's talking about the town we saw from the cliff, "not that far from here" isn't how I'd describe it. Especially not this early in the morning. "So, you walked there? How long have you been up?"

"A few hours. I knew it came out today, and I . . . I wanted to surprise you."

"You did that for me?"

He shrugs and looks away. "It's not a big deal."

Except that it kind of is. "You didn't have to do that."

"If I'd waited, they might have been sold out. They only had two copies. And by the time they got more, you might not have been here. I thought I could read it, too, and we could find out who she marries and get a chance to talk about it before we rescue your sister and you have to go back home. But if you don't want it . . ." He starts to take the book back.

I hold on to it, hugging it to my chest. "No, I do! I do want it!"

He seems relieved. "Okay. Good."

"Thank you."

"You'd think no one had ever given you a present before."

More like no one's ever put this much effort into it before. Not that I'm going to tell him that. "Just don't be surprised when she marries Orlando."

"Uh, no, she has to marry the prince."

"You're too biased."

"And you're not? How am I too biased?"

"Because *you're* a prince."

He rolls his eyes. "I'm also an outlaw. Though I guess I wasn't a bandit, and I've never solved any mysteries."

"You know what? I don't even need to read this book, because I know in my heart how it's going to end. So there."

"Well, if you're not going to read it—"

I push his hand away, keeping my grip on the book. "I didn't say that. I just said I didn't *need* to. Of course I'm going to read it. Don't be so grabby."

"Okay. But as soon as you put it down, it's my turn."

"Your turn for what?" I bring the book up to my nose and inhale, breathing in that new-book smell.

"To read. We'll switch off. That way neither of us gets too far ahead."

"All right. But you're not allowed to finish it before me."

He holds up his hands, like that thought hadn't even occurred to him.

I open the book, resisting the urge to flip through it, in case I accidentally catch any spoilers. "How about we go practice magic today, too?"

"Um."

"It's been a week and a half." We only practiced it that once, and it's not like I succeeded. And I know I was reluctant about it at first, but since I actually got some results, I kind of want to keep at it. But every time I bring it up, he makes an excuse.

"I . . . can't. I'm busy today."

"Really?"

"My father's having a court meeting later that I have to attend."

Sure he is. "This was your idea, you know. What about all that stuff you said about me needing to learn this *to save our lives?*"

He picks up a tiny feather that worked its way out of the mattress and twirls it between his fingers. "I know it's been a while, but I can't help it if I'm busy."

"It's funny how you're only ever busy when I bring up practicing magic. But you don't have to attend court or whatever until later, right? So we could go practice right now."

"I don't think—"

I hold up the book. "I'd even let you go first."

He hesitates, obviously tempted. "I don't want to risk stinking like magic in front of my father and the court. It would raise too many questions."

"Is that the only reason?" We both know it's not. I try to look him in the eyes, but he avoids me.

He yawns. "I also need to take a nap first."

Well, that part I believe, at least. I kind of want to go back to sleep myself, but there's no way I'm not starting this book right this second. I turn the pages until I find the first chapter.

Amelrik lies down next to me, not even bothering to get under the covers. He no longer makes sure he's as far away from me as possible, and I can't deny that we've gotten more comfortable with each other. I guess that's inevitable when you're sharing a bed with someone—or so I assume, since it's not like I have a lot of experience with it—but I don't know if it's a good thing, because it's kind of all I can do not to reach out and smooth the hair away from his face, or run my hand down his back, or something else equally embarrassing and inappropriate.

I settle for "accidentally" letting my foot touch his leg, but then I chicken out and move it back to my side of the bed, even though he showed no signs of noticing.

"Hey, Amelrik?"

"Mmm." He sounds like he's half asleep already.

"Nobody's ever done anything like this for me. Going so far out of their way like that, to get me something I really wanted. So . . . thanks."

His eyes stay closed, but he smiles and mumbles something that sounds like "Don't mention it."

I wait until his breathing is deep and even, and then I let my foot touch his leg again, and this time I leave it there.

27
SORRY DOESN'T BRING BACK PLOT TWISTS

"I hope you're happy," I tell Amelrik. "Since you got what you wanted." It's the next day and we're walking through the tunnels, on our way to get lunch. We're both about halfway through the book, though he's a little farther than me. In the part I just read, Princess Genevieve actually married Prince Liam.

He grins. "Don't blame me. It's not like I made it happen."

Two children in dragon form are chasing each other through the tunnel, one of them snapping at the heels of the other, not paying attention to where they're going. They run into an adult dragon, who chews them out in Vairlin, until they duck their heads and slink away quietly.

"I really thought Orlando was going to stop the wedding. That whole scene, I kept waiting for him to show up."

"He's wanted for murder. What was he supposed to do?"

"He's been wrongly accused." He was with the princess at the time of the murder, but since it would have ruined her reputation if she vouched for him and admitted they were alone together the night before her wedding, he took the fall. "And I wanted him to show up, anyway. It's not fair."

"Well, don't think I got what I wanted. Them getting married in the middle of the book means something bad's still going to happen."

"Like that she's going to come to her senses and leave him for Orlando? Once she proves his innocence. He's the love of her life."

He snorts. "Hardly."

"I thought you said you didn't care who she ended up with? As long as the series kept going?"

"I changed my mind. She and Liam are perfect for each other. She can tell him anything."

"Or he's just a really good *friend*."

"Why can't he be both? Like, when she tells him about the baby, and he knows it couldn't be his, but he says he's going to love it anyway?"

"What?"

"I'm just saying he's committed. Genevieve needs that, especially after that scene where she caught her father with one of the maids and her whole idea of marriage was shaken."

"*What?*"

"Because she found out it's been going on for years, and her mother knew about it the whole time? You can't blame her for feeling like she's . . . Why are you looking at me like that?"

"I haven't read that far!"

"Yes, you have. You're ahead of me." He hesitates. "Aren't you?"

"I think I'd remember this stuff! I can't believe you just spoiled it!"

A couple of dragons turn their heads when I start shouting, their eyes flashing green in the torchlight.

"Sorry. I thought you already knew. And it's not like the pregnancy thing was a secret, since it was heavily hinted at in the opening chapters."

"*Hinted* at. Not for sure! And you don't get to defend yourself right now. I mean, *seriously!*" I turn away from him and head down a side tunnel.

He hurries after me. "It was an accident! And where are you going?"

"To lunch. I'm taking the long route. *By myself.* You can meet me there."

"Come on, Virginia. Don't be mad."

"Too late."

"I said I was sorry!"

"'Sorry' doesn't bring back plot twists!" I turn down the next tunnel, just to try and put some distance between us. I'm still learning my way around this place, but I'm pretty sure it will reconnect with the main path that leads to the kitchens.

"Virginia, wait!" He's stopped following me, staying at the opening to the tunnel, like there's an invisible wall keeping him out. "I can't go down there."

"Great, because you're not invited."

"No, that's . . . *We* can't go down there."

"Still not hearing a problem." Other than that he doesn't want me to be mad at him, but he should have thought of that before he spoiled so much stuff. This tunnel isn't even guarded, and there's nothing here, so if he wants me to turn around, he's going to have to give me a better reason than "can't."

The tunnel twists to the right, so that now I can't even see him when I look over my shoulder. Meaning I'm completely alone, because there's no one else using this passageway. Which makes me think maybe it doesn't connect after all, but if that was the case, why didn't he just say so? Either way, I'm not going to turn back now—not after I made such a big deal about it.

But maybe I am slightly relieved when Amelrik catches up to me, because this tunnel's getting kind of creepy, and I could swear the torches are getting farther and farther apart.

"Virginia, come on."

"I thought you couldn't come down here?"

"I can't. I—I shouldn't have. And neither should you." He puts a hand on my arm, and I can feel that he's shaking.

This tunnel is creepy, but is it *that* creepy? "What's down here? Is it haunted or something?"

"Please. Let's just go back."

"You had no problem spoiling the book, but you won't tell me why you're so freaked out?"

He keeps glancing toward the far end of the tunnel, like he's afraid of whatever's down there. "I didn't mean to spoil anything. I know you're mad at me, but it's not worth this."

"Not worth *what*?"

"Did you hear something?"

"No. Did you?"

"We have to go. If that means I have to pick you up and carry you out of here—"

"Okay, okay! We'll go." If he's that serious about it.

He grabs my hand, practically dragging me.

But something else grabs me from the other side, tearing me away from him, and I scream.

"Virginia!"

I hit the wall of the tunnel with enough force to knock the air from my lungs.

A dragon looms over me, keeping itself between us so Amelrik can't get to me. "I should have killed you when I had the chance," it tells him. "They told me you were dead, but I knew if I didn't feel the life drain out of you myself that you'd be back. And so here you are, come to get your revenge."

Amelrik's voice doesn't sound like him. It's too small and too terrified to be him. "Mother, no."

Mother?

The dragon changes into human form. She's a middle-aged woman with wild brown hair and vivid green eyes. Her eyes are so like his that I wonder if I would have guessed who she was, even thinking she was dead.

Amelrik starts to move toward me.

His mother changes back into a dragon and lashes out at him with her claws, just barely missing him. "Don't lie to me! There's no other reason you would have come back here, and to bring a *St. George*? Did you think I wouldn't smell what she was?!"

"I didn't—"

"Of course you'd have to go to *them* for help. You disgusting, worthless excuse for a dragon! I should have done it then. The moment you slid out of me, I knew I couldn't allow something so *wrong* to live. You were small and weak—tiny, compared to a real hatchling. Even with the ring around my neck, I had the strength to destroy such a pathetic thing. No one would have known."

He cringes at her words. "Mother, I didn't come here to hurt you. I swear!"

"Liar!" She changes into a human again, then back into a dragon. It happens quickly, and I can't tell if she's just insane or if she can't maintain her form. "What did he promise you?" she asks me. "What did that creature who calls himself my son promise to give you in exchange for killing me?!"

She doesn't wait for an answer, just lunges at me, all claws and teeth. Paralyzing fear flows through my veins. I'm already against the wall, and there's nowhere to go. I should try to cast the binding spell, I know I should, but it all happens so fast.

Then Amelrik's in front of me, his mother's claws tearing into him. The force of the blow pushes him backward, so that he slams into me. Which hurts, but not nearly as much as getting mauled by a dragon.

"Run!" he shouts, putting a hand to his side, which is covered in blood.

I grab his arm, in case he has any ideas about not getting out of here.

His mother is about a million times stronger than me, though. She knocks him to the ground, pinning him with one long, deadly claw poised above his heart. "Transform," she says. "Show me how ugly you truly are, and this time I won't just break your wings, I'll rip them off!"

"Get away from him!" I don't know what I'm doing, but I know I can't let her kill him. Or *rip his wings off.*

"I'll tear every last scale from your body, one by one!"

It's like she didn't even hear me. And I know what he said about me being better than Celeste, but I kind of wish I was her right now.

I think about the binding spell, and about how much I want his mother to stop. No, not want, *need.* Because he can't die. He can't. And not like this.

The smell of sulfur fills the air. Magic tingles in my hands. The flash of red seems extra bright in the dark.

His mother screams bloody murder. I don't think the spell even worked, because she stays in dragon form, but she jumps away from him, hissing and cursing at me.

"Come on!" I grab Amelrik's hand, helping him up, and then we run like hell.

28

LOOK AWAY, VIRGINIA

The king is furious.

We're on our knees in front of him and his court—and maybe some extra onlookers, because it seems like there are a lot more dragons here this time—our heads bowed. Amelrik's skin is pale and his breathing is shallow. He's obviously in a lot of pain, and he has his hand pressed to the injury on his side, which is still bleeding.

His father doesn't seem to care about that, though. He stays in dragon form and yells at us, which is pretty terrifying, to say the least. "How dare you disturb her! What did I tell you when you came back here?!"

"That I was—"

"That you were not to have contact with her! She was not to see or hear or smell you. Six years you've been gone, and she's hardly had an episode. There are days where she's almost her old self, and now you've been back *two weeks* and you not only set her off, but you let your St. George torment her as well!"

I make the mistake of glancing up, right as the king's eyes focus on me. I still can't read dragons very well, but anyone could see how angry he is.

"I'm sorry, Father." Blood from Amelrik's wound trickles across the floor, staining the knees of my pant legs. He does *not* look good, and I'm worried he might pass out before all this is over.

"Do not think your concubine is so useful to us that you can allow her to get out of hand! Keep better control over her, or I'll gut her myself."

There are some murmurings in the crowd at that.

"It was my fault," Amelrik says. "Virginia didn't know."

I hate that he's taking the blame for me. And maybe I didn't know what was down that tunnel, but he tried to warn me, and I should have listened to him.

"Your behavior is unacceptable, Amelrik. *Unacceptable.* This is why I sent you away in the first place! Do you think I enjoy seeing my only son bleeding out on the floor of the Royal Chamber?! Do you think I enjoyed picking up your broken, misshapen body years ago, not knowing if you would live or die? If I'd realized you hadn't learned your lesson from that, I wouldn't have allowed you to return! You deserve every bit of the pain you're feeling right now, and you are not to go anywhere near your mother ever again. You or your St. George. And if you do, you'd better let her kill you, because if she doesn't, I'll do it for her!"

Amelrik flinches. "Yes, Father."

"Rise before the court."

He staggers to his feet. I try to help him, but he waves me off.

At least this is over.

"And let it not be said that the king of Hawthorne clan has no compassion for his idiot son. Heal yourself, Amelrik. Transform for all to see."

There are some gasps from the audience, both excited and horrified, followed by whispers.

Amelrik just stands there, bleeding. His shoulders are hunched, and he stares at the ground, his expression pained.

The king stays silent for a while, drawing out the humiliation, until finally he says, "If you're too ashamed to show your disfigurement, then at least stop bleeding on my floor. You are dismissed."

"Look away, Virginia."

We're back in Amelrik's room. He's taken off his shirt, and he's *so pale*, and I could swear his lips are turning blue. There are three gashes in his side, though one of them is deeper than the others. All three are still bleeding, and I'm surprised he made it back here without collapsing.

"I've seen you transform before."

"But you shouldn't have to." He stares at the ground, his eyes half closed. He glances up at me, then away again. "I don't want anyone to see me. I can't . . . *Please*."

He sounds so sad, and I don't want to cause him any more pain. I don't want to be yet another onlooker who stares at him or makes him feel like there's something horribly wrong with him. But if I look away like he wants, it would be like saying there really is something that wrong that he should be ashamed to be seen, even by the people who care about him.

I hate myself for ever making him feel like that.

"I'm not turning away. You're really hurt, and I . . . I won't do that."

He opens his mouth, presumably to argue some more, but then he just sighs.

There's the sound of flesh rearranging itself—a sound I never thought I'd be so relieved to hear. Amelrik's wounds knit closed, though his skin is still stained with blood. Scales appear down his sides, and his wings spring out from his back. His eyes turn yellow. Almost as soon as the transformation is finished, he wobbles and falls to his knees. He spreads his wings out and puts one clawed hand on the ground to steady himself. He puts the other hand to his head.

"Are you okay?" I thought he'd be better now, but he still looks so pale.

"It's just . . . it takes a lot of energy. To transform. And I . . ." He winces, and for a moment, he looks like he might throw up. "I lost a lot of blood. It takes time to heal from that, and I have to stay like this for a while. I'm sorry you have to see me this way."

"Don't be. I'm not."

He pushes himself to his feet and folds in his wings. He keeps his gaze averted, like he's afraid to look at me, or like he's afraid to see me looking at him. "I'm sorry about all of it. I should have just told you what was down that tunnel. You almost got hurt, because of me, and my father threatened you. I let you believe my mother was dead, because it was easier than the truth, and it almost got you killed. I'm . . . I'm so sorry, Virginia."

"Are you seriously apologizing to me right now?"

His eyes flick down to the ground. "You shouldn't have had to go through all that, and I know I can never make up for it, but—"

"No, I mean *I'm* the one who needs to apologize. I should have listened to you when you said not to go down there. You tried to stop me, but I did it anyway. You almost died protecting me." And I'm not convinced we're out of the woods on that one yet. "It was my fault we were in that situation. I'm the reason you got hurt." By his own mother, who would have tortured and killed him. "You're the one who shouldn't have had to go through all that, but I'm the reason it happened. And I'm sorry. I am *so sorry*."

"You don't understand. It's my fault, just like it was back then. I make her mad, and I wasn't supposed to be there, and then I was, with a St. George. It was the worst thing I could have done." He wobbles again, swaying on his feet, though he manages to stay standing.

"Come on. You should lie down." I lead him toward the bed.

"I have to explain first."

"No, you really don't."

"She doesn't like to look at me. She . . . she can't control herself." He's shaking now, and it takes me a second to realize he's shivering. "I knew that, but I . . . I thought she would be proud of me. I thought it would mean she didn't have to hate me anymore."

"That *what* would?" I shake my head. "It doesn't matter." I pull the blankets back from the bed, making a space for him.

He sits down and kicks off his shoes. He's wearing socks, but I can see claws poking out of them. "I . . ." He's shivering so hard, his jaw is shaking and his teeth are chattering, making it difficult to understand what he's saying. "I was fourteen. I'd . . . I'd never flown before, and she hated that."

"Just lie down." I try to put my hand on his shoulder, but he pulls away, not letting me touch him.

"'Even draclings can fly.' That's what she'd say. It made her sick to look at me. But one day I managed to get off the ground. My wings still worked back then," he adds.

Still worked? I glance at them, but he's got them folded behind his back, and I can't get a good look.

"I wanted to show her. I thought maybe if I could fly, she wouldn't get so mad. I mean, I *couldn't* fly, but it was a start."

"You don't have to tell me any of this. Please, lie down. You're freezing, and exhausted, and you lost *so much* blood, and you say you'll heal, but I—" I choke up a little, betraying just how worried I am.

He blinks, taking that in. Then he lies down on his back, pushing his wings out a little and tucking them in along his sides.

I pull the blankets over him.

His eyes fall closed, and I think he's finally going to let himself rest, but then he opens them. "I make her want to hurt me. I thought I could change that. I thought if I showed her that I wasn't worthless, that maybe someday I could fly, she'd . . ." He shuts his eyes again, and this time tears leak out. He wipes them away with his arm.

"She broke your wings."

He nods. His arm is still over his eyes, but I can see tears sliding down his cheeks. Some of them catch on the tiny scales that line the edges of his face. They follow the curve of them down to his jaw, while others slip into his hair. "She tried to kill me. If my father hadn't walked in . . ."

He's crying harder now, and he's really hurt, and no matter what he says, I know that what happened today was my fault. I caused this, and I don't know what to do. "Do you want me to get someone?" There's no way I'm leaving his room after getting chewed out by his father for wandering off, and there's no way I'm leaving him alone when he's this messed up, but I can ring the bell and ask one of the servants to do it. "I'll call for Odilia."

"No!" He reaches out for me when I move to leave, his clawed hand grasping my arm. It's the first time we've touched while he was in dragon form. His hand encircles the spot just above my wrist, his claws curving along my skin. He isn't hurting me, but he looks horrified when he realizes what he's just done and quickly lets go. "I don't want anybody else here, and I . . . I don't want you to leave." His yellow eyes are pleading with me—*Amelrik's* eyes—and I don't know how I ever thought they made him look like a different person.

"Yeah. Okay. I won't." The *Princess Mysteries* book is lying on the chest at the foot of the bed. I grab it and settle in next to him.

29
HOWEVER YOU GOT THAT WAY

I wake up a long time later with my arm draped across Amelrik's chest and my hand resting on his shoulder, my fingers brushing against the scales on his neck. I'm lying on my side next to him, and my forehead is pressed against his arm. I don't think he'd want me touching him while he's in dragon form like this, but he was having nightmares, and crying in his sleep, and I just wanted to comfort him.

I should move, before he wakes up. I know I should. But I like being able to feel his warmth and the rise and fall of his breathing. I like being so close to him, and feeling cozy and safe, and I just want to savor this moment for as long as I can, before I have to let go.

My fingertips explore the texture of the scales on his neck. They're smooth, and a lot softer than I thought they'd be, though there's resistance when I try to go against the grain.

He swallows.

I freeze. My face is still pressed against his arm, so I can't see his reaction to any of this, but I know he's awake. And that he felt me touching him.

"Virginia?"

I consider whether or not I can get away with pretending to still be asleep, but I don't think he'd be fooled. I pull away, retreating to my side of the bed before I can embarrass myself any more than I already have.

He sits up and stretches out his arms and his wings. One of them extends over me, and I get a glimpse of the splash of red scales at the base. Just for a second, and then he folds them back in and changes into human form.

I sit up, too. "I was just . . . You were having nightmares, and I didn't want you to be alone." I glance over at him. "Are you okay?"

The color's returned to his face, and he no longer looks like he's about to die. "Yeah. Mostly." He runs a hand over the bloodstains on his side, where his wounds were.

"Listen, about what happened . . . I know I already said this, but you were really out of it, so I'm going to say it again." I spread my hands out against the blankets, feeling the velvet squish beneath my fingers. "I'm sorry. Sorry that you ever had to go through any of that with your mother, and sorry that you had to relive it because of me."

"You didn't know. It wasn't your—"

"Please don't say it wasn't my fault."

His voice is quiet, almost a whisper. "Well, it wasn't."

"And don't say it was yours, either."

He's silent.

"Amelrik?"

"I should have told you about her, but I . . . It makes my stomach hurt, just thinking about what happened. It makes me feel helpless and alone, like I'm there again. Like I . . ." He slides his hands over his face, then lets them fall to his lap. "I was so upset when my father sent me away. It was supposed to be Odilia. She was the one who was supposed to be part of the hostage exchange. But after my mother tried to . . . After I was . . ."

He's shaking, and not from the blood loss this time.

"You don't have to tell me about it."

He squeezes his eyes shut, then opens them again. "After my mother almost killed me, my father decided it would be best if I wasn't around. For my safety, and because I set her off. She's mostly okay, as long as she doesn't have to see me."

Doesn't have to see him? "Um. I was there yesterday. I don't want you to take this the wrong way, but your mother is insane, and I don't buy that."

He looks down at the bed. "You saw her at her worst. Seeing me again, especially with a St. George, must have really freaked her out."

"I gathered that when she *tried to kill us*."

"I don't know what she was like before. My father says she's better when I'm not around, but . . ." He makes a face and rolls his shoulders, looking uncomfortable. When he notices me watching him, he says, "My wings ache."

I raise my eyebrows at him. "You can feel them when you're in human form?"

"Yeah. Sort of. They ache whenever I think about what happened. Or if it's going to rain. They never healed right."

"They didn't get better when you transformed?"

"Most of my injuries got better when I turned human, but I didn't have wings in that form, so they stayed broken. I could feel them hurting, but I would've had to change into a . . . I would've had to change again to fix them, and I . . . I couldn't do it. They were healing slowly, but I knew they weren't better, and they hurt *all the time*. But after what happened, I couldn't make myself take that form again." Tears fill his eyes, and he rubs them away with the backs of his hands. "Not for over a year, and by then it was way too late. They were never the same. Maybe I could have flown, *someday*, but not after all that."

I put a hand on his arm. "It wasn't your fault."

He flinches, but he doesn't pull away. "Physically, I could have done it. I should have. And I knew. All that time, I knew it was only going to get worse, but I . . ." His jaw trembles, and he wipes at his eyes again.

"I couldn't leave the barracks. I know it's not the same, but maybe it kind of is, because it's not like I couldn't walk. It's not like I couldn't physically go from one place to another, and everybody acted like leaving shouldn't be any different than that. And maybe it shouldn't have been, but every time I tried to do it—every time I even *thought* about it—I felt like I was going to die. I couldn't have left. Not on my own. And you couldn't have transformed."

He nods, but then he says, "I shouldn't have been there. I knew what she was like, and how much she hated . . . hated when I upset her. She can't stop herself when she gets mad, and I *knew* that. I'd made her mad so many times. I was always doing it, and I was so stupid, thinking she'd be proud of me for finally using my wings. But I should have known that she . . ." He sucks in a deep breath, fighting against the tears. It's a losing battle, and he covers his face with his arms and sobs.

"Wanting your mother to be proud of you isn't stupid."

He's crying so hard, it takes him a minute before he can talk again. "I just . . . I just reminded her of her shame. I made her mad, like I always do."

"You mean like you supposedly did yesterday? Because you didn't do anything wrong."

"I upset her."

"By what? Existing?"

"She has every right to be ashamed of me."

"Because you're not like everybody else? That's not your fault."

"I was *born*."

"So? I still don't see how you existing is a problem."

He shakes his head. "You don't understand. What I mean is, I didn't *hatch*. I told you my mother got captured by St. Georges, and they put a dragon ring around her neck. She was pregnant with me when they did it. She should have laid an egg, but she was stuck in human form, and so I was still inside her, incubating."

"Gestating."

"Right. That. They kept that ring on her for *months*. She couldn't transform all that time, and it drove her mad. It was cruel, what they did." He shudders and draws his knees up, wrapping his arms around them. "The ring kept me in human form, too. It made me . . . how I am. Eventually, she gave birth to me."

"And then what happened?"

"My father finally managed to rescue us not long after. But it was too late for her. She never really recovered all the way."

"Well, that explains why she's crazy, but not why you think it's your fault."

"I know, but—"

"You didn't put that ring on her." A St. George did. Someone I'm related to, even if I've never met them.

"It was the worst thing that ever happened to her. It *broke* her. She said she wished they'd just killed her, instead of letting her give birth to an abomination." He rests his arms on his knees, pressing his forehead to them. "My mother just wanted to come home and try to forget what happened to her, but she couldn't, because I was a constant reminder of it. My father thought maybe I would still develop more, that in time I'd get better, since I was no longer bound by the ring. But I didn't. And the whole clan knows what I am. They know what my mother went through, and all the ways that I'm a disappointment. She just wanted me to leave her alone, so she didn't have to remember any of it, but I wanted her attention all the time. I was always bothering her and getting in her way. I made her worse. That's why she hurt me."

"You mean when she tried to kill you?"

He's quiet for a second, keeping his face pressed against his arms and holding very still. "I mean all the times. But that one was the worst. I pushed her too far, and she just snapped."

"*You* pushed her too far? Do you know how ridiculous that sounds?"

He doesn't answer.

"Your mother's insane. She should be locked up. You get that, right? She shouldn't have hurt you. *Ever.* You didn't deserve that, and don't even try to tell me that you did, or that I don't know because I wasn't there. I don't need to have been there to know how wrong it was. And you didn't make her want to hurt you. If I ever hear you say anything like that again and mean it, I'm going to throw up. I'm seriously going to throw up—that's how messed up that is. Your mother is *insane.* That's why she did that stuff to you. And maybe she's somehow not quite as crazy when you're not around, but there is no way in hell that she's ever actually 'not crazy.' If she was, she'd be at court, or she'd live somewhere normal, instead of down some creepy tunnel nobody uses. What happened to her wasn't your fault, and just because you were involved in it doesn't mean she gets to blame you for it."

"It's complicated. She can't help—"

"She can't help what? Being abusive?"

"Being ashamed of me."

"Oh, don't get me started on that."

"There are a lot of reasons why—"

"No, there aren't. You don't have anything to be ashamed of. You can't help the way you were born, or even *that* you were born, or how your parents feel about it. And if your mother has a problem with you existing, she can take it up with me, because I happen to like that you exist. Not that you need my permission, or hers, or anybody's. And you know what else? I'm glad you were born this way, because if you weren't, we wouldn't have met. And you'd be just like any other dragon, and you wouldn't be *you*, and I . . . I like you the way you are."

He lifts his head and studies my face. His eyes are wet. "Don't say anything you don't mean, Virginia. I can't take it. Not from you."

"I wouldn't have said it if I didn't mean it. And I . . . I spent pretty much my whole life wishing I was like Celeste. She was always braver than me, and way more popular, and as we got older, it became clear that she had magic and I didn't. Everyone treated me like that meant I was worthless, and it only got worse after my mother died. Because it was my fault for being such a dud. For just standing there while a dragon ripped her apart."

"It wasn't your fault."

I nod. "I know that now, but only because of you, and I spent years wishing *so hard* that I could use magic and become a paladin. I couldn't take back what happened, but at least if I could use the family power like a real St. George, then maybe everyone would stop thinking I was so useless. They'd stop ignoring me and treating me like I wasn't good enough. And maybe my father would stop blaming me for my mother's death, and he wouldn't be ashamed of me. But being a paladin wouldn't have made me happy. That seems obvious now, and I don't even know if it would have changed anything. Everyone had already made up their minds about me, and I wouldn't have been able to forget all the years that they ignored me and looked at me like I didn't deserve to be a St. George. I couldn't have forgiven my father for wishing he only had one daughter, not two. He never *said* it, not out loud, but it was obvious he felt that way. And none of that would have disappeared just because I could use magic."

"You *can* use magic."

"And I'm totally going to rub that in everyone's face when I get home. But that's not my point. If I could have used magic all this time and had become a paladin, then I wouldn't be who I am, either. And you would hate me."

"Virginia—"

"No, you would. And you'd have every right to, because St. Georges tortured your mother, and they tortured you. And if I'd had magic, maybe I would have been one of the paladins who hurt you. Either way, we'd be enemies. Everyone at the barracks might think better of me if I was like them, but *you* wouldn't. You wouldn't like me if I was just another paladin, and we wouldn't have met. So I never thought I'd say this, but I'm glad I don't have magic. Didn't, I mean. And I'm glad you are who you are, however you got that way."

30

THE BRAVEST THING I'VE EVER DONE

It's the next day and we're outside. Odilia's in human form, showing us her section of the community garden. Well, showing Amelrik, anyway. She's mostly ignoring me. And who knew dragons had *gardens*? I mean, I wondered where they got the vegetables we've been eating, but I didn't know they grew them themselves.

"Do you still like radishes?" Odilia kneels down and pulls one out of the dirt.

Amelrik makes a face. "I *never* liked radishes."

"Yes, you did. You ate so many you threw up that one time."

"That wasn't me! That was Cedric."

She stands up and puts one hand on her hip, smearing dirt across her skin. The other hand's still holding the radish. "No, it was you. I remember you threw up on my stuffed boar, Tuskerbristle, and my mother said I had to get rid of him. I didn't talk to you for a week."

He grins. "Still Cedric."

"Who's Cedric?" I ask. "And also, I like radishes, if it's still up for grabs."

Odilia makes a point of chomping into the radish herself.

"Cedric's my cousin," Amelrik says. "Odilia's brother. He's off studying the migration patterns of humans. Right?"

"Uh-huh." Odilia rolls her eyes. "He says he's writing a book about it now. I can't believe my father let him do something so frivolous. I can't believe *your* father let him, either."

"But humans don't migrate." I think I would know, what with being one and everything.

They both stare at me like I just said something crazy.

"I just mean, it's going to be a really short book. Isn't it?"

"But humans *do* migrate," Amelrik says. "There's a mass exodus every year during the summer. Especially in larger cities. Not everyone, but a lot of humans migrate west, to the coast, and then they migrate back once the temperatures drop again. I know paladins are usually stationary, but you really haven't noticed?"

"Those are just *vacations*. Because it gets too hot in the cities. Nobody's migrating." That's ridiculous.

He raises his eyebrows, still skeptical. "Anyway, it was Cedric who ate the radishes and threw up on Tuskerbristle."

Odilia sighs. "I wish he was coming home for Eventide this year. And that he could see me in the games. Especially when my team *wins*."

"Well, I'll be there, and so will Virginia."

"You're bringing your whore to the games?"

"She's not my whore. And yes, I am."

Odilia opens her mouth to speak, but then scowls at something behind us. I turn to look and see another dragon approaching. She's in human form—there's not really room in the gardens for them to wander around in dragon form; at least, not without smashing everything—and she has wavy, dark brown hair, sharp features, and kind of a bitchy look on her face. And of course she's naked.

"Oh, great," Odilia whispers. "It's Bryn."

The other dragon—Bryn—calls out to her in Vairlin.

Odilia plasters on a fake smile and returns her greeting.

"Are we speaking in English these days?" Bryn asks. She must have heard us talking, though hopefully she didn't hear Odilia whispering about her. "Has your brother been gone so long he's forgotten his native tongue and feels the need to clothe himself?"

"This is my cousin, Amelrik. You've met him before, I think, when we were kids. My brother's still studying abroad. And Amelrik insists we speak English in front of his human, for some reason."

"Well, if you're her cousin, then you've been gone even longer."

Amelrik says something to her in Vairlin, I think just to prove that he can.

She laughs, says something back, and winks at him.

I want to strangle her.

Bryn looks down at Odilia's garden and gasps. "Odilia! *What* have you been doing to your radishes?"

Odilia is cautious. "Why do you ask?"

"No reason. It's just . . . Well, they're looking a bit small, don't you think?" Bryn's garden patch must be the next square over, because she gestures to the radishes there. The greens are really flourishing, and the tops of the radishes stick out a little from the ground. She doesn't even need to pick one for us to see that hers are doing much better than Odilia's, though she does anyway. "Maybe it's just because I'm used to mine being so healthy. I wouldn't worry about it. But if you're ever thinking about giving up your square, let me know. I'm always looking to expand mine, and I promise you I'd make good use of it."

Odilia speaks through clenched teeth. "I'm keeping it."

"All right. But the clan depends on these gardens, you know, and I'd hate to think you're neglecting yours or letting it languish. Osric tells me you've been practicing hard for the games. That must eat up a lot of your time, what with how much work you need to get ready. I hope you don't slow everyone down too much—they'll be so disappointed if they lose."

I nudge Amelrik, and we share a look.

Odilia glares at her. "I've been giving the team pointers on how to improve their speed. I'm surprised Osric didn't tell you that, but then again, we've been spending so much time together, I don't know when he would have had the chance."

Bryn turns up her nose. "Well, I suppose I'll see you at Godwin's after-party?"

"The after-party's only for participants in the games."

"And their dates. Osric must be getting tired of having to spend so much time with you, because he asked me to go with him."

Odilia's face falls. "He what?"

"You might have him during the day, but at night . . ." Bryn trails off, letting us imagine the rest of that sentence, and smirks. "Now, I really must be going, but it was wonderful talking to you again, Odilia. And please do come to the after-party, even if you can't find a date." She gives her a little wave, then saunters off.

"Wow," I say, once she's gone. "What a bitch." She's worse than Mina Blackarrow.

"Yeah," Amelrik agrees. "Don't listen to her."

Odilia bites her lip. "She only wants him because I do. And now I'm going to have to see them together all night at the party."

Amelrik shrugs. "You could just not go."

"No way," I tell him. "She *has* to go. She has more right to be there than Bryn does—she can't let her push her out. And," I add, to Odilia, "Bryn could be lying. Or exaggerating. Osric seemed really into you the other day."

She perks up. "You think so?"

"Yeah. And if he actually liked her, she wouldn't have so much to prove."

"Maybe I should go talk to him. Just as soon as I don't feel like I'm going to murder him." She flexes her hands, like she's imagining strangling someone, or maybe sinking her claws in. "Except . . . if he knew I liked him, that might make it weird when we have to see each other during practice. But if I wait until after the games, it might be too late." She considers that, then says, "What would you do, Amelrik?"

"What?"

"If you liked someone, but telling them might make things awkward between you, and you'd still have to see them all the time, would you do it?"

"I . . ." His eyes dart over to me, then away again. He swallows and looks down at the dirt. "I don't see how that's relevant."

"It's *relevant* because I'm asking for your advice. I really like Osric, and I thought he liked me. You know what? I'm just going to go find him. And then I'm either going to eviscerate him or make out with him. And Bryn's radishes might be bigger than mine, but they probably don't even taste good!"

She storms off.

I gape a little in awe. "She makes it seem so simple."

Amelrik's quiet for a minute. He looks like he's thinking really hard about something, but then he just says, "Yeah, she does."

"Maybe it is, though."

"Is what?"

"That simple," I say, and then I do the bravest thing I've ever done in my life.

I kiss him.

31
Very much on purpose

Amelrik kisses me back.

My heart races and my nerves tingle. I feel alive all over and invincible.

This is the best moment of my life.

Until he pulls away. "Virginia, wait."

Uh-oh. Did I say best moment? Maybe I meant *worst* moment. Maybe him kissing me back was just a reflex and he didn't really mean it. I put my hands over my face so he can't see how embarrassed I am. "I thought you wanted me to. I mean, *I* wanted to. I like you. And I thought you liked me, but I guess I had it all wrong. So please just forget I did that."

He touches my wrists and gently pulls my hands away from my face, so he can look me in the eyes. "You weren't wrong. I like you. I like you *a lot*. But we shouldn't do this."

"Why not?" It's a stupid question. I know why not—I just don't care.

He tilts his head. "I'm the prince of Hawthorne clan, and you're a St. George."

"And that matters to you?"

"I don't know. It's supposed to. And after everything that happened to me—to my family—because of St. Georges . . ."

"That wasn't me. I'm probably related to them, but I've never met them, and I wasn't even born yet. I've never even cast the binding spell. I'm not a paladin, and I'm not like them. And you're not like other dragons."

"My father's the king."

"So? Are you going to be king anytime soon?"

"I'm never going to be king. I already wasn't, even before they thought I was dead. Someone like me can't rule Hawthorne clan."

"Then what's the problem?"

"The problem is I'm still a prince. I still have responsibilities to uphold. And I've shamed him enough as it is."

"But he already thinks we're together, right?"

He shakes his head. "Not like this. If he knew how I really felt about you, he'd kill you, no matter how useful you are."

Which, so far, is not at all. And it seems like every little thing I do here has the potential to get me killed. "He doesn't have to know. *No one* has to know. What are they going to do, see us kissing? They already think we're lovers. I don't see how us actually being together would look any different."

"Maybe not. But . . ."

"What?"

"You're not going to be here forever."

"Oh, so I guess we shouldn't enjoy the time we do have, then. You know, if it's not going to be *forever*. Don't you want this?"

"I do—you don't even know how much. I've felt like an outsider my entire life. Like I never really belonged anywhere." He moves closer, so we're standing only a couple inches apart. "But you make me feel like I belong. With you."

Warmth spreads through my chest, and I smile at him. "Me, too."

"But I already don't want to say good-bye to you, and us being together is only going to make that worse. So much worse, and I can't . . . I can't handle the thought of . . ." He backs away, and I think that's it, he's made his decision. He's not going to do this.

But then he squeezes his eyes shut and mutters something to himself in Vairlin—something that sounds like an expletive—and changes his mind. He closes the gap between us and kisses me. Not softly and tenderly like he did the very first time, when we were in front of the court. This is more frantic, like he can't hold back anymore. He wraps his arms around me, and I slide mine around him. I'm kissing him just as desperately. I like the weight and warmth of his hands on me, and the feeling of being pressed up against him.

And I think maybe he's right—this is going to make saying good-bye so much worse. Because I already know that I never want this to end, and I already know that it has to.

Amelrik stands awkwardly next to the bed. We're in our pajamas, and I'm already under the covers. It should be like any other night, except it's not. He clears his throat. "Maybe I should sleep on the floor."

"What? Why?"

"You know why."

"So, what, now that we're together, I don't get to sleep next to you?" *That* sounds fair.

"I don't want you to feel uncomfortable."

He's the one who seems uncomfortable. "Do you *want* to sleep on the floor?"

He laughs. "Of course not. The floor is made of rock. And it doesn't have you."

I melt a little bit at his words, and I *do not* want him to sleep on the floor. "Just get in the bed, okay?"

He goes to turn out the last lamp, then crawls in next to me. Well, sort of next to me, because there's a gap between us. Not that that's new or anything, but I kind of thought we'd be closer. He's my boyfriend now, right? I finally don't have to worry about doing something stupid, like touching him inappropriately. I mean, *somewhat* inappropriately. Like his back or his shoulders or his chest. Not anything, uh, too intimate.

But if it's okay to touch each other, then why is he at the far end of the bed? We slept closer than this last night. "Amelrik?"

"Yeah?"

"You don't have to be all the way over there. If you don't want to."

"Okay." He shifts closer, then turns on his side, so he's facing me. "I've never done this before."

"Done *what*, exactly?"

"Slept in the same bed as someone."

"Uh, yes, you have. We've been sharing this bed for weeks."

"I mean someone I've kissed."

My stomach feels like there's a rock in it. I hate the implication that he's kissed other people. It's one thing to know it must be true, and it's another to have to hear it out loud. "Except for me. You kissed me before, remember?" He better not have forgotten. I know it wasn't supposed to be real, but it *felt* real, and maybe it meant more to me than it did to him, but he's still not allowed to just forget it.

"Of course I remember. But that was different."

"Because you didn't mean it?"

"Because you didn't want me to."

Oh. "I do now, though." I want him to do a lot more than just kiss me.

I want to know what it's like to have sex with him. Well, to have sex at all, really, but mostly how it would be with him. What kind of movements he would make. The sound of his breathing. How safe I would feel with the weight of him on top of me, his skin warm against mine, and what it would be like to have part of him inside me.

I imagine touching the muscles in his arms and his stomach. I think about running my hands down his back. And about kissing the outline of his jaw, and the place where his neck meets his shoulders. I want him to take his clothes off so I can explore every inch of his naked body.

Which probably makes me some kind of pervert, because it's not like he's thinking those things about me. And it's not even that I want to do all that right now. Which is good, since he told me he's never trusted anyone enough for that. There's no reason to think I'm the exception, and the last thing I want to do is find out for sure that I'm not. I mean, *I kissed a boy*, and he actually liked it. That's enough bravery for one day.

So there's no way I'm going to act on anything that I'm feeling right now. Just knowing what I was thinking would probably freak him out, and even though he's really close—close enough that I could "accidentally" touch his arm or something—I'm going to keep my hands to myself.

I turn over, just to make sure. And because I feel slightly less guilty for picturing him naked when I'm not facing him. Even though it's pitch-black in here and there's no way he could see me and guess what I'm thinking.

And then he moves closer and wraps his arm around me. His chest is pressed against my back, and I can feel his heart beating. He kisses my ear. "You were shivering," he whispers.

"What?" I don't know what he's talking about. If anything, I'm too hot.

"That first night we slept in the woods. We didn't have a fire, and you were so cold. I woke up at some point, and you were next to me, shivering. That's why I held you like that. When you asked about it,

I lied and said it was an accident, because I didn't want you to get the wrong idea, but it wasn't. It was very much on purpose."

Very much on purpose. His confession makes me feel warm and tingly all over. It makes me feel protected and wanted and happy. "I have to tell you, I'm kind of getting the wrong idea *now*."

He buries his face in my neck, and I feel him smile. "If you're worried about it, I could still sleep on the floor."

"Don't you dare," I tell him, and then I pull his arm tighter around me.

And all the things I used to be afraid of seem so ridiculous now, because I've never felt safer than I do in this moment, curled up with a dragon, in his bed, far away from the barracks.

32

AN IMPORTANT JOB

The games take place a few days later, on a drizzly afternoon. The sky is gray, and it's not exactly raining, but it's not exactly *not* raining, either. Despite the sort-of rain, hundreds of dragons fill up all the space on the cliff and around the edge of the lake. You'd think they'd be in human form, so there'd be more room, but Amelrik says it's because they can see a lot better as dragons. And because participants in the games have been known to crash, and nobody wants to get squashed.

We're watching from the opposite cliff—the one Amelrik took me to for my birthday. We don't have as good of a view over here, but there's no chance that an excited fan is going to knock us over with their tail or anything, either. Plus, we're alone. Which means we can make out, and I can rest my head on his shoulder, and he can put his arm around me and ever-so-casually let his hand graze the edge of my boob.

I want to tell him it's okay to actually touch me there, for reals, but I can't bring myself to say it. Because what if it really is an accident? I mean, it's not. I'm sure it's not. But what if calling attention to it scares him off? And even if he's not like other dragons, he still *is* a dragon, and maybe he doesn't even care about that part of me. And then I'll look like an idiot. Or like I want this more than he does. And he hasn't said anything about not wanting me to touch him, and he hasn't stopped me when I've dared to let my hand linger on his hip, or when I've brushed my fingers along the bottom edge of his stomach, but I can tell it made him uncomfortable. Not a lot uncomfortable—not like he didn't want me to—but enough that I didn't want to push my luck.

Actually, he seems kind of uncomfortable now, but I think that's just the rain. He said before that it makes his wings ache, and he keeps stretching out his arms and rolling his shoulders.

Above us, dragons whirl through the sky. Two teams of five compete at a time, racing in formation in specific patterns around the lake. The first team to finish goes on to the next round. Smashing into your opponents seems to be allowed, but only as long as nobody breaks formation. It's pretty intense, and we've already seen two teams get disqualified because one of their members fell into the lake. Actually, one of them hit the cliff first, then fell into the water, and a couple other dragons—who seem to have been posted around the lake in case of emergencies—dove in to make sure they got back out again.

After the round ends, a dragon shouts in Vairlin, announcing the next teams. I can't understand a word of it, but Amelrik nudges me and says, "Odilia's team is up."

This is the round we've really been waiting for—or at least that I have, since I don't know anyone else who's competing—but there are ten dragons on the cliff getting ready to take off, and I have *no idea* which one is her, or even which team I should be rooting for.

"Can you point her out?"

"Huh? Oh, right, I forgot your eyesight's not as good. She's the second one in from the left."

"It's not that. I just can't . . . you know."

"What?"

"Tell anyone apart. Not when they're in dragon form."

He frowns. "You can't? I guess you really only saw her for a few seconds as a dragon."

"Yeah, I'm pretty sure that's not it."

"Well, that's Odilia, and that's Osric right next to her."

"On which side?"

"Uh, he's the one who's not a girl?" He says that like it's super obvious.

"I can't tell that, either."

"Really? Okay. He's on her right. And Godwin's on the other side of him. And— Oh!"

All ten dragons leap into the air as someone gives the signal to start. Odilia's team glides into a V formation and takes the lead. The other team swoops in, clawing at them to get ahead. Odilia lashes at one with her tail, and Godwin swings his neck around and bites his attacker, nearly losing his place in the process.

We watch in silence, and I think Amelrik might even be holding his breath. It's a close race, and both teams fight viciously for the lead. I actually lose track of which is which, but I know Odilia's team wins because Amelrik shouts, "Yes!" when they cross the finish line. A cheer erupts from the crowd, peppered with some angry shouts from sore losers.

"This is so much better than last year," Amelrik says. "I was still at Elder clan. Lothar was competing, but no one wanted to win against him—not after what happened the year before—and it turned out to be the most boring games I've ever been to. He won the whole thing, of course."

"What happened the year before?"

"I wasn't there for that. I was, um, living in a human city at the time. But I heard all about it. It was the first time he'd competed, and when his team lost the second round, he beat the winner's captain senseless. And no one dared raise a claw to him—not to their prince."

"He sounds like a real prize. And just think, I almost married him."

Amelrik makes a face. "Don't even joke about that."

If I had, though, maybe Lothar wouldn't have abducted Celeste. She wouldn't be stuck at Elder clan right now. Amelrik said she'd be okay, but I can't help feeling a pang of guilt. After all, I'm here, with my new dragon boyfriend, and she's all alone, probably thinking no one's ever coming for her. But the Feast of Eventide is coming up soon, and then all of this will be over.

The thought makes my throat ache.

"I get why you hate Lothar," I tell Amelrik, "but why does he hate you so much?" Being a jerk is one thing, but advocating so hard to get him killed when the hostage exchange went bad is another.

Amelrik takes a deep breath. "It's complicated." He pauses, then shakes his head. "Actually, no, it isn't. His father was kind to me. He treated me like his own son—more than mine ever did. And that's why Lothar hates me."

"He's jealous?"

"The king saw us as foster brothers, but Lothar only ever saw us as rivals." He laughs, just a little. "It's a bit ridiculous. I never thought anyone would be jealous of me."

"No wonder you didn't like it there."

"I wouldn't say that."

"But you said you were upset, when your father sent you away?"

"I was. At first." He stretches his arms and his shoulders again. "It turned out to be a relief, living away from home. I didn't have to watch every little thing I said or did. I wasn't constantly looking over my shoulder, worried how my mother would react to me. It was like I could finally *breathe*. And it was different, over there. The Elder king never acted like he was ashamed of me. Neither did the queen. They knew what I was—everyone did—even though I didn't transform for so long. And I . . . I never told anyone what happened to me. Not until I told you. But I think they suspected."

"You really never told anyone?" I like that he trusted me that much, but I hate to think of him suffering alone all that time.

"No one, and I was miserable. I'd essentially been banished from my home, and I missed my cousins and being in a familiar place. I missed my father, too, even though I hated him for sending me away. My wings were broken, but I didn't want anyone to know. Not about what I had done to end up that way—"

"*You* didn't do anything."

"—or how I was just making it worse by not transforming. I blamed myself enough already, and I couldn't handle getting that from anyone else. I hardly ate, and I hardly spoke. I wouldn't let anyone touch me. It was probably obvious that it wasn't just homesickness. The king tried to ask me a couple times if I was all right. We both knew I wasn't, but I lied to him anyway and said I was fine. He couldn't make me talk to him, but he went out of his way to make me feel welcome there. He treated me like I was part of his family, and I always sat with them during the feasts. He didn't have to do that—no one would have missed me if I wasn't there—but he included me anyway. Lothar hated it. His older sister was living in a foreign court, and his other sisters were quite a bit younger than him, plus he was the only male, and his father's heir. He was used to getting special attention, and he was disgusted that his parents were reaching out to me."

I consider that, watching as two more teams take off across the lake. "So it turned out to be a good thing your father sent you there?"

"It was harsh, and I was so unhappy at first—for quite a while, actually—but overall, it was the right thing to do. I think it saved my life."

"Why did Odilia say that the Elder king exploited you?"

"Because she doesn't know what she's talking about. The Elder king made use of me. Most dragons can't stay in human form for more than a day at a time, but I can be like this indefinitely." He gestures to himself. "To my father, it was a shameful disability, but the Elder king saw it as a strength. After I'd been living there a few years, he sent me to infiltrate—" He stops himself, his eyes darting over to mine. "You don't want to hear about that."

"About how you tricked paladins and got them killed?" The words come out bitter and angry, and I didn't even know I was going to say them.

He stares at me.

"I'm sorry," I tell him. "I didn't mean to say it that way."

"You didn't say anything that wasn't true." He sighs. "I pretended to be human, and I got close to people, and they died because of it. It's not something I would have ever done on my own, and I'm not proud of it, but I still did it. And I . . . I hated paladins. If they hadn't hurt my mother, if they hadn't been so cruel, I wouldn't be like this. She wouldn't be ashamed of me, and she would have still been herself, instead of whatever she is now. I thought they deserved it at the time, and maybe they did, but the more I think about it, the less sure I am. I risked my life pretending to be human, and if anyone had ever guessed who or what I was, they wouldn't have stopped to ask questions—they would have just killed me. I was so afraid at first that I'd slip up, and I couldn't wait for my assignment to be over. But then . . . It wasn't easy, betraying the people I'd gotten close to. I hated that part."

"I can't picture you doing that." I know that he did, but when I think about the boy I've gotten so close to—the same one who holds me in his arms at night and whose smile makes me melt inside—I can't imagine him ever hurting anyone.

"I did what I had to. And I won't lie—on some levels, I liked it, because for the first time in my life, I felt useful. It made my foster father proud of me, and I . . . I'd never had that before. Lothar was more jealous than ever. He liked that I'd be gone for months at a time, and I can't say I was sorry to be away from him, either, but he hated that someone like me could be worth something, especially to his father. We fought all the time whenever I was home, about anything and everything. He tried to belittle the work I was doing, even though he knew how important it was."

"Important." The word feels heavy on my tongue. "If you'd infiltrated the barracks where I lived, I'd be dead right now, wouldn't I?"

He flinches at that, but he doesn't look away. "If I'd come to your barracks while I was still with Elder clan, then yes, there's a good chance you'd be dead. It makes me sick to think that, Virginia, but it's true, just like how if your sister could kill everyone here, she would. Only I doubt she would feel any qualms about it."

A shuddery feeling twitches down my spine, because he's right, she wouldn't. If Celeste had the chance to kill a whole clan of dragons, she'd take it. She'd murder them all, in cold blood, for no reason other than that they're dragons, and it wouldn't bother her. She'd come home, and my father would throw her a party and put some heads up on the wall, so everyone would know what a good job she'd done. And not that long ago, I would have thought slaughtering dragons made her amazing, too. But now it just kind of scares the hell out of me.

"We targeted the most dangerous settlements, the ones where the paladins were especially aggressive and relentless, and yours was about halfway down the list. I like to think I wouldn't have let anything happen to you, but I can't say for sure how things would have played out. It was an important job, but an awful one, and I've wrestled with my thoughts on it for a long time. What I did saved lives. The lives of dragons," he adds, when I give him a questioning look. "Ash clan was nearly wiped out by paladins. A whole *clan*, a society with its own culture and way of life. The humans there wanted to expand their hunting grounds, so they encroached on Ash territory and started picking them off without provocation. And I don't know if what I did was right or not, but I know that that clan still exists today because of me."

"Not all paladins kill dragons unprovoked."

"No, and not all dragons kill paladins out of self-defense. There's good and bad on both sides. I never killed anyone directly, but I don't know if that makes me better or worse than the dragons who did."

"You saved my life. You didn't have to. You could have let me marry Lothar, or you could have left me there to get ripped apart after you made him transform. And I know I'm not a paladin, but I'm still a St. George, and . . . My point is, Celeste would never save a dragon. No one at the barracks would. And they wouldn't think twice about killing one, let alone getting one killed. Before I met you, I wouldn't have, either. I'm not saying I like that you tricked people, because I don't, but I don't think you're a bad person. A bad person wouldn't struggle with it, or be bothered by it. St. Georges hurt you and your mother. They tortured you before you were even born, but you still saved me. And if the situation had been reversed, I can't say I would have done the same. Not back then."

He studies my face, his expression hopeful but wary, like he's not sure I mean that. "By the end of the second year, I wanted out so badly. Everyone who got close to me ended up dead, and I couldn't take it anymore. But the Elder king was adamant that what I was doing was right, and . . . If I'd insisted on stopping, I don't know if he would have forced the issue, but I also didn't want to disappoint him, so I didn't."

"But you were mostly on your own, right? Couldn't you have run away?"

"Not without putting my entire clan in danger. It would have destroyed the delicate peace we'd established with the hostage exchange. And it probably would have gotten Raban killed. Not that I knew him, and not that it mattered in the end, because he died and the peace was broken anyway, but I didn't want to be responsible for that. Not for his death, and not for potentially starting a war. It was complicated, so I stayed. Until it all fell apart, and the Elder king faked my death. After that, I lived on my own for six months, unable to go home or tell anyone I was still alive. I was free from having to betray anyone I got close to, but I didn't settle anywhere. I knew Lothar had been talking about capturing a St. George, and he'd been boasting that he could actually do it. I thought it was just something he'd said to try and show me up, but when I discovered he was at your party, I knew he must have meant it. I decided I wasn't going to let him succeed, and if I could get the paladins there to kill him in the process, well, so much the better. Then I met you, and you know the rest."

He falls quiet, and neither of us says anything for a while, though he keeps glancing over at me.

I think about how he got hundreds of people killed. *Paladins*, and others with paladin blood, like me and pretty much everyone I know. He was a dragon posing as a human and gaining people's trust, just so he could turn on them. He's the embodiment of everything I was so afraid of, the reason I couldn't leave the barracks all those years.

But he's also the reason I was finally able to leave. He's the reason I'm not afraid of dragons anymore. He taught me magic, and he's the only one who's never made me feel stupid for not being able to do it. He's the only one who's ever even *believed* me about not being able to leave the barracks. And he's the reason I no longer blame myself for my mother's death.

What he did was horrible, and being torn up about it doesn't change that. But hurting paladins saved dragons. Doing nothing would have meant more dragons getting hurt. No matter what, somebody would have died. And if I'd been in his position, if I'd had the opportunity to collect information that would mean Celeste and all the others could destroy the dragons who wanted to hurt us, wouldn't I have done it? And wouldn't I have felt useful, and like I finally mattered?

"Virginia," he whispers, his voice tight, "please say something."

But there's nothing to say. Nothing, and too many things, all at once.

So instead I put my arms around him, and I hug him like I'm never going to let him go.

33

HOW CAN YOU HOLD SOMETHING WRONG IF IT'S IMAGINARY?

Amelrik seems really nervous as we walk through the halls a couple days later, on our way to meet up with Odilia. We're supposed to watch her friend rehearse for a play, but I don't think that's what's bothering him. He keeps glancing over at me, looking like he has something to say, and then staring down at his feet instead.

He puts a hand on my arm when we get to the theater entrance, stopping me from going inside. "Virginia, wait. I, um . . . I need to tell you something."

"Okay." I pretend like I have no idea what he's talking about, as if I haven't noticed how preoccupied and fidgety he's been all day. Because whatever he needs to tell me, I get the impression it's personal. Like, just between me and him. And it's something that's obviously not easy for him to say. Something he's had to work up the courage for.

Maybe something he's never told anyone else.

"It's just, we've been together here for a while. And I've really enjoyed it. You. Er, not that I've *enjoyed* you, but . . . I'm not saying this right." He rubs his face with the heels of his palms. "You know how I feel about you. At least, I think you do, but that doesn't make it any easier to find the words for this."

"Come on, Amelrik. Whatever it is, you can tell me." Especially if he wants to elaborate a bit more on how he feels about me.

"What I'm trying to say is—"

"Finally," Odilia says, coming out of the theater entrance and interrupting him. And possibly the most important moment of my life. "I thought you were never going to get here, and then I find you standing around outside like an idiot." She shakes her head. "Slight change of plans, though. Your father wants to talk to you."

"Right now?" He sounds annoyed, but maybe also a little relieved.

"Yeah. He said to send you his way as soon as I saw you. You'd better go. It sounded important."

He sighs and says he'll meet us inside when he gets back.

While he trudges off, I follow Odilia into the theater. We come in from the side, in front of the stage, and my first thought about this place is that it's *huge*. I guess it has to be, since it needs to accommodate a whole audience of dragons, but still.

There are giant tiered steps carved into the stone to sit on, overlooking the stage, where Odilia's friend is rehearsing with a couple other dragons. We climb up a few tiers, and I wonder why we don't sit in the front row.

"So, Bryn was totally lying," Odilia says, a sly smile on her face.

I kick out my leg, letting my foot bounce back against the stone. "She wasn't going to the party with Osric?"

"Oh, no, she was. But only because she practically begged him to ask her, because she couldn't go otherwise. He wasn't interested in her—he was just doing her a favor." She pauses and shouts something in Vairlin at the stage. I have no idea what she just said, but it sounded encouraging. "I went right up to him and told him it was either me or Bryn. He had no idea what I was talking about. So then I bit the back of his neck."

"You bit him?"

She flips her hair over her shoulder. "My mother would say it's too bold, but I wasn't going to wait around for him to make a move. Besides, she wasn't there."

"So, biting is a good thing?" Is it the dragon equivalent of kissing? Or is it something more intimate?

Odilia squints at me. "Don't tell me my cousin hasn't— No, wait, never mind. I don't want to know." She makes a face. "My mother says it's not proper for a girl to bite a boy first, but that's so old-fashioned. And I wasn't about to lose him to Bryn. So I bit him, and he bit me back, and it turns out he's liked me for *years*. He was just too shy to do anything about it." She grins. "I don't even care that we came in second in the games. It's the best feeling, when someone likes you back."

I'm grinning, too. "Isn't it?" Especially when that someone's maybe about to tell you they more than just *like* you.

She gives me a funny look, like I just said something weird.

There's a flash of light from the stage, as one of the dragons breathes fire. And now I know why we're sitting this far back, because even though we're out of danger, I can still feel the heat. Goose bumps prickle along my arms. Other than at Celeste's party, this is the closest I've been to dragon fire since my mother died. It's amazing and terrifying.

One of the dragons switches to human form and darts into the middle of the stage. It's a girl, and I think it's Odilia's friend. She waves an imaginary sword at the others and says her lines.

Odilia cups her hands to her mouth and shouts something at her. Her friend nods, then starts over, louder this time.

"Is she supposed to be a paladin?" I ask.

Odilia nods. "It's Hild's first time playing a human. Amelrik's supposed to be here to give her some pointers. She's nervous about getting the details right."

"*I'm* human. And a St. George."

She looks at me like *Good for you?*

"I just mean that I could answer questions." I'm pretty sure I know more about humans than Amelrik does.

"You don't even know what they're saying."

"Right, because humans don't speak Vairlin."

Odilia waves that away. "In this story, they do."

"But that's already not authentic."

"It doesn't matter. Use your imagination."

"But if she's worried about getting the details right—"

"The *important* details." She rolls her eyes. "Just forget about it. Amelrik should be back soon, anyway."

An uncomfortable silence settles between us. Or at least it feels uncomfortable to me—Odilia doesn't seem bothered. I try to watch the rehearsal, but I have no idea what they're saying, and I can't follow it.

"So, did Bryn end up going to the party?" I ask, partly because I'm bored, but mostly because I'm dying to know.

"Yep. And she had to watch me and Osric together all night."

"Do you think you and him will . . . ?"

"Get married and have the most beautiful draclings? *Yes.* My father won't like it, because Osric's family isn't nobility, but Cedric's his heir, not me, so I think I can wear him down."

"I was getting at more like if you thought you'd have sex, but I guess that covers it."

"We already have, but . . ." She glances around, then lowers her voice. "Only in human form."

I swallow. "It's only been a couple days."

"Five days, and that's exactly what I mean! I know only doing it in human form makes me sound like a tease, but I'm not ready to go *all the way*. Besides, I don't want to get pregnant. If he wants it that badly, he can wait until our wedding night."

"You mean, that can't happen when you're in human form?"

She looks at me like I'm an idiot. "If I *stayed* in human form, then yeah, eventually. But obviously I'm not going to do that. I *can't* do that, and even if I could, I'd go crazy."

"But . . . if you're in dragon form, couldn't you just switch to human form, and, um, not get pregnant?"

"Wow." She blinks at me. "How do you not know this stuff?"

"I *do*." Mostly. "Just not about dragons."

"Well, it's possible, but it's not a sure thing, and, again, I'd have to stay human for way too long. But Osric said he didn't care what we did or didn't do—he's just happy we're together. Can you believe that?" She sighs wistfully.

We're quiet again for a while, only this time it's more of an easy silence. Eventually Amelrik comes back and sits down next to me. He usually seems upset after he talks to his father, but he has this big smile on his face, like something really good just happened and he can't wait to tell us about it.

"Well?" Odilia asks, when he doesn't say anything.

He starts to answer her, then frowns and points at the stage. "Hild's holding her sword wrong."

"It's an imaginary sword," I tell him. "How can you hold something wrong if it's imaginary?"

Odilia makes a frustrated sound. "You know that's not what I meant. What did Uncle Ulrich say? Or did you not end up talking to him?"

"No, I talked to him." Amelrik's hand rests next to mine in the space between us on the stone bench, where Odilia can't see. He moves his hand closer and absently draws circles on my skin with his thumb. "He's officially giving me a position on the court."

I raise my eyebrows at him.

"The court," Odilia says, "is all stuffy meetings and arguments. It sounds boring."

"He wants my opinions on things."

She seems skeptical. "Does the rest of the court know about this?"

"He announced it to them."

"And?"

"And a few of them expressed some concerns."

"In front of you?" I ask.

He shrugs. "My father told them the decision was final, and that they just have to accept it. He said I'm not a dracling anymore, and I'm his son, and that I have a lot to offer. That's what he said. About *me*."

Odilia stares at him in disbelief.

"Things are different now," he says, his voice barely a whisper. "It's not like it was before."

"And you actually want to be on the court?"

"Well . . ." He considers that. "It's what Cedric would be doing, if he was here."

"That's not what I asked."

"Okay, fine. No, I don't like boring meetings. And I don't like the way the rest of the court looked at me, when my father announced this. They were horrified. But he stood up for me. He's never done that before. He made them acknowledge me, just a little bit, and . . . Maybe it won't turn out to be my dream job—"

Odilia snorts. "You think?"

"—but I'm happy. *Really* happy." He smiles and secretly squeezes my hand, implying that I'm part of the reason why.

I smile, too. I want to put my arms around him and press my face against his. I want to kiss him so bad right now. But despite what I said before, about kissing not looking any different whether we're supposedly just lovers or actually together, I'm pretty sure that if I did any of that, it would be obvious that there's something more going on. So I restrain myself.

But even if I can't kiss him right now, warmth spreads through my chest, and all my feelings for him crowd together, until I think I'm going to explode.

And I wish, more than anything, that I could freeze this moment in time, and we could always feel this happy.

34

NOT. FAIR.

"Stop pressuring me," Amelrik says. "I'm reading as fast as I can." It's evening, a couple days later, and he's half sitting, half lying on his bed, finally finishing *Princess Mysteries #7*.

I'm next to him, with my head resting on his chest and his arm around me, sort of reading along, even though I finished the book over a week ago. "I'm not pressuring you."

"You asked if I was done with this page yet. Twice."

"Well, I didn't mean it in a pressure-y way. But you're almost done, and I really want to know what you think of the ending." After he spoiled part of it for me and then almost died, he kind of stopped reading it for a while. And even though he said it would be fair if I spoiled the rest of it for him, I wasn't about to do that.

I try to be patient while he finishes the book, focusing on how good it feels to be cozied up with him like this. I can feel his heart beat and the rise and fall of his breathing. Not for the first time, I wonder what he was going to tell me the other day, before Odilia interrupted. There've been a couple times since then when we were alone and he got really nervous and seemed like he had something to say, but he stayed quiet.

I mean, I think I know what he was going to say. Because he was talking about how much he's enjoyed our time here together, and about his feelings for me, and that can really only point to one thing, right?

Amelrik claps the book shut, startling me out of my thoughts. "Wow."

I sit up a little. "What did you think?"

"I hated it."

"*What?*"

"I mean, I loved it. But I also hated it."

"You mean, because of what happens to Liam?" At one point near the end, the murderer tries to kill Princess Genevieve, since she's getting too close to solving the case. But Prince Liam jumps in the way and takes a knife to the chest that was meant for her.

"All that, and they don't even get to be together!"

"But she knows he's her true love now." That has to count for something.

"That doesn't matter if he's dead! And what, because Liam takes the hit for her, she's able to catch the murderer and get Orlando out of jail?" He sighs. "Not. Fair. She's already having his baby."

"Yeah, but it doesn't matter if he's free, because she's heartbroken over Liam. *And* we don't know for sure that he's dead."

Amelrik scoffs. "There's no way he could have survived that."

"But it happens right near the end. We don't actually see him again. He might still be alive in the next book."

"Wishful thinking. And I thought you wanted her to end up with Orlando?"

"That doesn't mean I want Liam to *die*. Besides, I'm coming around to the idea of them being together."

"That's how the author wants you to feel! That's why she's killing him off."

"I guess we'll find out in book eight." Except it won't be out for another year. Will we even know each other then? I can't imagine not seeing Amelrik every day—not *being* with him—even if that's what's theoretically supposed to happen. And I know what he said, that being together like this was just going to make it hurt more when we have to say good-bye, but . . . Saying good-bye doesn't feel real, and I can't picture a future without him. I don't want to.

I bury my face in his chest, and he tightens his arms around me, like he knows exactly what I'm thinking because he's thinking it, too.

"Virginia, I . . . I have to tell you something."

"So tell me." Nervous excitement builds up inside me, and I feel like I'm either going to throw up or burst out laughing. Neither of which would be a very good reaction to him actually working up the courage to say what I think he's going to say, so I really hope I can control myself. "Whatever it is, it's all right."

"It's really not." He pulls away and stands up, so he's not on the bed with me anymore. "Don't hate me."

My heart beats faster, and an uneasy feeling settles in my stomach. "Why would I hate you?"

"Because I screwed up. I tried to tell you, I really did, but I didn't know how. Not when we should have left, and not after it was too late."

"What do you mean, we should have left? And too late for what?"

He glances up at me. His eyes meet mine. "Tonight is the Feast of Eventide."

It takes a second for that to register. "Tonight?! You mean, like, *tonight* tonight?"

"It's going on right now. We should have left for Elder clan yesterday. This morning at the latest."

I feel numb. "*That's* what you've been trying to tell me?!"

"I know it was wrong, but I just couldn't—"

"I thought you were going to say that you loved me!"

His eyes go wide, and he takes a step back. "*What?*"

Crap. Why did I say that? "I mean, I didn't know what you were going to tell me. But I didn't think it was going to be something like this!" I get up from the bed, on the opposite side of him, and pretend to be very interested in the carvings on the bedpost.

"Do you . . ." He pauses, but I'm too absorbed in this solid craftsmanship to bother looking up and seeing how freaked out he probably is.

But I'm pretty sure he was going to ask me if *I* love *him*, which is a question I'm not ready for. Because, for one thing, he was supposed to say it first, and for another, he wasn't supposed to have lied to me.

But then, thankfully, he clears his throat and says, "I never meant for this to happen."

"What? For me to find out? Did you think I wouldn't notice if the Feast of Eventide never came? Do you think I'm that stupid, or were you going to make up new lies to keep me here?!"

He flinches at that, and even though I'm mad at him, it still stings to know I've hurt him. "I don't know what I was thinking, only that these past few weeks have been the happiest of my life, and I didn't want them to end. Going to Elder clan is dangerous. We'd be risking our lives—I'd be risking *losing* you. And once we rescue your sister, this is all over."

"I can't believe I ever thought that you . . ." I wrap my arms around myself and stare at the floor. "That you were going to say you felt *that way* about me. It was stupid."

"It wasn't." He circles around to my side of the bed. "It wasn't stupid at all. And I never meant to lie. I just didn't know how to let go of you, Virginia." He reaches out to touch my arm, but I pull away.

"Why does rescuing Celeste have to be the end of this?" I gesture to the two of us, trying really hard to ignore the pleading look in his eyes.

"Because you're going home afterward."

"You could come with me." Celeste won't like it, but what can she really say about it? Of course, my father won't like it, either, and neither will anyone else at the barracks. But we can find a way around that. I think.

Amelrik's shaking his head. "If I could, then I would, but I'm a known dragon. I'd end up in your dungeon again, if I wasn't executed on the spot. And this is my *home*. I've been gone so long, and now I'm finally back, and my father's actually acknowledging me. It's what I've always wanted, and I . . . I can't just disappear."

"But . . ." But even though I knew this was supposed to end, part of me didn't believe that it would. I thought we'd find a way to still be together somehow. Because how can I leave someone who means so much to me?

"I can't go with you, Virginia, but you could come back here. To Hawthorne clan."

"As your concubine?"

"You could be more than that. You *are* more than that. And—"

"I thought you said your father would kill me if he knew how you really felt?" And I'm sure Amelrik wouldn't come out of the situation unscathed, either.

"He wouldn't have to know. Things could be like they are now."

"For how long? I don't care what your clan thinks about me, but sooner or later, someone's going to figure out the truth. That's going to be bad for both of us." I glance up at him. "And I still can't cast the binding spell. How long could I stay here before that came up?"

"I don't know." He presses his palms to his forehead. "All I know is that I want to be with you, but that's no excuse for what I did. I'm sorry I didn't tell you we were supposed to leave, but I've been thinking about it, and if we leave tomorrow, we can try to rescue her during the games. Elder clan always has theirs the day after Eventide."

"*Tomorrow?*"

"We'll set out early in the morning. It's not as good of a plan as sneaking in during the feast, and we'll have to hope that they leave Celeste inside during the games, because if they don't . . . Well, it doesn't matter—it's our best bet at this point."

He wants to leave in the morning. As in, *tomorrow* morning.

That means we've only got one more day together. It means tonight's the last night I'll get to sleep next to him in his bed. It means that a couple days from now, I won't wake up beside him. We won't have meals together, or talk about the books we've read, or talk about *anything*. Because after we rescue Celeste, we'll go our separate ways, and I'll never see him again. I'll never hear his voice, or kiss him, or feel his warmth.

And suddenly saying good-bye feels very, very real. Something in me breaks, and my eyes water, and a bitter taste builds up in my mouth as I start to cry.

Amelrik puts his arms around me, and I press my face into his shoulder. He holds me tighter and kisses the top of my head. And I get why it was so hard for him to tell me it was time to leave. It doesn't make it right, but I get why he couldn't do it.

"Virginia." There are tears in his voice. "About what you said earlier. About what you thought I was going to say."

"We don't have to talk about it." Maybe I don't want to know how he feels. Because either way—good or bad—I think I'm going to completely lose it.

"I want to. No, I *have* to, because I—"

A loud rumbling interrupts him. It shakes the walls, and for a second I think it's an earthquake. But it stops too quickly for that.

Amelrik's face goes pale. He doesn't finish what he was about to say. He looks toward the door flap instead, deciding something. "Virginia—"

"I'm not staying here. My whole life, whenever there's trouble, someone tells me to stay put, like I'm completely useless."

"You're not useless, and I'm not leaving you here."

Oh. "What's happening?" My voice is a whisper, as if it's a secret that something awful might be going on.

"I don't know," he says, taking my hand, "but it can't be anything good."

35

Blood debt

The noise is coming from the Grand Hall, which is where the feast is taking place. And I don't just mean the rumbling, but a lot of screaming and shouting. It's muffled by all the stone walls, so that I can't even tell which language it's in, let alone what anyone's saying. But I think it's a pretty safe bet to assume that they're not happy.

When we get there, it's obvious why. There are about a dozen purple dragons in the room, crashing the feast. The dragons from Hawthorne clan are seated around giant stone slabs that serve as tables. One of the tables has been smashed with a boulder.

The leader of the purple dragons—the one I'm certain is Lothar, even if I still can't recognize dragons very well—shouts orders at the rest of them. He's holding what looks like a big metal lantern, or maybe a cage, except that it's got metal plating all over it, hiding whatever's inside. He sets it down on the king's table, keeping one clawed, scaly hand on top of it protectively while he says something threatening to Amelrik's father.

At least, I'm assuming it's threatening. Because it's not like he's come here and crashed their feast and busted up one of their tables as a gesture of goodwill. Plus, even if I can't understand what he's saying, it *sounds* pretty threatening.

Amelrik's listening intently, his breathing shallow. I kind of want to ask him what's going on, but I also kind of don't, and then Lothar twists the lantern-cage thing a little, and I don't care what he's saying, because on one side of the cage is an open panel. Just big enough for whoever's inside to look out. And of course there's someone in it. Our eyes meet, and even though I can't see much of her face, and even though she's kind of far away, I *know* it's Celeste. I think I'd know her anywhere.

All the dragons must know who and what she is, too, because a lot of them are giving the cage wary looks. Lothar must be using her as a threat. Or maybe a weapon.

I nudge Amelrik, trying to get his attention, but he's too busy watching the argument play out between his father and Lothar. "Amelrik, the cage thingy, it's—"

Lothar suddenly snarls and shouts something at the king. His voice echoes through the chamber, so loud it hurts my ears.

Amelrik grabs my arm and pulls us both behind an outcropping in the rock wall. "He knows."

"He knows what?"

"Lothar knows that I'm here."

"He can't know that. He's bluffing."

"No, he figured it out. He told my father I'm still alive, that Hawthorne clan still owes Elder clan a blood debt, and when my father didn't seem surprised to hear that about me, Lothar put two and two together. He knew I must have come here, and now he's demanding that they give me up." He wraps his arms around himself and leans his head back against the wall, letting it hit the stone with a *thump*. "They're here because of me."

"They didn't even know you were here. And his father's the one who let you go."

Amelrik's shaking his head. "They're demanding a blood debt for Raban's death."

"It was an accident, wasn't it?"

"It doesn't matter."

"Lothar's known you were still alive for over a month. He didn't come here, on one of your biggest holidays, to settle a debt. He came to make trouble."

"Obviously, but—"

"He brought Celeste."

Amelrik glances over his shoulder, in the direction of Lothar and the cage, even though we can't see them from here. "You're sure?"

"Of course I'm sure. I only saw her for a second, but I know it was her. Besides, who else would it be?"

He pauses, thinking that over. "You're going to go get her." It's a statement, not a question, like he knows there's no way I'm not.

Even if the thought of going over there and trying to steal her out from under Lothar's nose is completely terrifying. "Yeah, but . . . how?"

"Lothar won't be looking. I'll make sure of that. He'll be distracted, and when that happens, get over there as fast as you can. I don't know how much time you'll have."

"What are you talking about?"

"I already screwed this up once. I'm not costing you another chance to save her. So just trust me on this."

"Amelrik, *no*. Whatever you're planning, you can't—"

"I made a promise to you, and I can't break it a second time. And I can't let them come here and cause trouble because of me. I can't let someone else die in my place. So . . ." He trails off, not having anything left to say, I guess. And before I can tell him again not to do it—before I can get in front of him and try to block his path—before I can do *anything*, really, he darts out from our hiding place.

Maybe no one would notice him if that's all he did, but he's shouting at Lothar. His voice isn't as loud as everyone else's, since they're all in dragon form, but he must get Lothar's attention anyway, because everything gets quiet all of a sudden.

Then chaos erupts, and there are a lot of voices, talking all at once. This is my chance. This is the diversion he bought me. I creep out from behind the rock, not nearly as confident about it as he was. Even though I'm pretty sure he's going to get himself killed.

But I can't think like that right now, even if it might be true.

"Come on!" Amelrik shouts. Not at me, but at Lothar. "I'm what you came here for, aren't I?"

Lothar snarls and lunges across the room. Amelrik's father shouts something.

I force myself to move, because otherwise I'd just stand here, watching, unable to breathe. I run along the edge of the cavern walls, trying to stay away from any lashing tails or stomping feet. When I glance over at the king's table, I almost have a heart attack because Celeste's cage is gone. But when I get a little closer, I see that it's just been moved. It's on the ground now, behind the table, in care of one of Lothar's friends. Whoever he is, he's paying more attention to the drama going on between Lothar and Amelrik than he is to the cage.

I creep up to the open panel.

Celeste gasps when she sees me. She presses her face to the opening, her eyes wide. "Vee?" she whispers, keeping her voice low.

"It's me." Tears prickle at my eyes, because maybe a small part of me—just a teeny, tiny bit—was worried it wouldn't be her somehow. That just when I thought I'd found her, it would all turn out to be a lie. Or that maybe I'd hallucinated the whole thing, because I wanted it to be her so badly, and the cage would just be empty.

"It can't be you. You're . . . you're outside of the barracks." She blinks at me, like me standing right in front of her isn't enough proof. "What are you doing here?"

"Rescuing you. I thought that was pretty obvious." I peer at the cage, looking for the mechanism to open it.

"No, what are you doing *here*? Did you get captured? Did they hurt you?" Her face gets all worried, even though it should be the other way around—*she's* the one who's been kidnapped for weeks.

"I'm fine." I glance across the room at where Amelrik is, but I can't see him. My heart speeds up. But Lothar's still talking, and surely if Amelrik had . . . if something had *happened*, the crowd would have reacted. They wouldn't just watch their prince get killed and not even blink, would they?

Celeste's eyes dart back and forth. "If you weren't captured, how did you get here?"

"Does it matter?" I fumble with the lock. It's not as simple as what would be on an actual birdcage—I guess so Celeste couldn't just stick her hand out the panel and unhook it—but I think I've figured it out. I have to press down on one spot while lifting the latch at the same time.

"How did Prince Amelrik get out of our dungeon, Vee?"

I flinch at her implied accusation, even though it's true. My hand slips along the part of the cage where I was pressing in, so that the latch sticks as I try to pull it open. "He's helping me. Us. He's probably getting himself killed right now, and you—"

"You *let him go*?! What the hell were you thinking?!"

"*Celeste,*" I hiss, motioning for her to shut up. And why does she have to jump to conclusions like that? Just because she's right doesn't mean it's not crazy.

"I told you to stay away from him! It wasn't bad enough that I got captured—you had to go and get yourself captured, too?!"

"I'm not a prisoner. You're the one in the cage." I press down with one hand as hard as I can while lifting the latch with the other. This time, it works, and the door swings open.

But too late. Celeste's shouting got the attention of Lothar's friend, who was supposed to be watching her. He swears and slams the door shut, knocking me back and sliding the latch into place with one claw. He grabs the cage and lifts it up onto the table, not even caring how much Celeste might be getting knocked around inside.

Then he turns his attention to me, and I know I should run, but I'm frozen in place. I had the door open. Celeste was free, even if only for a second. And now she's still right there, but she might as well be miles away, because I missed my chance, and this dragon's probably going to kill me.

It all happens so fast. He reaches out to grab me, and then there's a terrible roar followed by a scream. Not from him, or from me, but from Lothar. And Amelrik. The crowd gasps in horror.

All my blood turns to ice. I feel like my body's made of stone, even though I'm shaking all over.

The dragon guarding Celeste looks up to watch the slaughter, forgetting about me for the moment.

But I don't care. All I can think about is that Amelrik's dead. I couldn't save Celeste, and now he's *gone*, and nothing will ever be okay again. Tears slip down my cheeks, and a horrible ache rips through my chest.

Lothar's shouting orders, and the rest of the purple dragons suddenly can't leave fast enough. They grab the cage with Celeste and make their retreat. I guess Lothar got what he came for, and now he's getting out of here, fleeing the tension that's built up in the room, because it's obvious that the dragons from Hawthorne clan are *not* happy with him.

I still feel heavy and numb, but I run to the other side of the room, because I have to see him. No matter how horrible it is. There's a crowd circled around what must be Amelrik's body. I rush past them, squeezing through the gaps and scuffing my bare arms against their scales.

There's blood on the ground. That's the first thing I notice. But it's just blood. There's no one lying on the floor, dead. Amelrik's father's there, still in dragon form, despite the gashes running across his chest, dripping blood all over. He looks really pissed off, like he's two seconds away from killing someone. Several other dragons are fussing over him, but he waves them aside.

And then I see Amelrik. He sees me, too, like he's been scanning the crowd for me. The blood on the ground isn't his. He's not dead.

Fresh tears fill my eyes as relief floods my body. *He's not dead.*

"Amelrik!" I hurry over to him.

One of the dragons tending the king notices me and lashes a tail in front of me to block my path. It snarls something in Vairlin.

"It's *fine*," Amelrik tells them. "Let her through."

The dragon reluctantly moves its tail, turning its focus back to the king.

I rush forward, throwing my arms around Amelrik. I squeeze him tight, enjoying his breath on my cheek and the feel of his body crushed against mine—two things I thought I'd lost forever. "You're alive."

"Of course I'm alive." He hugs me back, somewhat stiffly, and jerks his head toward his father.

But I'm too happy to pretend I don't care. Besides, didn't he tell everyone that *I'm* in love with him? I think that means I can hug him all I want. "I couldn't see what was happening. I thought he killed you."

"He was going to," Amelrik says, leading me through the crowd and back out to the hallway, where we can talk. "He would have, if my father hadn't defended me."

"That's why he left?"

"He came here to cause trouble, not to attack a king."

"He still has Celeste. I couldn't save her in time." Not that he couldn't have guessed that, because it's not like I have Celeste with me or anything.

He nods, taking that in. "We'll get her back."

"But . . . I know I have to save Celeste, but I really don't want you to get killed in the process. And it seems to me that you going to Elder clan is just about the worst idea ever." It probably was to begin with, but even more so after what just happened.

"Yeah, it is. But I don't really have a choice."

"Yes, you do. Just because you made me a promise doesn't mean you have to kill yourself to keep it! I'll go. I'll figure something out. I'll—"

"No. I won't let you do that—not alone. And, anyway, it's more than that. The reason I don't have a choice. Lothar gave my father an ultimatum. He's got exactly one day to turn me in to Elder clan."

"Or else what?"

"Or else Lothar's coming back here, only next time he's bringing an army."

36

AT LEAST ONCE

It's our last night together, and I'm lying here in Amelrik's bed, *thinking* about him instead of actually, like, kissing him. Or touching him. Or even just talking to him.

But I don't want this to end, and all I can think about is how that's exactly what's happening. Huddling together in the dark, trying to cling to the last few moments we have together, would only emphasize that. It would just make me think about how final this is, and then I'd probably end up crying, and that's not how I want to spend my last night with him. So instead I'm over on my side, an arm's length away at least, sleeping as if I'm already alone.

Trying to sleep, that is. Well, *halfheartedly* trying to sleep, since all I can really do is think. My thoughts keep racing, showing no signs of slowing down.

Tomorrow, we're going to rescue Celeste. My sister's finally going to be free, and everyone at the barracks is going to feel pretty stupid when they find out that I was right.

And all that's assuming we actually succeed at our mission and don't end up dying horribly. Either way, I'm never going to see Amelrik again, and this is it. Our last night together, and I'm wasting it, because I can't handle this just being . . . *over.*

Not that he's exactly throwing himself at me, either. I miss the weight of his arm around me and the closeness of him pressed against my back. We've spent the last few nights falling asleep curled up like that, as if we had all the time in the world and this was never going to end, and now we're acting like it already has.

Unless he's asleep, but I don't think he is. I don't know how he could be. If he is asleep already, somehow, then I'm kind of pissed at him for caring so little that he could just drift off like everything's fine. That he could just drift off, *alone*, over on his side of the bed, as if I'm not even here. Is this what it's going to be like for him when I'm gone? Conking out instantly, while back home I'll be tossing and turning, missing him too hard to even sleep?

His hand finds mine in the dark and squeezes.

Okay, so maybe he's awake after all. Maybe this isn't so easy for him. "Amelrik?" I whisper, squeezing back. I don't know why I'm whispering, except that it makes it easier to pretend this isn't happening.

"My father forbid me to go to Elder clan," he says. His voice is quiet, just like mine. "He said we've never submitted to them before, and we're not starting now. And . . . he said there's no way in hell he's losing me again. He *said* that. My father."

I swallow. That's what he's been thinking about. I know I shouldn't be jealous, but I am. "You should listen to him."

He squeezes my hand again. "I'm not letting you go alone."

"But—"

"I'm *not.*"

Maybe I should argue with him more, but I know he means it, and I also know that I still need his help. I don't even know where Elder clan *is*, for one thing, and even if I'm worried about him, I'd be lying if

I said I wasn't relieved. "Don't do anything stupid," I tell him. "Besides coming with me, I mean."

He doesn't say anything.

"Amelrik?"

"Let's not talk about tomorrow."

"You're the one that brought it up."

"I know, but . . ." He shifts onto his side, so he's facing me. "I'm going to miss you so much, it's going to tear me apart."

His words bring a sudden ache to my throat, and I wonder if he can hear how close I am to crying. "I . . . I wish this wasn't happening."

"I love you."

And now I am crying. "You don't have to say that. Just because I thought you were going to say it earlier . . . You don't have to."

"I *was* going to say it earlier. Not when you first thought, but before Lothar attacked. And I mean it. I love you, Virginia. I don't know who I was or how I got by before I met you. I really don't. And I don't know how I'm going to face tomorrow, knowing that something could happen to you, and that even if it doesn't, I'm—" He chokes up. "No matter what happens, I'm never going to see you again."

I scoot closer, turning on my side, and put my arms around him. The ache in my throat spreads to my chest.

"But even if I don't want to think about tomorrow," he says, "I can't pretend I don't know this is our last night together, and I just had to say it. I can't stand the thought of you leaving, but even more than that, I couldn't stand it if you left and didn't know. That I felt that way. About you."

"I love you, Amelrik." I'm not supposed to love a dragon—especially *this* dragon—but I do.

He lets out a deep breath, like he wasn't certain I was going to say it back to him. As if there was ever any chance that I wasn't.

"You saved my life," I tell him.

"A couple times. Not that I'm counting."

"I mean besides that. I might not have been the one in the dungeon, but I was trapped. I was alone, and so unhappy. And maybe those aren't things that kill you—not right away, not for a long time—but they were eating away at me. Everyone kept telling me who I was, and I knew they were wrong, but . . . You're the only person who's ever seen me for who I am. Who let me *be* who I am. And that's everything."

And I don't know how I'm supposed to live without him. How am I supposed to go back to that life, as if nothing happened? As if there won't be a piece of me missing, stuck here with him, like we were fused together and then broken apart, so that I'll never be completely me, and he'll never be completely him?

He pulls me closer. We're pressed together, in his bed, on our last night together. And I know what I want to happen. I slide my hand down to his hip, lingering suggestively. I'll be mortified if he rejects me, but I'm pretty sure he wants this, too, and it's kind of now or never, so I pick now. Now, now, now.

He kisses me, hungrily, like he'll never get enough. I do the same, and it's not that we've never kissed like this before—just never in his bed. His mouth moves down to my neck, and he reaches under my pajama shirt at the same time as I run my hands along his back.

I don't ever want to forget how it feels to touch him like this. To feel the muscles moving beneath his skin, the shapes of his shoulder blades.

He tugs my shirt over my head. I do the same to him, and we undress each other, slowly, in between kisses. I wish the lamps were lit and that it wasn't pitch-black in here. I want to see him naked. I want him to see *me* naked, at least once.

My skin tingles where he touches me. His mouth trails a line of kisses down my neck and across my chest, leaving fire in its wake.

I can't believe I was supposed to do this with someone else, with someone I didn't choose, or trust, or even like. It seems so ridiculous, I almost start to laugh, even though this is just about the worst time for it.

I manage to stop myself, but Amelrik notices anyway. "What?" he says, hesitating before kissing me more. "Did I do something wrong?"

"No. It's nothing."

"If you want to stop—"

"I don't." I really, really don't. "I was just thinking about how I'm going to lose my virginity to a dragon, and how much that would piss off pretty much everyone I know."

"Are you sure you want to do this?" His voice shakes a little, his breathing heavy, and I think that's probably the last question he wanted to ask me right now.

"Yes, I'm sure." I pull him to me, so there isn't any doubt. "I've never been more sure of anything in my life."

"Good," he says, and I can feel the muscles in his face move as he grins, "because neither have I."

37

LIKE A CAT WITH A MOUSE

We make it to Elder clan the next afternoon, after sneaking out in the morning and walking through the woods all day. Though I use the term "sneaking out" pretty loosely, since I don't think anyone was worried about us going anywhere. Amelrik's father forbid him to go to Elder clan, but he didn't forbid him to go outside, and it's not like the exits were being guarded or anything.

Now we're hiding near a side entrance to Elder clan, one Amelrik says isn't used that much. Of course, as soon as we got here and he said that, two dragons came out of it, hurrying over to the games, or at least that's where it looked like they were going. So now we're staking it out and making sure we're not just going to get found out instantly, since that would be pretty stupid. I mean, the only thing worse than getting caught at all would be getting caught so quickly that we might as well have stayed home.

Home. That's kind of a loaded word now, because it doesn't make me think of the barracks—it makes me think of Hawthorne clan. It makes me think of Amelrik and hanging out in his room or climbing to the top of the cliffs and looking at the lake. And the really weird part is that that doesn't feel wrong. I know the barracks is home—that it's where I've spent almost my whole life—but it doesn't feel like it anymore.

Amelrik looks up as a team from the games flies overhead. They don't have the lake here to use as a race course, and there are only four dragons per team, but otherwise it seems pretty much the same as at Hawthorne clan.

And I know that the more dragons we see soaring through the sky, the less dragons there will be inside who might catch us, but it's still intimidating, seeing them flying over us like that.

"It's safe now," Amelrik whispers. "Nobody's around."

"You're sure?"

He hesitates, then nods. "Nobody's come out for a while, and I don't hear anything."

"So this is it?" My stomach feels like there are about a million butterflies in it. It was scary enough when I only *thought* we were going to Elder clan—when it turned out Amelrik brought me to Hawthorne instead—but this is so much worse.

"We'll go in, get Celeste, and leave. No one even has to know we were here. Not until they realize she's gone, and that will hopefully be much later, and, either way, it's not like they'll know it was us."

"You make it sound so simple." As if this isn't going to get us killed. "Maybe this was a stupid idea, coming here today. We should have come on a day when Lothar's not *specifically waiting for you* to show up."

Amelrik shakes his head. "He's expecting me to turn myself in. He has no reason to suspect I'd sneak in and try to steal their St. George. Er, your sister, I mean," he adds, when I give him a look.

"And if he does? If he's waiting for us inside?"

"He won't be. There's no way he's not participating in the games today."

"But if he isn't? If he catches us, what then?" I don't know what I want him to say, because it's not like I don't already know that Lothar catching us will be some serious bad news. But I can't decide if I want Amelrik to reassure me that it'll all be okay, or if I want him to convince me that we should go back home and try again tomorrow. Not that that's going to happen—we're here and we're doing this—but still.

"He won't," Amelrik says, though he doesn't sound like he completely believes that. "And this is our best chance at saving Celeste. So." He swallows and takes my hand. Both our palms are sweaty, and I wonder if he notices how fast my pulse is racing.

"All right," I tell him, because what choice do we really have? I didn't come this far to walk away, no matter how scared I am. Celeste is inside those caves somewhere, and I might have failed to rescue her last night, but not today.

I take a deep breath and squeeze his hand, as ready as I'll ever be. "Let's do this."

"Vee!" Celeste's face lights up when she sees me through the bars of her cell, but then her whole expression sours when she notices that Amelrik's with me.

I run up to her, putting my hands to the cold iron bars so that our fingers touch. Her cell is isolated, down its own hallway, away from any other prisoners, so it's just us here. We had to sneak past a couple guards at the entrance, but the way the hall twists around, they can't see us. Hopefully they can't hear us, either. "We're going to get you out. You're going to be free."

"I convinced myself what happened last night was a dream," she says, staring at my hand on hers. "It couldn't have really happened, because my sister hasn't left home in four years, and she . . . The Vee I know would *never* trust a dragon. She'd know better."

"Things change," I tell her, instead of what I'm really thinking, which is that maybe she never really knew me at all.

"You shouldn't be here," she says, though I can hear the relief in her voice that I am. "This place is dangerous. You can't save me. And didn't I warn you?" She tilts her head toward Amelrik.

Seriously? "Celeste. Come on. I wouldn't be here if it wasn't for him."

Celeste gives me a look, like maybe me not being here would be a good thing.

"We need to find the key," Amelrik says, coming up to us.

Celeste takes a quick step back. "Stay away from me." Her words are quiet, but steady, and full of conviction.

"Stay away from *you*?" Amelrik glares at her. "You're the one who tortured me. You put that ring around my neck. You broke my ribs! And yet here I am, helping Virginia rescue you. Not because you deserve it, because you don't, but because she asked. And you have the nerve to tell *me* to stay away from *you*?"

"You're a monster. And a criminal. You've—"

"That's enough." I give Celeste a stern look, which feels kind of weird, because it's usually the other way around. "We have to go find the key so we can get you out of here. We'll be back soon."

"No, you won't." She shakes her head. "He keeps it with him."

"Who does?" I ask, but my stomach drops, and I'm pretty sure I already know the answer.

"Prince Lothar." She glances toward the hallway, like saying his name might summon him. "He's afraid someone else might let me out and use me against him."

Lothar has the key. There's no way we could steal it from him without him noticing. I doubt either of us could even get close to him.

I look at Amelrik. He looks at me.

Celeste watches our silent exchange, her mouth twisting into a scowl of disapproval.

I ignore her. "There has to be another way. We can cut the bars—"

"Cut the bars?" Amelrik raises an eyebrow at me. "And how are we supposed to do that?"

"Okay, something else then! But we can't just—"

"Someone's coming." He keeps his voice low and motions for me to be quiet. He tilts his head, listening to something in the hallway.

My heart pounds as I glance around, looking for a place to hide. But there isn't one.

Amelrik's shoulders relax. "Never mind. I guess I was—"

There's a roar, and a flash of purple scales and claws. It happens so fast, I can't process what I'm seeing at first. And then Amelrik's on the floor, blood spreading out from a gash that runs along his side and across his stomach.

A purple dragon looms over him. Over us.

Lothar.

He laughs, his booming voice echoing through the chamber. "Did you think I wouldn't be watching?! That I wouldn't have instructed the guards to send word *the moment* they saw you?" He snorts, puffing smoke out of his nostrils. The key to Celeste's cell glints from a string around his neck, too high up for me to reach, even if I could get close to him. "I expected you to sneak in, coward that you are. But I thought it was my father you'd be going to see. Going behind my back and tattling to him, like you always did. But this? Trying to steal our St. George? That's grounds for war." He grins, showing off his teeth.

"Whatever your problem with me is," Amelrik says, wincing as he sits up, "it's gone on long enough." Wings rip through the back of his shirt as he transforms. The bleeding stops at the same time as his eyes turn yellow and black scales spread along his forearms and down the sides of his neck.

Celeste gasps in horror. A weird half-yelp, half-croaking sound escapes her throat.

Amelrik stands, keeping his focus on Lothar. "Let's settle this."

"You should have stayed dead the first time," Lothar says, "because unlike my father, I won't show you any mercy."

"*No!*" I step in front of Amelrik, holding up my hands. This is probably the stupidest thing I've ever done, but I can't just let this happen. "Don't move! I'm a St. George—I'll bind you if you don't leave him alone!"

Lothar peers at me, like he hadn't recognized me before. "If you were going to bind me, you would have done it by now." Then he lunges.

"Virginia!" Amelrik grabs me, pushing me out of the way. Lothar's claw clips his arm but only hits scale. Amelrik ducks as Lothar snaps at him with his jaws.

I turn to Celeste. "Do something!"

Her mouth opens and closes silently. Then she says, "I can't."

Lothar slams Amelrik with his tail. There's a crunching sound as he hits the wall.

Tears fill my eyes. "Because he's a dragon? You'd let him die because he's—"

"Vee, I *can't!*" She grips the bars of her cell. "I've tried, but there's iron here for a reason! It absorbs my magic, just like a dragon ring. They knew what they were doing when they put me here."

Amelrik cries out as Lothar hits him again, this time propelling him into the opposite wall. Lothar's playing with him—torturing him—like a cat with a mouse.

My eyes meet Amelrik's. His face is distorted in pain, but he mouths something at me: *Run.*

It's like the night we met all over again, except this time my paladin sister isn't going to save the day.

And I can't run. I *won't.* Because there's no way I'm leaving him here to die.

"What are you doing?" Celeste says. "Get out of here! He's buying you time, and you're just standing there, wasting it!"

One of Amelrik's wings hangs funny, obviously injured, maybe broken, and the thought of that happening to him again makes me sick. His yellow eyes plead with me, begging me to run while I still can.

It's because he's looking at me that he's off guard when Lothar slashes at him. Amelrik puts a hand to his chest as more blood soaks his clothes. Then Lothar knocks his legs out from under him with a sweep of his tail.

"Go!" Celeste shouts. "There's nothing you can do! You can't save him!"

"Yes, I can." I take a step forward, holding up my hands, which are shaking. I was bluffing before, when I threatened Lothar. But not this time.

"What are you doing?! You don't have magic!" There's desperation in Celeste's voice, like she thinks I've gone crazy and that it's going to get me killed. "You don't know what you're—"

"Doing? I'm so sick of hearing that. If you don't believe in me, then fine, but *shut up about it!*"

She goes silent, and just for a moment, I wonder if I've gone too far. Then I realize I don't care.

My whole life, I've tried to do things Celeste's way. I tried to learn magic, to be like her. To kill dragons like her, even if that's not what I wanted. But it never worked, and in the end, it wasn't Celeste who taught me magic. It was Amelrik, the dragon she told me to stay away from. The dragon I fell in love with.

The last time I tried to cast the binding spell, just the attempt was enough to scare off Amelrik's mother. But there's no way that will work on Lothar—it has to be the real thing.

And maybe I lied just now, because I'm not sure that I can cast this, that I can save him. But I have to.

Lothar presses a claw to Amelrik's throat. "Killing you is going to be even easier than killing Raban."

A shocked look spreads across Amelrik's face. He starts to speak, nearly cutting himself on Lothar's claw, and then stays silent.

I think about the binding spell, focusing all of my energy into it. I picture Lothar turning human.

There's a flash of red light, followed by the smell of sulfur. But those things have both happened before without it meaning anything. And Lothar's still in dragon form.

"At least he put up a struggle," Lothar says, and then slices his claw across Amelrik's throat.

Right as the binding spell works—it actually *works*—and there's the sound of flesh ripping and tearing as he's forced into human form.

Amelrik has his hands pressed to his throat. When he pulls them away, his hands are bloody, but his throat is intact, and I don't think I've ever felt so relieved in my life.

Lothar looks like he did the night I first met him—brown hair, blue eyes—except now he's naked. The string with the key on it lies sprawled on the floor. Amelrik moves to grab it, but Lothar tackles him.

They fall to the ground, and then everything happens really fast. Amelrik might be worn out and injured, but he's still stronger in dragon form. Lothar tries to hit him while he still has the upper hand, but Amelrik kicks him and twists out of reach. He punches Lothar in the face and then pins him down, and now it's Amelrik who has his claws to Lothar's throat.

"You murdered your own cousin." Amelrik's seething and out of breath from the fight.

"I had to! It was the only way to make sure that you didn't—" He stops himself from whatever he was going to say.

I grab the key off the floor and hurry to unlock Celeste's cell. As soon as she's free, I hug her as hard as I can.

"Didn't what?!" Amelrik shouts. He's shaking now, though I can't tell if it's from anger or from his injuries.

Lothar's face twists up in disgust. "I heard what my father had planned for you. Don't pretend you didn't know."

"I didn't. I *don't*. And whatever it was, it doesn't justify what you did to Raban, and what you tried to do to me!"

"He was going to bring Signy home and marry her off to you."

"What?"

"She's older than me. He could have picked one of my younger sisters—they're almost of age—but he didn't, and you know what that means."

"It doesn't mean anything! I didn't even know about it, and I certainly wouldn't have agreed to it!"

"Yes, you would have. Anything my father says, you jump up and do it, like some lapdog. And don't act like you wouldn't have loved for him to make you his heir."

"He wouldn't have! My own father doesn't want me to be his heir—yours definitely doesn't!"

"If not his heir, then at least his son! He liked you better than me. You, disgusting and half-formed and not even a real dragon!"

Amelrik glares at him and brings his claws in closer, his hand poised over Lothar's throat, clenched in anger. And there's a second where I think he's going to do it. Judging by the look on Lothar's face, I'm pretty sure he thinks so, too. But then . . . Amelrik hesitates. He pulls his hand away.

Another purple dragon rushes in from the hallway shouting, "No, don't!"

Amelrik backs off, unpinning Lothar and getting to his feet.

Lothar gets up, too. "Did you see that, Father? He attacked me—he and that St. George he brought!"

The Elder king looks from his son, who hardly has a scratch on him, to Amelrik, who's clearly injured. And I'm still not great at reading dragons' expressions, but I don't think he's buying it. He snaps something at Lothar in Vairlin, and Lothar scowls at the ground.

Amelrik shuts his eyes and takes a deep breath. He looks relieved. And like he might collapse.

I rush over to him and throw my arms around him. The blood from his shirt soaks into mine, but I don't care. "We did it."

He goes completely still, not hugging me back at first. And then slowly, being careful not to get me with his claws, he slides his arms around me and holds me to him. "Yeah," he says, not sounding all that happy about it, "we did."

38
Keep your opinions to yourself

It's a couple hours later when we say our good-byes. We're out in the woods, a little ways from Elder clan. Amelrik talked to the king for a while before we left, explaining who I was and that Celeste was my sister. It was all in Vairlin, but he gave me the gist of it afterward. Except I think he might have *actually* told the king who I was to him, because he seemed kind of nervous while he was gesturing to me, and his face turned red, and the king laughed a little. In a good-natured sort of way. I'm guessing. Since he didn't, like, kill Amelrik and lock us up or anything.

In fact, he let us go. He made an announcement, officially pardoning Amelrik, since he showed mercy to Lothar, even though Lothar totally would have deserved what he got. The king didn't exactly sign off on his son taking their St. George—er, I mean, Celeste—to another clan and trying to start a war. He made sure Elder clan knew that whatever Lothar had tried to start, it was over, and both clans were relinquishing their St. Georges as a sign of goodwill.

So, mission accomplished, and we didn't even get ourselves killed. I should be happy. Or at least I shouldn't feel like the whole world is ending, because this could have turned out a whole lot worse. But tell that to the hollow, aching feeling that's taken over my chest, threatening to rip me open.

"You're sure you're all right?" I ask Amelrik. "Because your wing—"

"I'll transform again when I get home." He's in human form now, and his injuries have healed, or at least most of them.

"You promise?"

"I swear I will."

We're both quiet, neither of us saying anything for a while. I'm painfully aware of Celeste standing only ten feet away, watching this. Probably wishing we would hurry up, so the two of us can start the trip back home.

"It's late," Amelrik says, and for one horrifying moment, I think he's about to say he has to get going. "Maybe you should stay the night. You could come back to Hawthorne with me and then leave in the morning."

I glance over at Celeste, who I know heard every word, and not just because she's glaring at me, like we will only be staying at Hawthorne clan over her dead body. "Celeste would kill me," I whisper. "And . . ." If I stay one more night, I don't know how I'll ever leave. "I can't."

He nods. "I thought I'd have so much to say to you, and now it's like I have too many things—a whole lifetime's worth—and I'm not saying any of them. It's too much for one conversation, and none of it feels like enough."

I start to tell him I know what he means, but then something inside me breaks. Hot tears fill my eyes and run down my cheeks.

He puts his arms around me. I press my face into his neck, breathing in his smell, and hope I never forget what it's like to feel this safe, or this loved. "I love you," I tell him, and it comes out choked and full of tears.

"I love you, too," he says, and his voice isn't any steadier than mine.

We stay like this until Celeste clears her throat, and when we finally pull away, Amelrik's eyes are wet. He wipes them with his palms.

I remind myself of all the reasons why I can't stay here, and why he can't come with me, and why it would never work out. And then I turn away, because one of us has to, and my heart snaps into pieces.

I hear him leave, but I don't turn around. My shoulders shake as I cry harder, and I think, *Please don't go. Please*, please, *don't go.*

I would give anything for him to come back right now.

But he doesn't. He has to go. And so do I.

"Come on," Celeste says, putting an arm around my shoulders. "It'll be okay, Vee."

It won't, but I don't tell her that.

"He's a *dragon*. You're a St. George! And you have the family power now. You've got a bright future ahead of you, and the last thing you need is to think you're in love with a dragon."

I shrug her arm off. "*Think* I'm in love with him? Did you seriously just say that?"

"It's not healthy, is what I meant. You had to be around him these past few weeks, so you could rescue me, and maybe it felt like you and him were—"

"Don't."

She sighs, like I'm the one being unreasonable. "You have choices. *Human* choices. You'll be better off without him. You'll see."

"No, I won't." I say that as coldly as I can, hoping she'll take the hint.

She doesn't. "I know he might have seemed human, but that's what he does. That's how he tricked all those people. You can't believe anything he—"

"You don't know what you're talking about."

"But—"

"Celeste? It's great to have you back and all, but if that's all you have to say, then keep your opinions to yourself. It's going to be a long enough trip as it is."

39

IF YOU NEED ANY HELP MURDERING THAT WEDDING DRESS

We arrive at the barracks a few days later. Everyone's shocked to see that Celeste is back, and that she's alive and well and not rocking back and forth in the corner. They're pretty surprised to see me, too. I think some of them even assume she rescued me somehow, until she claps me on the back and tells them I saved her.

As if it was just me, and Amelrik wasn't there. As if he didn't almost get himself killed so I could get my sister back. And I know he did it for me and not her, but still. She doesn't have to make it out like I did it all on my own.

Everyone looks at me differently after she tells them how I finally cast the binding spell and saved her life. Their expressions are full of disbelief and awe, like maybe they misjudged me. Even my father raises his eyebrows at me, like somehow his dud daughter got exchanged for someone worthwhile while he wasn't looking.

This is the part where I should be rubbing it in everyone's face, saying, "I told you so." But my heart's not in it. And even if they're all looking at me differently, none of these people are my friends. Me having magic doesn't change that. And I don't even see Torrin, the one person who *might* actually be my friend. Not that things really went so well between us the last time I saw him.

I leave Celeste to her adoring crowd and go to my room, where I can be alone. It feels weird to be here again. I mean, it feels weird to be back at the barracks at all, but it's especially strange to be in my room. It's exactly the way I left it, and yet it feels like it belongs to someone else.

The last time I was here, it was with Amelrik. The blanket on the bed's still wrinkled from where we sat together. My mother's hand mirror is on my nightstand, and I remember how I jerked it away from him, horrified that he touched it. It was only a little over a month ago, but it feels like another lifetime, like it happened to somebody else.

I glance at my bookshelf, remembering how I actually asked Amelrik if he could read. It's such a small shelf compared to the giant one in his room, and I feel pretty stupid that I could have ever thought that about him.

A pang of loss hits me when I think about the *Princess Mysteries* book he got me, and how I left it in his room. It didn't make sense to bring it to Elder clan with me, and then we never went back. It was the only physical thing I had to remember him by, and now it's gone, as if the last few weeks never happened at all.

Maybe the strangest thing about my room is that my wedding dress is still sitting on the dummy, waiting for me to put it on. I can't believe how close I came to marrying Lord Varrens. I wonder what he thought when I stood him up at the altar and how pissed Father was about it. Maybe almost as pissed as I was about having to marry someone against my will.

I grab a pair of scissors from my desk drawer. They're not sewing shears, but they cut the fabric anyway. I feel a little bad about destroying Mrs. Hathaway's work, but there's no way I'm ever putting this dress on. If I ever get married, it won't be in something Father had hastily put together, without even consulting me. And it won't be a marriage he arranged that way, either.

I attack the dress with the scissors over and over again, cutting it to pieces. I chop the ribbon roses into unrecognizable bits, exposing the chocolate stain. Beads skitter to the floor as I slice through the bodice and snip the sleeves.

I'm in the middle of tearing up the train when there's a knock on the door.

"Go away!" I shout.

The door opens anyway, and Torrin comes in, shutting it behind him. He stares at me, like he can't believe I'm really here.

Or like I'm sweating and out of breath and surrounded by cut-up pieces of the wedding dress his mother worked on for me.

"Vee," he says. "It's you."

I wipe a lock of hair away from my forehead. "I said to go away. I didn't say to come in."

His mouth turns down a little, hurt by that. "I'm sorry."

"For not going away?"

"For what I said to you, the last time we . . ." He swallows. "I just can't believe you're back. I thought I was never going to see you again."

"And?"

"And I . . . Is that chocolate on your mouth?"

"I stopped at the bakery on our way through town. I got those scones I like." The ones he usually gets me for my birthday. I wipe the chocolate off with the back of my hand. "They were hot and buttery, and the chocolate was all melted. I hadn't had them like that in years."

He looks like I just kicked him. "I tried, Vee. You know I did."

"Was there something you wanted? Besides gawking at the fact that I'm still alive?"

"That's not fair. The last time I saw you, you were with a *dragon*. It just . . ."

"Wasn't like me?"

"I didn't think you were coming back. You said you were going to rescue Celeste, but I thought maybe it was something else. That you and him . . ." He clears his throat. "It doesn't matter now. You're back, and I heard you cast the binding spell. That's amazing."

"Yeah, sure." It is—I know it is—even if it doesn't feel like the victory I thought it would be. "I mean, thanks."

"I really am sorry. About all those things I said."

I study his face, not sure if he means it. Or at least not sure if he means it *enough*.

"I know I was a jerk," he says, "but I'm really glad you're back. And if you need any help murdering that wedding dress . . ."

I almost smile at that, but I don't want him to think I'm forgiving him, because I'm not. "I don't need any help. I just want to be alone."

"Oh. Right. Okay." He hesitates, then starts to leave.

And I don't know why, but the words just spill out of me. "Torrin, wait. It was like that. Between me and him." I clench my fists, fighting back the bitter taste that's filling my mouth, but it's a losing battle. And as much as I don't want him to see me cry right now, I also have to say this. "I love him. He's a dragon, and I'm a St. George, and I know how wrong that sounds to you, but it doesn't change anything, because *I love him*, more than anything, and I'm . . ." A sob interrupts me, choking off the words, and when I do manage to speak, my voice is high and squeaky. "I'm never going to see him again."

Torrin takes a step toward me. He reaches out a hand, pausing before putting it on my shoulder, like he's afraid to touch me. But when

I don't bite his head off for it and just cry harder, he puts his other arm around me, too, and says, "It's okay, Vee."

"No, it isn't."

"All right, no, it isn't. But it's going to be. Maybe not anytime soon, but someday. And I meant what I said. About being sorry. I really, really am."

Celeste beams at me when I meet up with her and Father in his office. We've only been home for a couple of days, but they're both "eager to talk to me about my future," or at least that's how Celeste put it when she told me about it.

Father actually gets up from behind his desk when I walk in, which is a first. He comes over to me, not quite looking as excited as Celeste, but still proud, I guess. It's been so long since he looked at me with anything other than shame and disappointment that I'm not sure how to take it. This is what I've been waiting for, ever since Mother's death, but it feels hollow and superficial. He knows I somehow infiltrated Elder clan and rescued Celeste after everyone else had given her up for dead, and that I cast the binding spell, but he doesn't really know *me*. And I really doubt he'd be looking at me like that if he knew I'd shared Amelrik's bed for weeks—even if we only actually slept together that last night—or that I was in love with him.

"Great timing," Celeste says. "I was just telling Father that we should start your paladin training right away."

"We?"

Father smiles at me. It's not exactly a warm smile—not like the kind he'd give Celeste—but it's an improvement. "Celeste's offered to train you herself."

"You're way behind everyone else your age, but with one-on-one lessons, I think you can catch up."

"Thanks, but I don't want to be a paladin."

Celeste's smile falters. "What? Of course you do."

"I thought I did, but it turns out I don't."

Father scowls at me. That didn't take long. "Your sister's offering to take time out from her important work to teach you herself. You should treat that like the honor it is."

"And by 'important work,' you mean hunting dragons?"

"Vee," Celeste warns, shaking her head.

"I don't want to do that, so I don't see the point in training to be a paladin."

They exchange a concerned look, one that tells me Celeste's already told him about me "thinking" I'm in love with a dragon.

Father sighs and rubs his temples. "I was looking forward to having two paladin daughters, but there's no shame in going straight to preserving the bloodline."

Celeste still looks disappointed that she won't be training me in all things paladin. "You're sure about this, Vee? It won't be like last time," she adds, giving Father a scolding look—way too little, way too late, if you ask me. "We'll find someone more suited to you this time. *Right?*"

Father nods, though he seems reluctant about it. "After all the trouble you caused, I can't believe we're back to this. But after everything you've been through, I can see why a quiet life might be more appealing, and . . ." He takes a deep breath, steeling himself for this. "Maybe I was too harsh with you before. You deserve some choice in the matter."

"Wrong." I glare at him. "I deserve *all* the choice in the matter. And just because I don't want to use my magic to help you murder dragons doesn't mean I'll get married, either."

Father throws his hands up and lets them fall to his sides. "Those are your options, Virginia. I don't know what else to tell you."

"She doesn't have to decide right now," Celeste says. "You can think about it, Vee."

But I shake my head. "I don't need to think about it. I'm not getting married, and I'm not becoming a paladin."

She gives me a worried look. "Then what are you going to do?"

I shrug. "I have no idea. But whatever it is, it'll be my choice. And if you guys don't like it, that's just too bad."

40

A PRETTY GOOD START

It takes a week for Father to plan our welcome-home celebration. I think by "our" he really means "Celeste's," but the refreshments table has both of our favorite foods, the banner stretched across the courtyard entrance has both our names, and, despite what I said about not getting married, there's a noticeable number of eligible bachelors at this party, all of them around my age.

I don't know if inviting them was a hopeful gesture or a pushy one, but at least this time he didn't tell me what to wear, and it's not a silent auction for some cheap St. George stock. It's not an auction at all.

But even if my father's not trying to marry me off, and even though several guys here have actually tried to strike up a conversation with me, seemingly genuinely interested, it feels so much like the last party that I can't help scanning the crowd, half expecting I'll spot Amelrik.

"You shouldn't be dancing with me," Torrin whispers.

We're dancing together because Celeste said I couldn't just stand by the buffet all night, ignoring our guests. And Torrin's technically one of our guests, even if he lives here at the barracks, so I think dancing with him counts, even if I know that's not what Celeste was getting at.

I roll my eyes at him. "Not you, too. You should consider yourself *lucky* to get to dance with me."

"There are a lot of other guys here."

"That's exactly my point."

"I just mean—"

"I *know* what you mean," I snap. "You think if I give someone here a chance that I'll just forget about Amelrik." It's what Celeste and my father are hoping for.

"Not forget, just move on. I'm not saying you're going to fall in love with anyone tonight, but you could at least try talking to some of them."

"It's only been a week."

Torrin frowns and looks like he's going to argue about that, even though it's true, when some guy comes up to us and says, "Excuse me? You're Virginia, right?"

He's one of the guys my father invited, and if I'm being honest, he's not exactly hard to look at, and he has a bright, slightly crooked smile.

"Can I have the next dance?"

Where was he two months ago? "I'm sorry," I tell him, "but—"

"She'd love to," Torrin says. "We're just friends. No need to wait for the next dance—you can cut in." He practically shoves me at this guy.

I glare at him and speak through clenched teeth. "Gee, Torrin, how nice of you."

He disappears into the crowd, and I'm about to tell the new guy that there's been a mistake, but he looks so excited to be here with me, like a puppy who just found out he's going on a walk, that I don't have the heart to just brush him off.

"Is it true?" he asks, once we're moving in sync with each other. "Did you really sneak into *Elder clan*?"

"Yep. I had help, though."

He grins, shaking his head a little. "That's still really badass."

"Thanks," I tell him, surprised that I actually mean it.

"I'm Devon, by the way. Devon Waters."

"What, like the prince?" Even if I'd never met one before Lothar and Amelrik, I at least know the names of the royal family.

He clears his throat. "That's me."

I gape at him. "You're serious?" And what's with me and princes?

"I heard about what you did, and I wanted to meet you."

I take a step back, so that his hands aren't on my waist anymore and we're not dancing. "I'm not really a paladin. I cast the binding spell *once*. So whatever you think I am, whatever my father told you—"

"Whoa. That's not . . . I know you're not a paladin. That's what makes what you did so amazing."

"I . . . I have to go."

"Wait! I'm sorry if I said something to offend you. I just—"

"You didn't. It's not you."

Or maybe it is him, because he's cute and charming and actually interested in me for me, not because of my St. George blood. And there's no reason why I shouldn't spend the rest of the night getting to know him, except that it doesn't feel right, and all of a sudden, I don't know what I'm doing here. I don't know why I'm letting anyone dance with me, or letting my friends and family try and push for me to meet someone new. All I know is that I can't spend the rest of my life looking for the right person—not when I know I've already found him—and I can't spend another minute here.

Devon's still trying to ask me what's wrong, but I abandon him on the dance floor and run out of the courtyard. The cool night air feels good, and I take a deep breath, relieved to finally be away from the party.

I don't know if I'll be able to find Hawthorne clan again, and going into dragon territory on my own is probably a really bad idea, and there's a good chance I won't even make it there, but . . .

But I can't take this feeling, like something vital's been ripped out of me. And I know that there's no reason why it should work out between us. Maybe it can't. Maybe my heart's just going to get even more broken somewhere down the line, and it'll be that much worse, because I got to be with him for a while. But I don't care.

Because even if I can't be with him forever, I can't stay here and not know how things might have turned out. I might get lost along the way, or killed by a dragon, or I might make it there only to have Amelrik turn me away. But letting him go was the biggest mistake I've ever made, and I have to fix it, no matter what the risk.

I just have to stop by my room first and grab some supplies. And leave a note. Not that saying I've run off to go find my dragon boyfriend is going to reassure anyone that I'm okay, but still.

I dart around the corner, hurrying to my room before anyone thinks to come find me. I'm so busy going over the list in my head of everything I need to bring that I don't look where I'm going and accidentally slam into someone. Though to be fair, I didn't expect anyone else to be out here.

"*Ow.*" I put a hand to my forehead where it just banged into someone's chin.

"Virginia?" The sound of Amelrik's voice sends a shiver up my spine.

I'm almost afraid to move my hand and see if it's really him. Because it can't be him. He's far away, and I just really, really want to see him, badly enough that I'd imagine he was here, and—

And suddenly his lips are on mine, and I have no doubts about whether it's him or not. "What are you doing here?"

"I couldn't . . . I mean, I tried, but . . ." He swallows. "Were you going somewhere?"

I grin at him. "I was coming to find you."

"How did you know I was here?"

"I didn't. I was going to Hawthorne clan."

He smiles and puts his arms around me. I thought I'd never get to do this again, to be this close to him, and the relief that washes over me brings tears to my eyes.

"I'm still a St. George," I whisper.

"And I'm still the prince of Hawthorne clan."

"So, nothing's changed."

"Except that I don't know how I ever thought I could live without you. I love you, Virginia. More than anything."

"But I don't know how we're going to make it work." When I thought I was heading off to find him, figuring this out seemed like a distant problem. Now that he's standing right here in front of me, it seems obvious that there's still no solution.

"I'll tell you how."

I raise my eyebrows at him, skeptical, but hopeful, too.

He leans in close, his breath soft against my ear. "Like this," he whispers, and then he licks the side of my face.

I shriek with laughter and surprise—I can't help it—and punch him playfully in the shoulder. "That's not a real answer!"

"Yes, it is. Less than a minute ago, you didn't even know that dragon spit has the same mood-enhancing quality as human spit. Obviously, there are a lot of things you don't know, so how can you be so sure that we won't figure this out? Besides," he adds, "now that I've got you back, I'm never letting you go."

"That's your plan?"

"It's working so far. Good luck getting rid of me."

I laugh. "I'm *never* getting rid of you."

"Then I guess we're stuck together."

"That's not a real answer, either, though."

"Maybe not," he says, leaning in to kiss me again, "but it's a pretty good start."

Acknowledgments

I hate to admit this, but once upon a time, I didn't love this book. I had the first six chapters or so, almost exactly as they appear here, and I thought they were terrible. Which seems crazy now, because I love them, and they're probably some of the best chapters I've ever written. I read that first chapter now and am like, "How did I ever think this was crap???"

But I did. For a long time.

I don't know if it was my thyroid being at an all-time low (this was before I'd found a website called stopthethyroidmadness.com), which made writing anything almost impossible, or if I really just wasn't ready to write this story yet, but I put it aside, thinking there was very little chance I'd come back to it. Actually, I thought that several times, as I picked it up and set it aside again and again over the years. I couldn't make it stick, but I couldn't just let it go, either.

Fast-forward to now, when I've still got a fair amount of health issues but am mostly on the mend. Well, okay, don't fast-forward to *now* now, but early 2015, when I was trying to figure out what to pitch to my editor and started thinking about *Dragonbound* again. I remembered that what I'd written before was complete and total crap, so I came up with plans to overhaul the idea and make it into something worth working on. Thankfully, while I was working on these new plans, I decided to actually read what I'd written before. This wasn't the first time I'd reread those chapters, but it was the first time I fell in love with them.

I loved the writing. I loved the characters. And all the things I'd convinced myself were wrong with it before . . . didn't actually exist. (Brains are funny that way. And by "funny," I mean more like "annoying.")

So many thanks are in order to the people who believed in this book before I did: Holly Root, agent extraordinaire, who loved this idea from the very beginning and never gave up on it; Karen Kincy, who kept asking when I was going to finish it, no matter how many times I claimed I wasn't; and Chloë Tisdale, who discussed every nuance—maybe even every sentence—of this story endlessly with me.

Huge thanks also go out to my editors, Miriam Juskowicz and Robin Benjamin, who were not only crazy enthusiastic about this project, but amazingly patient and understanding when it took me longer than originally planned.

You guys are all the best.